FATAL ENDINGS

ANITA WALLER

Boldwood

First published in Great Britain in 2024 by Boldwood Books Ltd.

Copyright © Anita Waller, 2024

Cover Design by Head Design Ltd

Cover Images: iStock and Adobe Stock

A CIP catalogue record for this book is available from the British Library.

Paperback ISBN 978-1-83533-914-5

Large Print ISBN 978-1-83533-915-2

Hardback ISBN 978-1-83533-913-8

Ebook ISBN 978-1-83533-916-9

Kindle ISBN 978-1-83533-917-6

Audio CD ISBN 978-1-83533-908-4

MP3 CD ISBN 978-1-83533-909-1

Digital audio download ISBN 978-1-83533-912-1

This book is printed on certified sustainable paper. Boldwood Books is dedicated to putting sustainability at the heart of our business. For more information please visit https://www.boldwoodbooks.com/about-us/sustainability/

Boldwood Books Ltd, 23 Bowerdean Street, London, SW6 3TN

www.boldwoodbooks.com

To our new great-grandson, Alfie James David Kitchen,
born 2 June 2024

For life and death are one, even
as the river and the sea are one.

— KAHLIL GIBRAN

Ask for me tomorrow, and you shall
find me a grave man.

— *ROMEO AND JULIET*, WILLIAM
SHAKESPEARE

1

Matt Forrester picked up his newly poured mug of coffee and opened the patio doors. He quietly moved the metal garden chair and sat down with a sigh. It was a beautiful morning. Not quite sunrise yet, but the sky was already a stunning shade of red, enhanced by the odd cloud or two. The weather forecast had promised a fine mid-March day, and his mind ran swiftly through the jobs he had to do that were definite ones, and debated if he could make them indefinite. Maybe then he could devote some time to getting the garden into shape...

He looked up with a smile as his life partner, Karen Nelson, stepped through the doors to join him.

'Just wow,' she said, staring at the vista of Ridgeway spread out before them, and all of it tinged by the red sky. 'This is worth getting up early for.'

'Certainly is, but if you've to be in work for six you can't sit there for long.'

She frowned. 'Hate it when the top brass come, but I'll be home early. What time you getting Harry up?'

Matt laughed. 'Maybe I should start anytime now. His last words as he went to bed last night were that he didn't think it was worth going back to school for the last couple of weeks of term, that Easter was 9 April, and he expected everybody would bully him for running away in December. Of course, he had all sorts of reasons carefully thought out for not returning to school, but he's missed so much already, and he's twelve now, such an important age for learning. I know he needs to go back. He's been so ill with that blessed pneumonia, but now he's been given the all-clear, so back to school he goes.'

Karen checked her watch. 'Want me to go and wake him?'

'No, I'll give him another half hour, promise him a bacon sandwich for breakfast if he gets up straight away, and I'll run him to school. I'd like to watch what happens when he goes into the yard, just check there's no silliness. I don't think there will be, but he's obviously worrying about the possibility, so I'll keep an eye on things. I'll pick him up tonight as well, so if I'm not in when you get home, that's where I'll be.'

Karen nodded. 'No problem. Maybe we could go to McDonald's or something tonight, it's Harry's favourite. See if Steve and Herms want to join us, celebrate Harry's return to full health.'

'Good idea. It might help ease things for him.' They both watched the sun climb a little higher, sipping at their drinks, and thinking about the boy that had caused them so much worry when he had run away from home. Fortunately the reason behind his need to escape – Superintendent Brian Davis – was no longer a valid one, as the man was now living in London, almost divorced from Harry's mother Becky, and completely out of their lives.

Karen drained the last of her coffee, and stood. She walked around to Matt, kissed him and left him to enjoy the red sky before his own day started. She was in the kitchen when her phone rang. She spoke quietly, gave a couple of instructions and returned to the back garden.

'Problems?'

She nodded. 'Body found. Thought I'd better tell

you, so you don't expect me home early. I'll keep you informed. Early-morning meeting moved to this afternoon, I'm heading straight to join the team at the site.'

'Take care. Ring if you need to talk.'

She smiled, blew him a kiss and left to start her job. He suspected the trip to McDonald's might not happen now.

* * *

Matt called Harry from the bottom of the stairs, and waited for some sort of response. There was a grunt. He called again, and the grunt was increased to two grunts. His son sounded stressed.

'Harry! Final warning. Next stop is water torture.'

'I'm up,' was Harry's response. 'Listen.' There were bangs on the floor that were meant to sound like footsteps, so Matt followed up with the warning that the bacon was almost ready, and unless he liked cold bacon sandwiches, he needed to be downstairs in five minutes. The footsteps changed to real ones.

* * *

Harry's hair resembled a hedgehog in attack mode.

'Morning,' he mumbled. 'Have I really got to go to school?'

'You have. Uniform is in your wardrobe, and I would highly recommend a shower first to try to tame that hair. Breakfast in one minute, orange juice poured. Want anything else?'

Harry pulled his dressing gown tighter around him and sat at the kitchen table. 'No, I'm good.' He gave a deep sigh. 'I think I'm scared.'

'And I understand,' his father said, while dealing with the safe delivery of the bacon sandwich. 'But you'll probably turn out to be the star of the school, because you managed to evade capture all the time you were on the run. It was only illness that forced you to contact me. Look, you'll have your phone with you, and if anything becomes unbearable, text me. Or even text Karen, but it seems she's dealing with a death so she might not be available.'

Harry used both hands to pick up the overloaded bacon butty. 'Thanks, Dad. This looks good. A death? At this time in the morning?'

'It doesn't mean the person is newly dead. They could have died last night but only just been discovered.'

Harry thought about it, then nodded. 'Suppose so. I've a lot to learn before I join your business, haven't I?'

'The main thing you've to learn, young man, is you don't run away from anything, big or small. I know you thought you were protecting me, stopping me from hammering Brian Davis, but I'm the adult. And I'm old enough to make my own decisions. And it didn't work, because I still hammered him anyway.'

Harry allowed a small smile to cross his face. 'We won though, didn't we? He's gone now. Mum said the divorce is nearly done, and he wants nothing to do with Florence.' Mention of his baby half-sister brought a further smile to his face. He finished his breakfast and downed the last of his orange juice. 'Okay,' he said, 'shower, dressed and sort out my hair.'

'Good lad. And I'll take you to school.'

'You want to make sure I go?'

'I do. You've got prior convictions in this happy family for just disappearing, so I'm taking you. Besides, I want to. At one point we thought we were losing you, so I'm taking good care of you from now on. I'll probably pick you up later as well, but if anything happens to stop me, I'll text and you can catch the school bus.'

* * *

Matt remained in the car and watched as his son turned and gave a hand salute that meant he could go.

He smiled to himself. He'd go when he was sure Harry was safe.

Within a minute, Harry was surrounded, and Matt watched the flurry of high fives that Harry received. He breathed a sigh of relief. He had expected this welcome, but had wanted to see for himself that Harry wasn't likely to experience thoughtless bullying as a result of his escapade. He waited a minute, heard the bell to summon the pupils into classes, and drove away.

So far, so good. He continued his journey to his office at Gleadless, seeing the welcoming lights on inside the premises that told him Carol Flynn was already there and hopefully brewing the coffee.

Carol was just about to enter his office as he opened the front door. 'Morning,' she said, handing him the three envelopes she held in her hand. 'I've kept the generic ones, but these are all personally addressed to you. Coffee is ready. And how's Harry?'

'I dropped him off at school and everything seemed okay. I'll breathe a sigh of relief if I get through the day without a text message from him. He was really nervous, but from what I saw it seemed he was the hero of the hour. He did what I imagine 50 per cent of the kids at that school have wanted to do at some point in their lives. Harry didn't do it to escape trouble, though, he did it to stop me getting into trouble.'

'He'll be fine. The first day is always the hardest, tomorrow will be just another school day. You ready for a coffee now?'

'I am. My last one was out on the patio about six this morning, with Karen. She had an early meeting, but as she left she got a phone call from the station with reports of a dead body. You heard anything on the news?'

She gave a slight nod. 'Sort of. Just something along the lines of a lot of police activity near Crystal Peaks, and the area around the shopping mall has been closed off. It didn't say why. I'll check Facebook, there's always somebody on there who knows exactly what's happening. I'll get your coffee, then fill you in on your day.'

'Steve's not in today,' he reminded her.

'They've had a good time?' She knew his colleague Steve and Matt's sister Hermia had spent the weekend in Stratford-upon-Avon to give them a much-needed break before the birth of their baby, as they waited out the last couple of weeks of her pregnancy.

'From the amount of photos they've been sending us, it seems they have. They're off to see something Hermia only thought about last night, then travelling home later. The message also involved a picture of the huge hotel breakfast they were eating at the time. It made our bacon butties look sad. That reminds me, I had a phone call last night while I was helping Harry sort out his stuff he would need for today, but I'd left the phone downstairs. I heard it, but left it, figuring they would call me back if it was urgent. The number wasn't one I recognised, they didn't leave a voicemail, and I didn't get a return call.' He held out his phone for Carol to see it. 'You recognise it?'

She looked at it for a moment. 'I'll do a quick run through on WATSON, see if it throws up anything.' WATSON, their own private version of HOLMES, the police Home Office Large Major Enquiry System, held details of anything that had ever passed through the files of the Forrester Detective Agency, going right back to its inception with Matt's father, Dave Forrester.

'Thanks. I know I could call it back, but I don't want to get involved with anybody trying to sell me investment opportunities.' He grinned at her. 'I'll get us those coffees now, shall I?'

She scribbled the phone number on a piece of paper and handed his phone back. 'I'll do this while you're doing the coffee. We've got new mugs.'

'We have?' He headed through to the tiny kitchen area where the new mugs stood proudly on the side.

There were two that said Boss, although in different colours, and one that said Slave. He filled two up and carried the Slave to his desk, taking the Boss one through to Carol. She was staring at the screen of her computer.

'That number,' she said hesitantly, 'I thought I almost recognised it. We removed it from our phones. It belongs to Susan Hunter.'

2

'Susan Hunter?' Matt's look of surprise flashed across his face. 'I thought she'd disappeared out of our lives. Wonder what she wants. I'm not convinced we want or need her back, I tend to think of her when she occasionally flashes across my mind, as an evil witch. And we certainly cleared everything up some months ago with her so-called case.'

'You want me to get her for you?'

He shook his head. 'No, if she really wants us for a genuine reason, she'll ring back. And it can't be that urgent because it was nine-ish last night when she rang, and as I said, she didn't leave a voicemail. She's not rung the office?'

Carol shook her head. 'No, I've already checked our messages. Nothing there at all.'

'Well, I'm not keen to get reacquainted with her, so we'll ignore it until, or if, she tries again.'

'Okay. You in the office all day?'

'Probably. I decided not to put anything in the diary just in case there is some sort of issue with Harry, but if everything is good it will all be back to normal tomorrow.'

Matt disappeared into his own office and Carol smiled. All of them had felt a sense of relief that Harry had been cleared to return to school. Matt's sister Hermia had taken on the role of home tuition, but the birth of her baby was drawing ever closer, and she was showing the tiredness that she was obviously feeling. Yes, Carol acknowledged, it was time for her favourite people to get back to some form of normality. Although Carol was an employee since the agency's early days, she considered herself to be a presence in the Forrester family, and felt their various woes and happiness almost as strongly as if they formed part of her own family.

* * *

Steve and Hermia arrived home just before lunchtime, and Steve sat back with a sigh. 'Is that it?'

'Is what it?' Herms looked and sounded puzzled by the question.

'All our gallivanting done until our child is safely delivered into our arms.'

She gave a gentle laugh. 'It is. Not sure I have enough energy for even one more gallivant, not even to the shops, and you might need to remember we have no milk. Or bread. Or chocolate.'

She opened the passenger door and breathed a sigh of relief. 'Mmmm, chocolate.'

'Come on, we'll go and get the kettle on, then I'll take a jug to Matt's and raid their fridge for milk. If you live next door to the brother-in-law, you have to take full advantage.'

'Smart thinking,' Hermia said, wincing as she straightened her spine after the long car journey. 'But that won't solve the chocolate issue. You might have to nip along the road to the Co-op.'

'I'll go later, give you time to make an actual list. My priority is getting you inside, on that sofa with your feet up, and a cuppa in your hand. That sound okay?'

'It sounds perfect,' she said, smiling at him. 'I'll message Matt to tell him we're doing a milk raid of his fridge, but we'll buy him a bottle to replace it when you go to the shops.'

Steve carried their suitcase through to the house, leaving it at the bottom of the stairs for transport to the bedroom later, grabbed a jug from the kitchen and hurried across to the Forrester home to get enough milk to last them until he went on his shopping expedition.

Hermia clicked on the kettle, took down two mugs and moved into the lounge. She really felt tired, and the pains her midwife had confirmed were merely Braxton Hicks were really becoming a little bit more than annoying. Why did nobody mention the side effects of a thoroughly enjoyable night of unprotected sex? Braxton Hicks should be top of the list.

She lay back on the sofa and closed her eyes. Experience had taught her how to deal with the irregular contractions, and she relaxed. By the time Steve carried the two mugs of newly brewed tea into the lounge, she was fast asleep.

* * *

Matt opened up the file on his laptop that always seem to surprise him every time he inspected it. They had diversified into security almost by accident, after getting several requests for help with choosing the right systems for businesses in their area. They had partnered with the company that set up the Forresters' own high-level office security system and it had proved to be an excellent relationship. It was now taking on a life of its own, and most days saw a new request for a consultation and a quote.

Carol did the initial work, setting up a file for each query, complete with all relevant information that had arrived with the primary email document. It was then forwarded through to both Matt and Steve, where they decided between them who would deal with what, depending on their current workload. It had panned out remarkably well, and Matt saw there were three new businesses requiring help. He sent off a quick response to each one, assuring them they would be in touch within twenty-four hours, and thanking them for their contact. He then moved onto the emails he had sent out the previous Friday, promising contact on Monday, and listed the four names in his notebook.

Having seen the original queries the previous Friday, he had earmarked one he considered would be right up his street, the Birley Spa Bath House. It seemed that a small group called Friends of the Bath House had received a lottery grant to up the security on the Victorian building, and they had approached

Forresters following a glowing reference from another small business in the area who had been very satisfied with the work undertaken by the local detective agency.

He had been down the path that led off Birley Spa Lane and ended at the Bath House many times, both as a child and an adult, but the building itself never seemed to be open. Surely he could get sight of the inside of it if they were wanting quotes for security on it? And would it look completely unprofessional if he took Harry with him? He knew the answer to that thought almost before it floated around his brain. He would take Harry, but only at some future time, once they had received agreement for the work to be done.

He picked up the phone and rang the number.

* * *

Once appointments for all four of the Friday emails had been sorted, he sat back, trying to remember how it had all happened with Susan Hunter. She had managed to get into their office because their security had been pathetic, and it had prompted a massive upgrade of cameras and alarms. The work had taken place over about a week, and the van parked outside had stated they fitted full security systems. It seemed to have grown from that, and now there was even talk of taking on an extra person, to deal solely with that side of the business.

He drained the last of his cold coffee and pulled forward the invoices Carol had completed. She insisted either him or Steve check them before she sent them out, saying they might spot an omission from the original work sheet, so he opened his diary file, and began the somewhat boring job of checking something he knew would be accurate to the ultimate degree.

There were six in total and he initialled each one before heading out into the reception area. He passed the paperwork through the sliding window.

'Everything okay?' Carol asked.

'Absolutely fine. If you stick stamps on the envelopes, I'll nip across and post them.'

She laughed. 'You're bored.'

'Of course not.' He hesitated. 'Yes.'

'Matt, Harry will be fine,' she said gently. 'And if the school, or even Harry, needs you, they can get you on your mobile. Now go and do something.'

'Tyrant,' he grumbled, and heard her laughter as he closed the glass pane.

Sitting at his desk didn't help, neither did spending money on Amazon. He needed to know Harry was okay and buying a new iPad wasn't going to give him the answer.

He rang school, knowing he wouldn't settle until somebody confirmed his son was fine – and hadn't decided to run away from any problems again.

The school secretary was more than helpful. 'I've just seen him in goal, he's out on the pitch and I swear there's about fifteen kids in each team, girls and boys. Harry's always been their first choice for goalie, and he's there today. I stood watching them for a bit, never seen so many high fives as have been given to your son, so stop worrying, Mr Forrester. We're taking care of him. The kids are as well. In fact, seems to me he's a bit of a legend.'

He thanked her and disconnected. Carol, of course, laughed at him for giving in and checking with school, then handed him the small batch of envelopes, duly stamped. 'We're running low on stamps. Here's twenty pounds from petty cash. Can you bring as many as you can get for that money, please? It won't be many, but make sure you get a receipt. You still don't want to send these via email?'

Matt shook his head. 'No, it's all about creating an impression. It's good to feel quality paper, a quality letterhead, in your hand. Quotes and invoices we'll continue to issue like this, anything else is email.'

He gave a small salute in acknowledgement, and let himself out of the front door. He waited for the tram to go by, then hurried across the road towards the post office. One or two people said hello, and he felt good that the neighbourhood was getting used to their presence. The business was thriving and he frequently wondered how his dad would have reacted to the many changes they had made since his death. He slid the newly bought stamps and receipt into his inner pocket and left the shop.

He heard his ring tone and pulled out his phone. His relief was palpable as he saw Karen's name on the screen.

'You in the office?' she asked.

'I've just been sent out on junior duties, posting envelopes and buying stamps. Heading back now. You want me to pick you up a sandwich for lunch?'

There was a momentary hesitation. 'No, that's fine. I won't be staying long. I'll be there in about ten minutes. Wait for me.'

They disconnected and he ran across the tram tracks. Karen had sounded stressed, and he put on a fresh pot of coffee for when she arrived.

Carol wasn't impressed by the small number of stamps he'd managed to exchange for the twenty-pound note. 'Not good enough,' she said. 'I'm sure there must be a cheaper way of posting things. I'll look into it.'

'I've put a fresh pot of coffee on. You want one? Karen should be here any minute.'

Carol shook her head. 'No, I'm good, thanks. I've got water. We've got scones though,' she added, and flourished a plastic box.

'That's probably why she's coming.'

He turned at the sound of a car pulling on to the shop forecourt, and went out to meet her.

Karen wasn't alone. DS Ray Ledger was in the passenger seat.

'Good to see you, Ray.' He shook hands with the man he had known for several years.

'And you, boss,' Ray replied.

Karen and Matt exchanged a smile. Matt would always be 'boss' to Ray despite the length of time Matt had now worked in the private sector, well away from South Yorkshire Police.

'I'm assuming you're here for a reason. I've got a fresh pot of coffee and Carol's made some scones. Let's go through and be civilised for ten minutes.'

'That's about all the time we have,' Karen confirmed. 'The dead body I was called out to this morning has actually led us here.'

They went into Matt's office and sat down. Carol

appeared immediately with the box of scones, and asked what they wanted to drink.

They all said coffee and as she left the room Karen asked her to return to sit with them. Carol nodded.

Within two minutes they were all seated around Matt's desk, and Karen spoke.

'The body at Crystal Peaks was found at the top of those stairs that connect the retail park to the main shopping centre. Know where I mean? Round the back of T K Maxx.'

Both Matt and Carol nodded.

'We've identified her, and found her car in the top car park, parked outside Boots the Chemists.'

Matt's intuition kicked into overdrive.

'You're about to tell us it's Susan Hunter, aren't you?'

3

Karen frowned. 'You did it?'

'No,' he said, surmising she was joking. 'It's against the law. Seriously though, her name cropped up this morning. It was actually just a wild guess. And now let me guess something else. You've got her phone.'

'We have. It was underneath her body when the forensic people moved her. We managed to get into it because it's fingerprint activated. The last call she made was to you at nine last night.'

'I didn't answer it. I was sorting Harry's uniform out and I heard it ringing, but my phone was downstairs. She didn't ring back or leave a message. I haven't heard anything since then.'

'You knew it was Susan?'

He shook his head. 'No, I removed her number from my phone. Don't like the woman, and didn't imagine I'd ever hear from her again. Carol checked it for me this morning, and obviously her contact details are in WATSON. I decided not to ring her back, figuring if she really wanted to speak to me, she'd try again.'

'When did she die?' Carol asked quietly.

'We've only had a rough estimate. We'll know a little more accurately after the PM, but between nine and eleven last night was mentioned.'

'Well, that's a relief,' Matt said. 'I've got the best alibi ever. I was with the SIO of the case.'

Ray shook his head. 'We didn't think for a minute you'd done it, boss. We were more interested to find out if you were working a case that involved her. We've nothing on CCTV that will help, because the camera that covers those stairs has been smashed, conveniently for the killer.'

'Well, you can scratch me out,' Matt replied. 'I haven't heard anything from her for months. It's definitely murder, then?'

'It is. Knife into her stomach, and she bled out. One of the Crystal Peaks security men found her. Rattled the poor man a bit, I can tell you.'

'I can't remember much about her, but we can let

you have sight of the file we do hold. She had connections with some of the lowlife of Sheffield, and she seemed a bit desperate for money, but that could all have changed.' Carol frowned, and opened the box of scones. 'After I'd threatened to smash her face into the steering wheel, she sort of disappeared off our radar.'

Karen sighed and picked up a scone. 'You do know we knew you had no connection, don't you? We only came on the off chance there would be scones.'

Ray took a bite from his scone and stared at Carol. 'Threatened to smash her face into the steering wheel?'

'It's a manoeuvre I was taught in my previous job.'

'I thought you worked with some high-ranking politician?'

'I did,' she said and grinned. 'And don't ask me to demonstrate.'

'Not bloody likely,' Ray said, taking a second bite of what he considered the best scone he'd ever tasted.

* * *

Carol and Matt stood side by side at the open front door, enjoying the slight breeze and the warmth of the sun. They waved as Karen and Ray drove away, then turned and headed back inside.

'Strange,' Carol said.

'It is,' Matt agreed and Carol looked at him.

'I mean strange that she's tried to contact you. You think she was feeling threatened and wanted some help?'

'Possibly. I feel guilty for not answering now.'

'Your phone wasn't glued to your hand, Matt. It was downstairs and you had gone to Harry's bedroom. You can't blame yourself.'

He nodded, acknowledging her words, but she didn't miss the frown across his forehead.

* * *

Harry walked out of the school gates, deep in conversation with a boy his father didn't recognise.

Matt waved as Harry lifted his head. He climbed back into the car, then sat waiting patiently for the conversation between the two lads to end. Harry eventually slid in beside him.

'Okay?' Matt asked.

'Yep. He's new.'

'The lad you've just been chatting to?'

'Yes, he's called Isaac. Smashed me in the face with a football.' Harry turned his face towards his dad and pointed to the red mark high on his cheek bone.

'Ouch.'

'He said sorry, and the ball didn't go in the net, so it's all okay.'

'Oh, good. I'm pleased he didn't score.'

'We're both trying out for the school team next week, because after September we're old enough to be in it.'

'So today's been good then?'

'It's been ace. Glad I came back, now.'

The journey home was driven in silence, and as they pulled onto the large driveway, Harry leaned forward. 'Aunty Herms and Uncle Steve are home.'

'They are. Don't go bounding in, just in case Aunty Herms is having a rest. She messaged earlier to say she felt tired, it had been a long journey.'

'I'll go round after we've eaten. Will Karen be home late?'

'No idea. The death I mentioned this morning turns out to be unnatural causes.'

Harry was halfway out of the car, and he swung himself back in. 'What?'

'It's death at the hands of somebody else, so it depends on what they've discovered during today as to what time she gets home. The plan originally was to go to McDonald's tonight, to celebrate your return to school, but it's highly unlikely that's going to happen now.'

'So are you cooking?'

'I am. What do you fancy?'

'McDonald's.'

* * *

The family conference involving Steve, Herms, Matt and Harry decided to order in a takeaway McDonald's, and somehow Matt found himself logging into the app on his phone. He stared in amazement at the price of four Big Mac meals and four McFlurries, and ordered them quickly, to avoid dwelling on the amount disappearing out of his bank account.

'My treat,' he whispered, and pretended to wipe sweat from his brow.

'Well, I can't afford it,' Steve said. 'I took your sister to Stratford for a few days, and she used our credit card.'

'She's not my sister, she's your wife.'

'So she's solely my responsibility now?'

'She is.'

'That can't be right. That wasn't in the marriage vows, was it?'

'Oy, you two.' Hermia wagged her finger. 'Pack it in, I'm worth every penny. Have you heard from Karen?'

'Not since she left at lunchtime. The first day on a murder case is always a long one.'

'Is there a touch of nostalgia in your voice?' Hermia smiled at her brother.

'Not likely. I miss the people, but I don't miss the job. Funnily enough we always seem to be on the periphery of the major crimes though.'

Steve came through from the kitchen carrying various condiments. 'That could be something to do with sleeping with the lead detective of the Major Crimes unit. Does Karen talk in her sleep?'

'Only to nag me. We do tend to discuss her bigger jobs though, I must admit. And as this one involves an ex-client of Forresters, there's half a chance it will be our topic of conversation tonight. I'm a bit puzzled as to why Susan Hunter rang me, although I do have to say that even if I'd known the call was from her, I probably wouldn't have answered it. I don't suppose we'll ever know now.'

* * *

Karen attended the delayed meeting, took no part whatsoever in it, and left as quickly as she could. They could talk drug reduction as many times as they wanted, it would make no difference to the lowlifes in Sheffield who ruined so many lives, and it seemed as soon as they managed to send a bunch of the top dealers to prison, there were more waiting to step into their shoes.

The crime scene was only a five-minute walk from the police station, but she opted to take her car. She'd bring her new team member back with her. PC Rachel Quixley hadn't been introduced to the rest of the team, and had been thrown in at the deep end in a spectacular fashion.

Karen knew the young PC had requested a move to Major Crimes a couple of times, and she had received the transfer notification on Friday. When Karen had said to the desk sergeant she wanted her team calling in to attend the crime scene, Rachel had been on the list. They had all arrived within a few minutes and she had watched Rachel's face lose its colour, as she had first sight of the copious amounts of blood surrounding the body. Forensics were erecting the tent, and now the goriness was hidden from view, it wasn't only Rachel who felt better.

When Karen asked that someone remain with the forensics team until they had finished their work,

Rachel volunteered. But now, as SIO, Karen felt it was time to head back, taking Rachel with her, see if anything further had been discovered, and arrange for a member of the afternoon shift to take over from the uniformed constable who was currently supporting the forensics team at the crime scene. Maybe then she could get to know Rachel a little better, and introduce her to the rest of the team who were trying to piece together anything they could find about the victim.

An officer held up the crime scene tape blocking off the entire bottom section of the car park, and she drove through. None of the shops had been allowed to open, and it seemed strange to see so many empty parking spaces. The white tent was still in place, and a coroner's van was standing by with its rear doors open. Rachel had moved to one side, away from the tent entrance.

The two women turned to each other.

'Rachel? You okay?'

Rachel nodded. 'Yes, I'm fine. Bit of an initiation by fire, but I'm over it, thank you, ma'am.'

'Call me boss, Rachel. The rest of them do. I've arranged for a couple of officers to be here overnight until we get the site cleaned up, so I'll be taking you back to the station with me when they arrive. Do we know any more?'

'They're ready to move the body. It's apparently taken longer than normal because they've done loads of the tests that they needed to do with the lady in situ. They've found her bag in the bushes, with her contact details and £180 in notes plus some change in it, along with a prescription of antibiotics she had just collected from Boots' evening collection window. So it doesn't seem as if she was mugged for money. They have the phone, of course. A truck came and took her car for forensic examination about an hour ago, so I just took notes of the time anything happened, and tried to not get in the way.'

'Good girl, that was the right thing to do. I'm sorry I threw you in at the deep end; I thought I'd be able to introduce you to the team first thing, get you mingling with them, that sort of stuff, but we didn't even start off at the station. So once Ms Hunter has been removed, we'll head off back to Moss Way. You had anything to eat and drink?'

Rachel smiled. 'A cheeseburger and a bottle of water. A crime scene virtually next door to a McDonald's...'

'Good. An early start like this usually means we all miss out on breakfast, although I have to admit I didn't. The call came through just as I was leaving home this morning for a crack of dawn meeting.'

There was a flurry of movement inside the tent, and the two women stepped back. They stood with respect and watched as the body of Susan Hunter was loaded into the coroner's van.

4

Everyone was sitting silently, waiting for Karen to sort through her notes before addressing them.

She eventually looked up and thanked everybody for their patience. 'Before we go into the case itself, I want to introduce you to our new team member who has been on duty down at the crime site all day. Would you believe she actually applied to work at Major Crimes?'

Without exception everyone shook their heads, as if in amazement at such a folly. 'Her name is Rachel, PC Rachel Quixley, she's moved here from uniform and after today we no longer treat her as the new girl. She's a valued member of our team, and she wasn't sick when she saw the victim and all the blood this morning so she's definitely passed her first test. Rachel, we have a team of five including me, you now make us a team of six. The others are DS Ray Ledger, DC Kevin Potter, DC Jaime Hanover, DC Ian Jameson, and me, DI Karen Nelson. Our DCI is Daniel Armitage, and our Superintendent is Carl Granger. You'll not remember all our names at first, but I prefer "boss" anyway. Welcome to the team, Rachel.'

Rachel gave a slight nod of acknowledgement and sat back to take in her first briefing. Reading crime books hadn't prepared her for anything that had happened today, and she had no idea what to expect.

Karen looked back at the whiteboard, with a picture of Susan Hunter attached to it.

'This was a brutal murder. At the moment we have no idea of the motive, the perpetrator, the weapon he or she used; in fact, we know very little. She made a phone call at nine last night, and was killed shortly after. For those that don't know, the phone call was to my partner, Matt. He didn't answer it because he didn't have his phone with him, but Susan Hunter was a previous client of the Forrester Detective Agency. Rachel, Matt Forrester, my life partner and owner of the Forrester Detective Agency, used to be DI in the Major Crimes Unit. You probably remember him from that time, he worked out of Moss Way.'

A look of surprise flashed across Rachel's face, but again she confirmed she understood by giving a brief nod.

'So, Jaime, I want to know everything there is to know about Susan Hunter. I can tell you that she was in Australia for five years but returned to her roots here in Sheffield sometime last year. She was a temporary client of the Forrester Agency, but after she attacked a member of their staff, they dumped her. According to Matt they've heard nothing from her since then, and he'd removed her from his contacts list in his phone. He had no idea the strange number in his call log had come from Ms Hunter until he turned up at the office today, and his PA tracked it back to Susan Hunter.'

'Am I okay to contact Forresters?' Jaime asked.

'Yes, of course. I suggest you contact Carol Flynn, she's definitely the smart cookie there. She's put in place their own HOLMES system, called it WATSON. It's an amazing set-up, and everything that happens within the business is logged into it. She's taken it right back to the first day when Dave Forrester opened the business, so it's a massive resource for them, but what's more important is that it's accurate. She just put the random number from Matt's phone into WATSON, and it came up with an immediate answer for the caller, along with the link to all information they held on her. I'll message Carol and tell her you may be calling her.'

'Thanks, boss.'

* * *

Jaime sat back and breathed a sigh of relief. It was always easier when the way forward was cleared for them, and she was feeling a little out of sorts, wanting the day to be over so she could crawl back into bed and sleep. The previous night's pregnancy test result had thrown a huge curveball into her life, and sleep hadn't really happened at all.

Her tiny one-bedroom flat had felt suddenly claustrophobic, and she had hurled the testing stick into her bedside drawer and headed out of her home, the home that now felt violated. Two hours of walking hadn't helped. It had produced a huge blister on her heel, but nothing seemed any clearer.

Jaime listened to the rest of the briefing in a mildly befuddled state, then opened up her computer as everybody stood to follow up on jobs that had been allocated. She felt somebody move to stand by her, and looked up to see Rachel.

'Can I help?'

'I don't know what to do.'

'Then welcome to the team. Half the time we don't know what to do, but miraculously we've never had a cold case. We've solved them all, either by good luck or ignorance. The biggest piece of advice I can give is do what I did when I joined Major Crimes – stick with the boss. In my case it was Matt Forrester initially, but when he left I simply transferred my allegiance to Karen. She'll talk you through everything, and she'll have your back when you balls something up. Just try not to kill anybody, it's frowned upon.'

Rachel laughed. 'I'll try. I've worked hard to get this transfer, so to use your words, I don't want to balls anything up.'

They watched as Karen's office door opened, and she headed towards where the two of them were watching her. 'Okay, Rachel, we're going back down to the crime scene. With the body out of the way, we can have a proper look around. I'll tell you anything that looks a bit off to me, and eventually you'll learn what to look for, not just in death cases, but in all major crime cases.'

* * *

They parked in the taped off area, and sat for a moment watching everything still being meticulously checked by the forensics team. The temperature was dropping and Karen shivered.

'That spring sunshine during the day certainly fools you into thinking warmer weather is on the way. Come on, let's go and see what we can see, and get back to the station.'

The Crystal Peaks shopping mall was separated from the retail park by a hillside and a main road. This resulted in the top of the access steps linking the two shopping areas being in the retail park, and the bottom of them being down in the car park of the shopping mall, linked by disability-friendly ramps and a long tunnel traversing under the main road.

Susan Hunter's body had been found at the top end, and the two police officers stood and simply looked.

'It's pretty, isn't it, when it's looking normal?' Rachel said quietly, her mind visualising the scene that she knew would never leave her, the one with a dead body and so much blood.

'It is, and I must confess I had never seen this little area tucked behind the shops before. That stainless-steel monument thing is stunning, and the two round seats with the plaques in the middle of them bear the names of children who were at the local school when this area was constructed back in 2004. It has such a peaceful vibe to it. Who would have thought...' Karen's tone faltered as she too remembered the scene from earlier in the day.

She turned at the sound of Martin Moore's voice behind her. It was only the second time she had met the new pathologist and she had liked his no-nonsense attitude from the first case they'd worked on together.

'Nasty one, this,' he said. 'I feel she was running away from something, and I suspect she didn't realise she couldn't get far because that tunnel, which goes under the main road, has a locked gate across from this side every night, once all the Peaks shops are closed. Whoever was chasing her would have easily caught her.' He paused. 'Like a rat in a trap.'

'And the PM?' Karen asked. 'I'd like to be there for it.'

'Eight o'clock tomorrow morning. I already have one in to do, so I'm heading back for it now, but I'm hoping it's straightforward. Ms Hunter, of course, is definitely murder, so anything but straightforward.'

Karen smiled at him. 'Thank you. If you do have to delay it, can you message me?'

He nodded. 'Of course.' He turned away with a wave of his hand and headed towards his car.

'He's nice,' Rachel said.

'He is. Not been with us long, so we're working on a smooth working relationship. It's always best to keep on the right side of the person doing the post-mortems,' Karen said, turning back to the area now looking blood stained but naked. The tent had been removed and initial forensics had been done in the immediate vicinity of where Susan Hunter had been found, but the two women took care to skirt around the edge of the contaminated area.

'So, let's go investigate.'

They walked past the grassed area where the steel monument was sited, with Rachel slowing to get a closer look.

'Wonder why they put this round a corner where you can't actually see it from the retail park?' she mused. 'It's a stunning little area. Strange...'

They continued to walk on a circular route until they reached the combination of steps and disabled ramps giving access to the tunnel. The gate had been re-locked following the discovery of the body, and the crime scene tape stretched across it to delineate inaccessible areas.

The gate had already been locked at the time of death, and neither Susan nor her killer could have gone beyond that point. Rachel and Karen peered through it just because they could, then walked back up, this time taking the more circuitous route of the disability ramps instead of the shortcut of the steps. They walked slowly, their eyes travelling from side to side, but found nothing to hold their attention except a pretty blue convolvulus flower near the top. It seemed to be the only flower surviving amongst the green hedges and shrubs lining the walkways.

'Nothing,' Karen said, 'but I'm glad we walked this part because I feel I know it now. I bet Susan Hunter thought she could get down to the safety of Crystal Peaks, that there would be people there, but she didn't even get to the tunnel. I wonder if she knew her killer to run from him like that, or if she just sensed she had a problem. Tomorrow we'll head to her home, do a thorough search and hope we can find a link to something that will tell us more. At the moment we have nothing. I'll take you, Ian and Ray. We'll go after the PM. You'll be okay at a post-mortem?'

'We'll find out tomorrow,' Rachel said, smiling at her boss. 'I have to do it, it's part of the job, and if I thought I couldn't handle death and all that goes with it, I wouldn't have even entered the police force. Honestly, I've loads to learn, and today has been a memorable starting point. I'll be in the office tomorrow by seven thirty, because I've never been to the morgue so you'll have to take me this first time, but for any after that I'll be able to meet you there.'

'That's fine.' They reached her car. 'Let's get this day over with, and I'll organise having Susan's keys made available tomorrow for us. A good first day?'

'A cracking one. I can't believe I thought I would be led gently into Major Crimes. How wrong can somebody be?'

5

The football was on television when Karen walked through the front door, and she heard the raucous shout of 'goal' from her partner and his son. These two always made her smile, and hearing them enjoying their football together was one of the best things in her life.

'It's me!' she called, but realised very quickly that she came second to the football. She headed for the kitchen, popped two slices of bread into the toaster and rummaged around in the cupboard until the chocolate spread came to light. Tonight she needed chocolate spread.

With the toaster popped, the chocolate on the

bread and the toast on a plate, she headed into the lounge. They both looked up in surprise at her entrance.

'Hi, sweetheart, didn't hear you come in,' Matt said, attempting to rise from the sofa.

'Stay where you are. Somebody had just scored a goal as I came through the door, so you didn't hear me. I'm going to sit over here and eat this toast, then possibly go to bed. Early start tomorrow again, and I've had a full-on day today.'

Matt looked at her, concern etched on his face. 'You okay?'

'We'll talk after the match.'

Matt took this to mean they'd talk after Harry had gone to bed. He gave a brief nod, but stood anyway to go make her a cup of tea to go with the toast. He suspected she hadn't managed to summon enough energy to feed and water herself, so he could do that for her.

* * *

Harry disappeared upstairs to finish some English homework temporarily abandoned when the football started, and Karen moved to sit by the side of Matt. 'I feel strangely knackered,' she said.

He nodded sagely. 'We should go to bed.'

'So I can feel even more knackered?' she asked.

'Did I say that?'

'No, and if not, why not? I only said I was knackered, not tired to the point of exhaustion. I think I need some closeness anyway. It's been quite a frustrating day. We have nothing to indicate why this has happened to Ms Hunter. Nothing was stolen that we're aware of, even her car was still there. Her phone was underneath her, and I think she threw her bag in the bushes in a sort of reflex action, because it wasn't hidden, it was just on top of a small laurel bush.'

'I've had Carol print off everything we have on her, which makes for some strange reading, I can tell you. Don't forget we never really got to the bottom of why she claimed to be very close to Dad, yet he never mentioned her, and seemed pretty relieved when she took herself off to Australia. Take it into work with you in the morning and have Jaime go through it with her eagle eyes.'

'Thanks, Matt. That's one job we can cross off for tomorrow. She okay to ring Carol if she has any queries?'

'Of course. Always happy to be of help to our police force.'

They sat quietly while Karen munched her way

through her food, enjoying the closeness of finally sharing moments after the stress of the day.

Her new PC, Rachel Quixley, had appeared to be quite level-headed and adaptable, and had definitely been thrown in at the deep end with her first day in Major Crimes. There had been significant blood loss from the victim, but Karen always felt it was the glassy-eyed stare of a body that was even more unnerving, especially to someone new to the team. She made a mental note to check that Rachel hadn't simply put a brave face on it, and she was truly as level-headed as she appeared to be.

'So Harry is okay?'

'He's fine. Seems to have palled up with a new lad, Isaac somebody or other, and they can try out for the school football team in a few weeks. It seems we have a bit of a goalkeeper in the family, which I'm dead chuffed about. Dad was a goalie back when we had a police team. A good one.'

'I've seen the photo on the canteen wall. Thought it was your dad. I'm glad Harry has a new friend; it'll hopefully make the return to a normal life easier. You taking him tomorrow?'

'He's asked me not to, so I've reluctantly agreed. Steve and I are going down to the Bath House tomorrow, sort out a quote for their upgrade on their security, so I can make an earlier start if I don't take him.'

'Thank goodness they're taking security a bit more seriously. We have uniforms down there a couple of times a week, There's always some attempted vandalism. It's such an old building, such a history-filled place, and it attracts thugs and vandals constantly. But I am envious. I've never been inside the place, have you?'

'Many years ago when they allowed schools to visit. What it really needs is a properly staffed building with paid workers, rather than the voluntary group that takes care of it. If it could be opened once again as a community resource it would be amazing. Can't see that happening though, I doubt the council could afford it.'

Karen stood and carried her plate and mug back into the kitchen, then returned to kiss the top of Matt's head. 'Come on, tiger, let's go to bed. And make sure Harry knows it's lights out time. He'll never get up for school if he doesn't sleep soon.'

But Harry was asleep already. Matt smiled as he looked at him, all too aware how close the pneumonia had been to taking away this precious boy. He gently closed Harry's bedroom door, and headed back down the short flight of stairs to his own room.

Karen was curled up, on her side, also fast asleep.

* * *

Tuesday arrived with the rain overnight continuing to the morning hours. The sunrise was non-existent, more of a dark cloud-rise, and Karen drove into work feeling optimistic that today would see some sort of breakthrough in the case. She knew the shops that had been forced to close because of the crime scene would be opening today, and she needed to speak to the pharmacist who had been on duty on Sunday night.

She briefed her team on everything they knew, which was precious little, then allocated Rachel to Jaime for a couple of days, once the post-mortem on Susan Hunter was completed. She would leave her newest recruit with each person for two or three days; they all worked differently, yet came together as a co-hesive unit when it was needed, and she wanted Rachel to see that side of teamwork, and to understand that sometimes she would be out in the field, at other times glued to a computer.

The post-mortem was over in just under an hour. Cause of death was a stab wound that had seen the victim bleed out very quickly. She wouldn't have lived for long after the penetration. The knife hadn't been serrated. Karen checked that Rachel was okay after seeing her first PM, then dropped her off to rejoin Jaime at the station.

She drove down once again to the retail park, and headed for Boots the Chemist. The night service window was locked and hidden by an internal blind during the day, but she walked over to inspect it. Medication was available via this window until 11 p.m. almost every night, but the shop itself was closed to customers at differing times. One thing was for sure, at 9 p.m., the time Susan Hunter had been in the area, she wouldn't have been able to access the shop. Only the window.

It was a large shop, and the pharmacy side of it was down at the bottom end, the furthest point from the entrance. She showed her warrant card and asked if the pharmacist who had been on duty Sunday night was available.

He had obviously heard her request, and walked from the sectioned-off glassed area where the dispensing of the medications was done.

'I am,' he said, holding out his hand. 'David Adams. If you go through that little door at the end, it leads to my office.'

* * *

They sat facing each other, and it occurred to Karen that it was about the same size as her own office. Diminutive.

'Thank you for seeing me,' Karen began. 'I wasn't really expecting you to be in, knowing whoever I needed to see had done a late shift on Sunday.'

'When I do a late shift I make sure the following day is left free for me to stay at home. I did that yesterday, and this week I'm working all days, which I prefer. It meant I missed it all yesterday. I kept getting little updates from the staff all day though, and finally heard we could open today, so I figured somebody would be contacting me. And here you are.'

'Here I am. I was down here most of yesterday, a pretty horrific scene, so just be grateful you missed it.'

She removed the photograph of Susan Hunter from her bag and showed it to him.

'This is our victim, Ms Susan Hunter. Did you see her on Sunday night?'

He took the picture from her and looked carefully at it.

'I did. I even spoke to her. She was pretty desperate for a prescription and she apologised for troubling us on a Sunday night but she said she had been ill with cystitis since Friday and her doctor had emailed a script through to us for her to collect. We also had her repeat medication here awaiting collection. She kept apologising. She said she'd hoped she could wait till the Monday morning but she was in so much discomfort and she was crying whenever she had to go for a wee, which was frequently because of the infection. I tried to reassure her, told her it was ready for her, and went to the prescription drawers to get the cystitis medication and her routine meds.'

He looked at her picture again. 'It's hard to believe she's dead now.'

'We believe she was attacked within a couple of minutes of leaving your window.'

'But...' A look of horror flashed across his face as he digested her words.

'What medication did she collect?'

'The one for her cystitis was a standard antibiotic for targeting that particular nasty infection, but her repeat prescription medication was for pain relief. She collected a two-month supply of Gabapentin and also Tramadol. She also collected a low-dose anti-depressant, which she has on repeat, Amitriptyline, plus she bought paracetamol and ibuprofen tablets because when the pain is extra bad, she can top up between doses of her normal drugs with the others.'

'Wow. Heavy-duty stuff.'

'She has... had... ME. Sufferers of this experience

pain all over their body at different times, it's a singularly unpleasant illness that doctors are really only just beginning to accept and recognise. ME stands for Myalgic Encephalomyelitis. It used to be called CFS, standing for Chronic Fatigue Syndrome, but now that has been replaced by ME. We talked for some time at the window because I was concerned. She really looked washed out, and she kept apologising for troubling me at an out-of-hours window. In fact, we have a camera on that window every night, you could actually see her.'

'Thank you. That will be a huge help. I'll get one of my tech colleagues to come down and do the download.' She sent a quick text to her colleague, DS Ray Ledger, knowing he would organise somebody to be at the pharmacy within ten minutes.

'So she had quite a package of medication. One bag held it all?'

'I believe I gave her a small bag with the cystitis meds in, and her repeat prescription was in a separate, larger bag. She also had a smaller bag with the paracetamol and ibuprofen in it. The repeat prescription had been awaiting collection for about four days.'

Karen stood. 'Thank you for your time. If you remember anything else, please give me a call.' She handed him a business card. 'Any time.'

He nodded. 'I will. And take care of the medication, it's powerful stuff she takes.'

'If only we could. She had none of the strong medication with her when we attended her body next morning, only the antibiotics. So, it seems we have found a potential motive for her murder, even if we have no suspect as yet.'

6

Matt and Steve travelled in to work in convoy. They had debated going in one car, but Steve needed to go out at some point to quote for a complete garden makeover for his landscaping business, and the decision was made to take both cars.

They did, however, take Matt's car down to the Birley Spa Bath House. They parked in a layby immediately opposite the entrance to the tarmacked track that led down to the building, and walked across the road. Matt had grabbed a small voice recorder as they left the office, and he now took it off automatic voice recognition, and put it on manual.

They walked slowly down the driveway, Matt commenting on anything that would present an opening for vandalism or theft, and by the time they reached the building itself they simultaneously reached agreement that to enclose the entire building in a twenty-foot-high fence would be the best thing to do. It was accessible by teenagers with a penchant for scaling ten-foot-high fences, which currently surrounded the house. It needed to be non-accessible. It was an unmanned building, and that left it wide open to anything nefarious such as rattle-can painting on the walls, and damage to any part of the exterior. It was a gift to drug dealers in the area as it was completely hidden from the main road, well known to the police as such, and Matt found himself hoping that the lottery grant was a substantial one, because this historic and fascinating place was more vulnerable than even their own office had been a year earlier.

'Isn't it weird how your memory of a place is completely different to the real thing, and yet it isn't this building that's changed. It must be me. I thought it was pretty big, but it's not really. When we come back to meet one of the volunteers tomorrow, we'll be able to get inside and see the pool. I also have a memory of that, but I now think it could be a false memory. I do vividly remember having a sip of the water and feeling scared in case it poisoned me, but it was beautifully cold and fresh. The pool itself is round in shape, with steps at the front that lead you down into it.'

'It's fed by a spring, isn't it?' Steve asked. 'Continuously freshened, I guess. And cold all the time. I've never been inside, so I'm looking forward to it. I think you were right to come and evaluate the outside first though, because we needed to do this without suggestions from the people who look after it. This one is special, isn't it?'

'The entire area is covered in springs, not just this Victorian bath. It can be a bit of a pain, but generally I think people enjoy the idea of having a spring that occasionally bubbles up in their garden.'

Steve took a few steps back and looked up at the roof. 'Vulnerable up there as well,' he said.

Matt nodded his head slowly, and continued to dictate their thoughts into the recorder. 'You ever been down to the ponds?'

'Never been here at all. How many are there?'

'Two, if I'm remembering correctly. When it was first built, one was for pedal boats, very popular place. It was a day out during school holidays and the like. Not sure what they're used for now, but watch where you put your feet because dog walkers come down here.'

* * *

They sank back into the front seats and Matt started the engine. 'Impressed?'

'Very. I can't believe I've never been to it before. It is a bit hidden from view in all fairness, but it's not advertised either, is it?'

'They occasionally have an open day, but I'm not sure they can now because that roof definitely looks dodgy. And putting that spiked fence round it doesn't really help. Kids can get over that. It needs to be taller. The whole place needs to be much more secure, but if they're going to allow the building to degenerate even further, is it worth it? The council tried to sell it a few years ago, but there was uproar in the community so they stopped the sale.'

He set off and headed over towards the office, with both of them discussing what they could do to the place if they owned it. Both decided they would need a lottery win of some magnitude to be able to afford to even repair the roof. It had been a truly memorable visit.

* * *

Carol was immersed in completing the input of the previous week's work as Matt returned. She looked up as the door opened, feeling quite startled.

'You're back!'

'And I made you jump,' he said, unable to stop smiling. 'Steve's not in this afternoon. Today he's a gardener. Got a quote to do over at Ecclesall for a full rework of the garden, and so he's going round to the other projects, just show his face and check everybody's happy. I'm going to put together some thoughts about the Bath House, things that have already occurred to us from this initial inspection, then tomorrow we're meeting up with one of the volunteers who takes care of the place. We're meeting her at ten so I'm hoping there's nothing to bring either of us in here first?' He raised his eyebrows in query.

'No, you're free until the afternoon tomorrow. Your first appointment is two o'clock, then you've a Zoom meeting at three o'clock with the alarms people. I confirmed earlier that it's still on, and it is.'

'Good. I need to talk to them about the Bath House, because this is going to be big. It's a mess, but totally daft putting any sort of security in place unless the roof is repaired first. Have you ever been?'

Carol shook her head. 'No, but I'd love to see it. Maybe I can go with you one day?'

'You certainly can. If our quote for the work is acceptable, they'll have to give us a set of keys and I'll take you down. Its biggest problem is that it's not visible from the road and therefore vulnerable to damage, as you'll realise straight away when I take you.'

She handed him his mail, and he turned to go into his own office.

* * *

Ray returned to his desk with the download of the CCTV from the dispensing window camera, and watched it through carefully. Then he called Karen.

'Already on my way,' she said. 'I was coming back to the station to collect a team, to go search Susan's house. Five minutes, and I'll be there.'

Temporary traffic lights on Birley Lane extended her five minutes to six and a half minutes, but she figured it wouldn't make a deal of difference. It was rare in policing to actually have a victim that you knew, and although Susan Hunter hadn't crossed her path as a product of her work, she had known of her because she had been a client of sorts for the Forrester Detective Agency. It made the case a little more personal, and being at the post-mortem had hit her harder than it usually did. It was definitely the least favourite part of her job.

She headed into the briefing room to find Ray, Jaime and Rachel there, with Kevin and Ian both out doing follow-up work on a recent drugs arrest that had suddenly escalated.

'Any news from Kevin and Ian?' was her initial question.

'They've requested a custody van, so I'm guessing it was well worth their surprise visit.' Jaime smiled as she spoke, but then switched off the smile. It was as if a light had gone out, and Karen felt herself shiver. She hoped Jaime wasn't considering moving on from her team, but for the past few days she hadn't been her usual self. She had to make time to talk to her.

Her eyes moved to Ray. 'Do we have something?'

'Kind of. We can actually see somebody by her car. Look on the wall screen, it might be clearer than on the small screen.' He pressed a button and the wall screen lit up. They all swivelled, and Karen walked towards it. They watched the entire six minutes and thirty-five seconds that Susan Hunter had been at the night window before leaving to go back to her car. She then appeared to swerve, and was suddenly out of range of the shop CCTV. No one spoke, until Karen said, 'Replay, please, Ray.'

She asked that it be paused four times in total then at the end turned to face them.

'Thoughts?'

'Somebody was definitely by her car.' Jaime spoke first, then nodded in agreement of what she had said, as if stressing she knew it was fact and not an imagined thing.

'Definitely.' Ray and Rachel spoke at the same time.

'And she saw whoever it is, because she swerved away from the car as she reached it. Sensed danger?' Rachel continued to stare at the screen. 'Can we see it again, Ray?'

He repeated it, letting it run through until Susan disappeared from the scene.

'Does it go further, Ray?' Karen asked.

He continued for a further minute then stopped it. 'It shows nothing once Susan leaves the area.'

'But whoever stabbed her had to come back. Let it run for a further ten minutes. He or she couldn't get down those stairs into Crystal Peaks because the gate was locked, so he had to come back towards the retail park after he'd stabbed her. And how the hell did they know what drugs she had just collected? Was it just a lucky hit? Did she tell her attacker she had

Gabapentin and Tramadol then try to give them to whoever it is, in order to save her life?'

They continued to watch and just as Ray was about to stop it, a shadowy figure appeared. It moved around the driver side of Susan's car, briefly ran a hand along the bonnet, then ducked down and disappeared, now out of the range of the camera.

'That's him,' Ray said quietly. 'And it's a him.'

Karen nodded. 'I agree. And I'd say a youngster. It's a start, but we'll get him. I know we don't have an explanation of why she rang Matt Forrester, but I'm kind of leaning towards it being an accidental call. Her phone was found underneath her, and her contacts list is small. I know Matt is concerned that he didn't answer her, but I genuinely think she was possibly already dead or very close to death when it called Matt.'

'I think you're right. If the time on the CCTV is accurate, the two happenings are only about a minute apart. Wrong place, wrong time for this victim.' Ray sighed. 'Tomorrow I'll go down and do a timing check on the CCTV system at the pharmacy so that when this comes to court we have the answers.'

'Rachel, I don't think we're going to find anything at the Hunter house that will give us any lead on this, but we'll go across there now. The two of us can handle it, I believe. Ray and Jaime, just watch this again, very slowly. Any tiny detail... but I don't need to tell you.'

7

Susan Hunter's home was one of a small huddle of houses on a cul-de-sac of eight dwellings built around 1930, with most of them having been modernised and brought into the current century with ease. It was a pleasant, quiet neighbourhood, and Karen and Rachel walked through the front door, both of them snapping on gloves automatically as soon as they entered the hall.

Karen's intuition was telling her Susan's death had been about getting the drugs off her, and she truly didn't expect to find anything of consequence at this address, but it had to be ruled out.

Everything was clean and tidy. There was a glass on the draining board, but other than that there was nothing out of place in the kitchen. Karen checked all cupboards and drawers, then moved into the lounge, a compact room that held a two-seater sofa and a matching armchair, a small coffee table and a television on a stand in one corner. On the back wall was a small bookcase with around thirty paperbacks on it, and Karen knelt in front of it, systematically removing one book at a time, shaking it and replacing it.

They were all crime novels, and she took care to put them back in the same order – Susan had kept them in pristine condition and alphabetised by author surname. A brief flash of envy passed through her – how she would love a little more organisation in her own life. Their own bookcase was full to overflowing, with odd books now having to lie on top of the upright ones.

This pale green room was calm, and Karen took a moment to enjoy the pleasant feel that Susan Hunter seemed to have created. It felt a little sterile, almost as if nothing was allowed to be out of place, and she thought once again of the lounge she shared with Matt and Harry; its sometimes chaotic feel held little resemblance to this haven. She preferred her chaos. This small lounge was a room for one person.

The hallway had a tiny room attached to it, and a couple of coats were hung up. Karen quickly checked the pockets, made a mental note that there was just one pair of knee-high boots and a pair of Nike trainers, before closing the door behind her. Rachel was coming down the stairs towards her, and she saw her shrug her shoulders before speaking.

'There's nothing.' Rachel's face held a slight frown. 'She's so tidy. The bed was slightly ruffled, as if she'd lain on top of it, but we know she'd been feeling ill with cystitis so that was probably why it was a bit un- tidy, but even her towels in the bathroom were on the towel holder. Everywhere up here is spotless. The second bedroom has a desk, so I brought the laptop.' She held up an evidence bag. 'I couldn't get past the password bit, so I'm assuming we need to take it to somebody who can.'

'You went through the desk?'

'I did. Just stationery. It seems she likes notebooks. About half a dozen, but all blank. She probably likes to stroke them.'

Karen laughed. 'Stroke them?'

'Yes. Don't you stroke books?'

'I write in them.'

'Oh.' Rachel decided it was time to shut up, but it was too late.

'Go on then. You stroke paper?'

'Everybody does who likes notebooks. It's a thing.

I've got lots of them. People buy them for me for all sorts of odd reasons because they know I like them. I've got some quite expensive ones. Mum and Dad bought me one for Christmas, and because I chose it, I know it was over £70. I'm not sure I'll ever dare write in it, but it's the most beautiful thing.'

'Good lord.' Karen's voice was faint at the thought of a notebook costing that much. 'And this is something other people do, just collect notebooks?'

'Yes. I'm pretty sure our victim simply collects them. She had one on her desk that she wrote in, a log for the books she had read since January. She must have started it about fifteen months ago, because it starts the previous January then she ruled it off in December. Started a new list this January. She makes a note of whether a book is on Kindle, or a paperback. So I guess somewhere she probably has a Kindle, but it wasn't upstairs anywhere.'

'We'll check with forensics. It may have been in her car, in case she had to wait any length of time to get her prescription. Are we done here?'

'There's a shed in the garden. I could see it from the office room. Should I go and look?'

Karen handed her the bunch of keys. 'Yes. I'm just going up to the office, I need to see these notebooks. Stroke them,' she added with a laugh.

And stroke them she did. She tried to get inside the late Susan Hunter's head, tried to feel what she probably felt at the acquisition of a new notebook, but Karen knew it was beyond her. It was simply paper. And she found herself thinking that whoever cleared out this house, which Susan would never again enter, should treat these notebooks with respect.

Rachel reported that there had been very little in the shed; a lawn mower and a few hand tools. And a huge spider.

They returned to the station, Rachel handing in the bagged laptop to forensics before heading up to the briefing room.

* * *

Karen looked around, hoping everybody was there, then moved towards the whiteboard where she scrubbed off the house visit they had just completed. She waited for Rachel to join them before she checked around the rest of her team for any reports.

There was very little that anyone could say. Jaime had gone through the file sent over by the Forrester Agency, then spent a pleasant fifteen minutes or so chatting to Carol Flynn, who had filled her in on the way she had felt stalked by Susan, after Susan had seen her at the graves of Dave Forrester and his business partner Johnny Keane. Although Jaime hadn't known Dave Forrester in person, only his name as an ex-DI who had been seriously injured on duty, Carol had made him come alive as she had spoken of him with such fondness. It seemed Susan had believed he had cared for her, but Carol had vetoed that idea, saying they had Dave's journal and that told a different story.

Jaime finished repeating all she had discovered to the rest of the team, with the occasional nod from Karen as she recalled the Susan Hunter issues from a few months earlier, little bits she had forgotten.

Ray reported he had been down to Boots and confirmed the timings on the CCTV camera used at the night window, and it was accurate to a couple of seconds, so they could take it that everything they had seen on the recording was spot on.

Kevin and Ian had been back down to the crime scene to give it one final detailed inspection before allowing the removal of the tape and the opening of the locked gate at the end of the tunnel linking Crystal Peaks shopping mall with the retail park where the murder had occurred. They had followed up this activity with a trip to Susan Hunter's doctor, Sarah Chambers.

She had proved to be more than helpful, having seen reports of her patient's murder. She confirmed the medication for the cystitis had been prescribed via a telephone call rather than a personal visit, and it had been faxed to Boots Pharmacy on the retail park, as all of Susan's prescriptions were dealt with in that manner. She also confirmed that Susan's repeat prescription, obtained every two months, had been dealt with in the same way, three days prior to her request for antibiotics. Her ME caused her considerable pain and fatigue and had progressed to the stage where she could no longer work, hence the high dosage levels of her pain relief medication.

They had thanked Dr Chambers – she could have refused her help, they both realised that. But she held up a hand. 'I liked Susan. Why anybody would want to do this to her I really don't know. If there's anything else I can help with, please contact me.'

Karen was impressed. Some doctors simply closed them down, but others helped as much as they could. Today they had been lucky.

She turned to Rachel. 'Okay, Rachel. Our turn now. You go first.'

She saw the deep breath taken by her youngest member of the team, and tried not to smile. She knew the next time she asked Rachel to report, she wouldn't think twice about it, but the first time is difficult.

Rachel spoke clearly and concisely, basically saying she had found very little upstairs. It was extremely clean and tidy, she had bagged and tagged a laptop that she had dropped off with forensics, and she had found a very large spider in the shed.

Karen's report was almost the same – how tidy it was, how clean, almost as if the person who lived there did nothing inside her home except sit quietly and allow the world to pass her by. 'I suspect,' she added as an afterthought, 'that Susan has a cleaner come in to take care of her home. If she is as ill as the doctor is suggesting, and the strength of her medication does confirm that, then keeping that house as clean as it is would probably be beyond her. Maybe we should have crime scene tape across her door with a message on it asking anybody requiring entry to contact South Yorkshire Police. If a cleaner does turn up, it will stop her going in, and hopefully get her to contact us.'

'Good idea,' Kevin said. 'I'll call and do it on my way home. I live quite close to where she lives.'

Karen nodded her thanks and asked Jaime to produce a notice for the door. Jaime spun her chair around and faced her computer, then stood and leaned both hands on her desk. She suddenly moved, and almost ran out of the room.

The others looked at one another, obviously puzzled.

'Is Jaime okay?' Karen asked.

'Not sure,' Ian said, 'but she proper snapped at me this morning when I asked what had happened to her smile. I was joking, but she has been a bit snarky for a couple of days. She said something about only smiling at people who were important to her. I was a bit taken aback by it, because we've been partners at work for a couple of years now, but clearly I'm not allowed to overstep some mark I didn't know existed.' He shrugged. 'Should I...?'

'No, I'll go and find her,' Karen said. 'Ian, can you cobble together a notice for Kevin, then everybody can get off home. We've had a long day, back here for eight tomorrow unless you hear otherwise.'

* * *

Karen walked down the corridor and into the ladies' toilets. If Jaime wasn't in here, the next port of call would be the canteen. After that she figured tracker dogs might be her next idea.

The tracker dogs weren't needed; Jaime was indeed

in the ladies' toilets, leaning against one of the sinks, and splashing cold water onto her face. Her eyes were red, suggesting there had been tears that required washing away.

'We need to talk?' she asked, slipping an arm around the younger woman's shoulders.

Jaime's head slumped and she took a huge breath. 'I think so. I know I'm upsetting everybody, but it's because I'm bottling stuff up. We're Major Crimes, and that says everything really. Most crimes these days are major, and we just have no time for the personal stuff. But I've got personal stuff, and I don't know where to turn.'

Karen pulled her closer. 'I've sent everybody home. I'll go make us a cup of tea, and we'll sit in my office and talk about what's wrong. Give it five minutes to make sure everybody's left. That okay?'

Jaime nodded. 'That's okay. And thank you, boss.'

8

Karen smiled at Kevin, Ian and Rachel as she passed them in the corridor, saying good night to each of them. She reached the office to see Ray was still there.

'Do me a favour, Ray,' she said quietly, 'and don't ask any questions. Will you go home? I need an empty office at the moment.'

He nodded. 'Course I will, boss.' He picked up his jacket from the back of his chair and turned to leave. 'And tell Jaime if I can do anything to help...'

'Thanks, Ray. See you tomorrow.' She smiled at the man she trusted as much as she trusted Matt, and knew he wouldn't say anything to anyone until he knew what the situation was. And even then he would keep it to himself, if it was possible.

She went into her office and switched on the kettle. Jaime walked through the door as she was fishing tea bags out of the cups.

'Okay?' she asked her ashen-faced colleague.

Jaime nodded. 'I have to be. You've guessed?'

'That you're pregnant? I half guessed. You don't look well, yet you hadn't said you were feeling poorly. You hid it.'

The sound emanating from Jaime was half hiccup, half moan. 'I didn't want to tell anybody...'

'How far on are you?'

'Nearly three months. I've an appointment for an abortion for Wednesday. I intended booking a few days' leave, but now this case has cropped up.'

'Woah! Let's start at the beginning. That's a big step to take. Is that really what you and the father want?'

'There is no father,' was Jaime's short and terse response.

Karen waited a moment, her mind racing in circles. 'No father? Let's go back to December. Christmas? You met somebody around Christmas?'

'I was stupid. Incredibly stupid,' was Jaime's muttered reply, her head down, her hair hanging in front of her face.

Karen moved to stand by her side, holding out Jaime's cup of tea. 'Here, you look as though you need this. And you are not stupid. Far from it. Tell me what happened. Then I can help you get through whatever you choose to do.'

Jaime lifted her head, moved her hair back from her face and sipped at the tea. 'Thank you,' she said quietly. 'I need this, my stomach is churning.'

'Begin at the beginning. I'm here for as long as you need to talk.'

'Remember us all going to the pub for those Christmas drinks?'

Karen nodded. 'I do. Matt and I went, and everybody on the team at various times. Lots of uniforms in there, and even the Super popped in as well. It was a good night.'

'It was. I got chatting to some of the uniforms I knew from when I was with them, and we had a pretty loud and over-the-top night. I decided to walk home, to try to sober up a bit, and one of the uniforms, who I'd known for about three years or so, said he was going in my direction so he'd see I got safely home.'

Karen waited quietly while Jaime wiped away tears.

'You invited him in?'

Jaime nodded. 'I'd pretty much sobered up, and he asked to use my toilet before carrying on to his own home. After he came out of the bathroom, he asked for a glass of water, and I went to get it for him, pouring one for me as well. He carried them into the lounge and we sat for five minutes, just chatting and sipping at our water. That's the last I remember of that night.'

'He drugged you?'

'I believe so. Next morning I woke up with him standing by my bed, getting dressed. He assured me nothing had happened, but I had suddenly gone to sleep so he helped me upstairs, then slept on the other side of the bed to make sure I was safe. Would you believe I actually thanked him for taking care of me?'

'Oh, Jaime. And I have to ask this. You haven't slept with anyone else?'

'Not since this time last year in Lanzarote.'

Karen tried to hide the smile at the woebegone expression on Jaime's face, failing miserably. 'Don't laugh at me,' Jaime said. '*That* was sex worth having. This wasn't, obviously, if I can't remember it.'

'So it was non-consensual sex. It was rape, let's not pretty it up with legalese. You're going to get the bastard?'

'I have made some decisions. I'm not going to report it. I'm going ahead with this abortion, but I will need a little time off, boss. I'm sorry. If I report it, I have no proof. I showered that morning in an effort to get rid of the stinking headache, and of course my clothes were washed within a couple of days.'

'You didn't feel sore?'

Jaime shook her head. 'Not at all. He's probably only got a little dick.'

The tension vanished and Karen hugged Jaime. 'That's my girl. Now, I don't want you in tomorrow. The others will only be nice to you if they suspect there's something wrong, and you'll end up telling them, so let's take that away from the equation. Take sick leave, tell them you're going to stay with your mum in Leeds for a few days, and only come back when you feel you can. I mean it, Jaime. Don't come back too soon. It's quite a major operation. I'm sorry to be so blunt, but that's what you're doing and you need to take care of your health. But now tell me what you've got planned for the little scrote with the tiny dick. Because I've known you for a long time now, Jaime, and I know you won't let this go.'

When Jaime smiled, her face always lit up. Suddenly it resembled a beacon. 'I am still at the decision stage. Don't ask me any more, boss, and I promise you that whatever I do, it will be legal. Almost, anyway.'

She finished her cup of tea, and carried the cup towards the small sink at the back of the room. 'I'll go to my mum's for a few days. The clinic is in Doncaster, so I can get there easily from Leeds.'

'You'll tell your mum?'

Jaime nodded. 'I will. She'll be as angry as I am, so I'll take care not to reveal his name.'

'Can I have his name?'

Jaime hesitated. 'Leo Hampton. Although you could just inspect every male uniformed officer's dick, and whoever has the littlest one, that's probably him.'

* * *

Karen watched through her window as Jaime walked across the car park. She ached for the girl; such a massive decision on such young shoulders. She would need careful monitoring when she came back to work, and Karen decided that it was maybe time to book her in for the IT course that was on offer to start in October. Jaime's eyes had lit up when she had seen the email, and had mentioned it a couple of times since. If she had a definite booking for it, it would give her something to look forward to, and maybe take her away from the planning of whatever she intended doing to the man who had violated her, then lied about it.

Karen had grown to know and care for Jaime over

the couple of years they had worked together, and she was in no doubt that Jaime could be, and probably would be, merciless. PC Leo Hampton needed to permanently be casting a glance over his shoulder at least twenty times a day.

She waited until Jaime had driven out of the car park before gathering together her bag and coat. She knew she would tell Matt; he had a wise head on his shoulders, and would probably come up with something to ease her own troubled thoughts. She hated not being able to say anything to Ray Ledger, but for the first time ever she had to keep something from him. He would immediately want to rush off and protect Jaime with everything in his power, because that was the way Ray handled everything, full on and caring.

In fact, she guessed her entire team would want to give their support when she told them the following day that Jaime was taking some time off on doctor's advice. She would ask them not to try contacting her because she was spending a few days away in the country with her mum; hopefully that would satisfy their natural curiosity.

She drove home with a deep feeling of sadness. Jaime had learnt a very valuable life lesson and Karen's heart ached for her. Now Karen had to decide what to do next – PC Hampton was a bent copper, and bent coppers weren't wanted or needed in her world.

As she entered her front door, she could hear gales of laughter coming from the lounge, and knew Matt and Harry were in there watching something on television. She popped her head around the door and felt her senses lighten a little. 'Pizza and a few chips?'

Both said, 'Yes, please,' at the same time, and she held up a thumb in acknowledgement, before heading into the kitchen and ferreting through the freezer. Being late home meant a quick meal, she knew the men in her life would be hungry.

And as if on cue, Matt joined her in the kitchen. 'What can I do?'

She smiled at him. She always wanted to smile at him. 'Frozen chips and frozen pizza? Nothing to do. We'll eat at the kitchen table, so if you want to find some drinks and plates and stuff, that would be good.'

'You fancy wine?'

'How did you know?'

'Your voice. Something's happened. To do with Susan Hunter?'

'No. Nothing to do with her. We'll talk later when Harry's in bed. And let's not have a heavy wine. A white zinfandel, maybe?'

Matt set the table, opened the wine and replaced it in the fridge until the meal was ready.

'Harry's away this weekend. He's going to his mum's straight from school on Friday, and she'll take him in on Monday morning. I think he's missing baby Florence.'

She nodded. 'I'm sure he is. He mentioned her a couple of times on Sunday, and I was going to suggest he might want to stay at his mum's for a few days. I'm glad he's decided to do it. I know we've never set up a strict agreement for Harry spending time with his mum and baby sister on a regular basis, but he must miss her. And thankfully that bloody Brian Davis is well out of the picture now.'

Matt frowned. 'Last time I spoke to Becky at any length, she was saying his child support payments for Florence were intermittent, and he was a considerable sum of money behind. I'm keeping out of it, obviously, but she certainly needs to get it put on a more official footing, rather than him saying he'll pay her a certain amount each month. If the police knew...'

'He'd be in serious bother,' Karen finished off. 'Right at this moment in time I'm a bit fed up with police officers that shouldn't be in the police force, but are.' She shuddered. 'More later on that subject.'

She opened the oven door and checked on the pizzas, then lifted them out on to the side, moving the tray of chips to the top rack to finish browning. 'Give Harry a call, will you? I'll just cut these up, and we can eat. And for goodness' sake, let's have some of that wine poured out. I need it.'

9

Josh Earnshaw had had a shit-awful day. He'd spent two hours in the sick bay at school because he'd had a bad asthma attack and it took some controlling, then to his horror one of the teachers had taken him home, deeming it unsafe for him to be in school with his breathing being so erratic. This meant Mr Jackson saw his mother in all her drugged-up glory, uncombed hair, glassy-eyed and almost incomprehensible in her speech. He'd never felt so fucking embarrassed in all his life, and everything got a lot worse when Mr Jackson passed him a bit of paper with his telephone number on it, whispering if he needed any help, he'd to ring him and he'd get help to him. He'd been glad to see the teacher go, but then he realised his brother

Freddie wasn't anywhere around, and he began to worry about things going pear-shaped with the asthma. It was a sure thing his mother wouldn't be able to handle it if things got bad again, like they had been just after he'd got to school.

His spray had been neither use nor ornament and he guessed it was maybe time for a doctor's visit to get his breathing checked. It seemed a long time since his mother had been stable enough to organise it, so he reckoned he might have to do something about it himself. He'd never been to the doctor's on his own, first time for everything, he decided. His chest felt tight and he used his spray again, but it eased it only slightly. He couldn't understand why he was feeling so bad, it was months since he'd had anything like this.

His mother seemed to have disappeared – he knew she didn't like visitors to her home, didn't like having to attempt some sort of control over her movements. He went upstairs, and found her fast asleep on her unmade bed, the curtains closed and a strange smell in the room that he knew was probably today's drug of choice, and made by Freddie. It was starting to become concerning that Freddie was giving his mother drugs that she didn't know she was taking, sipping at her cup of coffee without thinking too much about the strange taste other than to guess maybe the milk was a little off. He took a blanket from the end of the bed and pulled it up over her, then quietly closed the door. He checked out Freddie's room but it was only to confirm what his mother had said about her elder son being out. He could try threatening Freddie with him going to the police to tell them what he knew, but he was a bit scared that Freddie would start drugging his drinks too, and then who would take care of Mum?

Despite his thoughts and convictions about what his brother was up to, Josh felt uneasy not having Freddie at home. Although he had tried bravado as a cure for his breathing difficulties, the earlier attack had been scary. There had even been talk of sending for an ambulance, but he'd managed some limited control and the alternative had been to get him home safely and into the care of his mother. He snorted at that thought as he remembered their words. The care of his mother. Every day he expected to find her dead when he got home.

Josh went to his own room, set the alarm on his phone for thirty minutes just in case he fell asleep; he needed to keep a close eye on his mum. He couldn't cope if she popped off. She was the only one who seemed to have some control over what Freddie was asking of him with certain deliveries, and he knew he'd got major problems if she wasn't around to handle his brother.

When the alarm went off, he forced open his own eyes and went to see if there was any chance of his mother opening hers. There wasn't. She was fast asleep, emitting small snores, and he smiled. At least she hadn't died.

He returned to his own room and once more rested his head on his pillow. That was when he heard the front door open and close, and recognised Freddie's footsteps as he moved around the lower rooms.

There was absolutely no reason for Freddie to know he was there, Josh reasoned. He'd stay quiet and hope Freddie would go out again. That seemed to be the pattern now built into his brother's life, in and out, in and out, never saying where he was going, keeping secrets.

He heard Freddie climb the stairs, then discerned his footsteps passing by his own door and along to their mother's room.

'Mom,' he heard Freddie say quietly, then the bedroom door closed once again. Clearly his mother hadn't answered her son. Josh figured she was still unconscious.

Freddie went back downstairs, pottered around for ten minutes or so, then Josh heard the front door open and close. He ran to the bathroom, peered out of the window and watched as Freddie headed down to his car, the red Astra he loved so much. Josh breathed a sigh of relief, returned to his room and finally closed his eyes to seek the sleep his body was telling him he needed.

* * *

Josh headed to the kitchen around six, made himself some beans on toast and took some upstairs to his mother. She smiled at him as he touched her shoulder to wake her.

'Josh,' she said. 'You okay, lad?'

'I'm fine, Mum. Think you can manage some beans on toast?'

She struggled into a sitting position, and he laid the tray across her knees. 'I'll be back in quarter of an hour,' he said. 'Eat as much as you can. I'm going back down to get mine now.'

She smiled her thanks, and he wondered if she would be able to stay awake long enough to eat more than a mouthful.

Freddie returned some ten minutes later, and he clapped Josh on his back.

'I need you tonight for a little job,' he said, and Josh

felt inordinately angry that Freddie assumed he would do whatever was asked of him, without it actually being asked.

'To do what?'

'Just need you to take this package across to the Bath House. A minute's job. Worth a tenner to you. Hand it over to the feller who's meeting you there, he'll give you an envelope to bring back to me, and job's a good 'un.' He handed over the white paper bag, sealed with Sellotape, to his brother.

Josh doubted that very much. Job was probably a bad 'un. Job probably was a handover of drugs.

'Why can't you do it?'

Freddie paused as he was leaving the kitchen. 'Why can't I do it?' There was a silence in the room, and Josh felt more than a little uneasy. 'I can't do it because I've to go to Doncaster tonight, to see a man about a shipment. Then I'm going straight to an overnight party.' Freddie grinned at the thought. 'But I've promised this package to Kingy, so I need you to drop it off for me tonight. And don't ever fucking query it again, Josh. Just do as I say, deliver it and get back home. Ten minutes tops. Okay?'

He growled the last word, and Josh shivered. He felt the tightening in his chest and he reached into the back pocket of his jeans for his inhaler. He used it, and said a very quiet, 'Okay,' to Freddie.

'He'll be there for nine, so don't be late. I'm off now, see you tomorrow. Take care of the mother, she looks well out of it.'

'She's okay,' Josh muttered. 'I've taken her some food up.'

Freddie stared at him for a moment, perhaps wondering how his younger brother could have possibly come from the same parents as him. Then he raised a hand in salute, turned and left the house. 'See you tomorrow,' he called from the front door, 'and put that envelope under my pillow.'

Josh walked into the hall and slid the white paper bag into the pocket of his school blazer that he'd hung on one of the hooks at the bottom of the stairs when Mr Jackson had brought him home. It was as safe a hiding place as any, he reckoned.

He trailed upstairs to find his mother had eaten most of the slice of toast, a few of the beans, and had drunk the full glass of water. The tray was at the bottom of the bed and she was asleep once more.

He carried the tray downstairs, ran some hot water and washed up the few dishes he had used for the two of them. Halfway through he felt the now familiar tightening in his chest, and he took out the inhaler, sat at the kitchen table and breathed in the medication. He placed it on the table, then dropped his head onto his arms and just rested for a few minutes before returning to drying the dishes and putting them away.

* * *

He checked on his mum just before he set off and she was awake, but opted to stay in bed. She said it was hardly worth the effort of going downstairs, so she'd get up in the morning, feeling much better.

'I'll only be ten minutes or so, Mum. Just got a little errand to do for Freddie, then I'll come back, get everything locked up and make you a nice cup of tea if you're still awake. If you're not, I'll see you in the morning. Mum... if Freddie comes back and makes you a drink, do me a favour and don't drink it. Ever, not just tonight.'

'You're a good lad, Josh,' Lynn Earnshaw said, wondering how on earth she'd managed to produce such different kids. 'Hurry up and come home, won't you? And then you can tell me what you mean by not drinking Freddie's drinks.'

'I will, Mum, don't worry.'

* * *

The Birley Spa Bath House was literally two hundred yards away from the council house shared by the Earnshaws, and Josh crossed the main road and headed down the quite steep path leading to the historic building. He walked around the side, then halted as he reached the back. There was nobody there, and he glanced at his phone to check the time. Five to nine.

He leaned against the railings and waited, but when he heard approaching footsteps coming up from the pond area below the building, he straightened.

He recognised Kingy, and took the white paper bag out of his pocket. He walked across to the man he had learned to detest through making previous deliveries for Freddie, and handed it to him. 'You've got an envelope for me?'

'Hang on a minute, kid. I need to check this is the genuine stuff.'

He ripped off the Sellotape and took out some white boxes. He opened them, throwing the small cardboard pieces on the floor. 'Oh, yes,' he said, quietly, and smiled.

'Don't chuck the rubbish on the floor,' Josh said. 'Envelope, please,' and he held out his hand. He felt more than a little uneasy, wanted to get home. And his chest was tightening by the second. He reached for his back pocket but it was empty, and he had a momentary flashback to the kitchen table, where he'd placed his inhaler during his pot-washing session.

Kingy approached him, and grasped him around his throat, forcing him backwards, pushing and pushing until he smashed Josh's head into the iron railings.

Josh tried to scream, but his breath simply wasn't there. He felt the pressure of Kingy's hand increase, and then everything went black. He wasn't aware of the blood pouring down the back of his head, wasn't aware as Kingy's foot kicked him hard between his legs, wasn't aware that he wouldn't be making his mum a cup of tea at any time in the future.

Kingy stared down at him, stamped hard on his foot, and walked away, shouting instructions to Josh to pick up the damn rubbish himself if he was that bothered about litter picking. He'd give the damn envelope of money directly to Freddie Earnshaw, and tell him not to send kids to do a man's job next time. In the meantime, he had the Tramadol, the Gabapentin, the Amitriptyline, all drugs craved by his girls and difficult to get a hold of. He didn't know how Freddie Earnshaw had got them, but he'd slip an extra tenner into the envelope as a bit of a bonus. Freddie'd maybe give it to the lad for making the delivery.

He walked down past the ponds, threw all the

white pharmacy packaging away as he walked, and exited the area onto Dyke Vale Road, where he'd left his Jaguar. He got into the driver's seat, drove without exceeding the speed limit, and gave himself a pat on the back as he reached his home without having broken the law in any way on the journey.

10

Wednesday dawned, a slightly different outlook to the previous day. The intermittent drizzle of Tuesday had disappeared, and by seven o'clock the rain was torrential. Karen offered to drop Harry at school to save Matt doing it. Harry, of course, grumbled that he wasn't a little kid any more and could go on a bus, but both his father and Karen stared at him without speaking. They didn't need to say anything.

By the time Karen and Harry left the rain had eased a little, and negotiations with reference to Harry returning from school via a bus ride had been completed. He would be allowed to do it from that day onwards, and they would see how the return journey went before agreeing to a bus ride to school in the morning rush hour.

Karen dropped him off, blew him a brief kiss to save him the embarrassment of having a real one, and grinned as she drove away. She loved that kid, she mused. He had his dad's sense of humour and good looks, and she suspected he would go far in this world. They needed to play their part in getting him backwards and forwards to school safely. His three-day absence when he'd left home had been the worst time of their lives, and something they would never forget.

She drove into the police station car park, grabbed her umbrella and ran for the door being held open for her by Ray Ledger.

'Lousy morning,' she said. 'Let's hope we've got indoors work today.'

'I'll second that,' Ray agreed. 'But you ever heard of sod's law?'

* * *

Matt had a full day planned. He had arranged to meet Steve at the office, then they would go in his car over to the Birley Spa Bath House, where the plan was to meet up with someone from the volunteers who took care of the place. A senior member of staff from the alarm company, Sam Bonnington, would also join them to give advice on what was needed, and where, and then the three of them would go somewhere for lunch, have a brainstorming session and come up with some costs to send to the volunteer group. The lottery grant had provided for the initial overhaul of the security of the place, plus ongoing costs for three years, and Matt and Steve were keen to see a good deal offered to the group.

Steve arrived five minutes after Matt, and Carol thrust a coffee into his hands. 'You'll need this to fortify you against this awful weather. Sometimes I envy you being able to get out and about, but there's no envy there today,' she said with a laugh. 'I've booked you in for lunch at twelve, for three of you, at the Vicarage. If you need to add to that, they said it will be fine. Just let me know by text and I'll give them a ring. I've explained it's a business lunch, and they're putting you on a corner table so that you can talk as much as you want. That okay?'

'Carol Flynn, what would we do without you?' Steve shook his head, then sipped at his coffee. He already felt cold and damp, and he'd only walked from his car.

'Let's get on our way,' Matt said. 'We hopefully will be first there, gives a good impression. And today I'm hoping we get inside the place, and don't take a tumble into that pool.'

Steve grinned. He'd been waiting to see the inside ever since the job had arisen, and he could take a bit of rain as well, he reckoned. He waved his cup around. 'I'll take this with me. I promise to bring it back again,' he said.

'You'd better do, young man,' Carol said.

'Pinky promise,' Steve said.

'Oh, that's different then, if it's a pinky promise. Matt. Make sure he returns it.'

The two men were laughing as they got into Matt's car, and both of them waved as they spotted her watching them.

She shook her head, and returned to her desk. It still amazed her every day that she had landed on her feet with such a job, and the camaraderie between the three of them was a joy. She pulled the jobs completed ledger towards her, and began the day's invoicing, ready for when Matt and Steve returned and they could check them. It would be a quiet day without either of them popping in and out, and she wanted to give the reception area a bit of a clean and a polish if she could make time for it. She pulled up an invoice template and began to type.

* * *

Matt parked on the main road and the two men got out. Their first action was to look over the metal railings that separated the building at the bottom of the hill from the main road.

'It needs at least two cameras trained on the access lane,' Steve mused. 'They need to be too high for anyone to reach to damage them, and preferably too high for anyone to see them to know they're there.'

'Agreed. The biggest issue is: will the recordings be clear enough to identify anyone? This is a priority for discussion with Sam at lunchtime.' Matt turned his head. 'But just take a look down the road to the corner of the next road on the left. There is a tonne of new equipment, new technology, all very recently installed. This whole area has just had new cables, new Wi-Fi stuff, and all the corner of that road is where the controls are. Well protected. We could maybe talk to them about placing a camera high up on their mast. It's worth a shot. If not, we're going to have to put in a high pole or two ourselves. Seems a shame to have to have a camera in plain view when we could effectively hide it in amongst all the technology in that little area.'

Steve walked a few yards further down the road and

saw the collection of brand-new equipment, concealed inside equally brand-new white containers. It all looked very smart, but also very secure. They needed to research just who they needed to contact, but he guessed Sam Bonnington might have the answers they needed.

He walked back to Matt. 'No idea what that lot's all about, but my guess is we need to talk very nice to them. Come on, let's get down the hill, there might be a bit of shelter. We can at least stand under a tree.'

They headed down the narrow lane leading to the Bath House and circled the perimeter of the railings. It was as they reached the front of the property that they saw the body.

* * *

Matt knelt and felt for a pulse. He knew it was a waste of time, but he had to do it. He looked at Steve's white face, and shook his head.

'Okay, you ring Carol. Tell her to cancel Sam, cancel whoever is coming from the volunteer group, and cancel the Vicarage. Thank God we came early. I'll ring Karen.'

* * *

Karen was in the morning briefing when her phone rang. She was shocked to see Matt's name – their unwritten rule of communication by text was strictly adhered to, and she knew something was definitely wrong. Her first thought was Harry, and she waved her phone at the others. 'Back in five,' she said. 'I have to take this.'

She stepped into her own office and closed the door behind her. 'Matt?'

'I'm ringing you as DI Nelson,' he said. 'Steve and I have just got to the Bath House, and there's a body. No pulse, young lad about maybe fourteen or fifteen. I've checked for life, but definitely extinct. Need a tent urgently or this bloody rain is going to wash everything away. We'll stay here but obviously won't touch anything.'

'Be there in five minutes,' Karen said. 'We're all at the station. You know the lad?'

'No. And I've not checked pockets or anything. He may have ID on him. He's so young, Karen.'

'Five minutes,' she repeated and disconnected.

She re-entered the briefing room, and within a minute everyone was on their way. They took police vehicles, using blue lights and sirens, with Karen requesting urgent forensic back-up with a tent to protect the scene. She also requested two uniformed constables to monitor comings and goings at both entrances to the Grade II-listed building, which would have to have crime scene tape sealing it off from dog walkers and anyone else wanting to get out for a walk, rain or no rain.

They parked their cars behind Matt's car, and Karen, Ray, Kevin, Ian and Rachel headed down the lane. Matt and Steve stepped back, allowing Karen and Ray access to the body. Karen repeated Matt's actions of confirming lack of pulse, and turned to cast a look at her partner. She shook her head, then stood. She moved towards him and he wanted to take her in his arms and hold her. He didn't. He knew what she was thinking – this young lad was a similar age to Harry, and now he was gone.

'What can we do?' Ian asked.

'Nothing until forensics get here. Martin Moore is on his way. He'll say what's what, where we can go, but we can't risk contaminating the scene. Rachel, contact the station and see if we've any missing teens been reported overnight.'

Rachel held up a thumb and took out her phone. She spoke for a couple of minutes and then disconnected. 'Only one,' she said, 'and that was a girl who has now been found. It makes it even worse that nobody has missed this poor lad, doesn't it?'

Karen nodded. 'It does. What the hell was he doing here? And who was he with? There's blood underneath his head, and his neck has some hefty bruising on it. I'm pretty sure Martin will be confirming murder when he gets him back to the autopsy suite. Right, I need to talk with Matt and Steve, just to confirm their actions once they found him.'

Ray was already with the two private detectives, but he walked away as Karen approached. 'See you later, boss,' he said, and Matt threw his arms up in the air.

'I can't get through to him I'm no longer his boss,' he said, and Karen grinned.

'We all wish you were,' she said. 'So, talk me through you arriving at this point.'

'Not much to say. We had a meeting planned, a meeting about security at the Bath House. We arrived, did a bit of surveillance from up top, actually on the main road, then walked down the lane. When we got to the bottom we saw the body. I immediately checked for a pulse, Steve stayed out of the way so there was no transference from him, but I had to check. I couldn't just assume...'

Karen touched his hand. 'I know,' she said softly. 'I'm going to need you to come into the station to give a statement, but it shouldn't take long. We've got top and bottom access points sealed off with tape now, and a PC stationed at both points, so you'll have to sign out when you leave.' She turned at the sound of the pathologist's voice.

'I have to talk to Martin,' she said. 'I'll see you later. You and Steve are free to go, but maybe tomorrow for your statements?'

'You'll let me know when you find out who he is?'

'Of course. Oh, thank goodness the tent is going up. Maybe some answers will be arriving soon. I'll ring you, I promise.'

Steve and Matt began the trek up the incline back to the main road, gave their names to the constable standing at the top, and ducked underneath the tape.

The journey back to the office was travelled in complete silence.

11

The rain had lessened by the time the body was removed. Martin had decided he could find out more by getting the young boy back to his autopsy suite, because he didn't appear to have any identification in any of his pockets.

Underneath the body he found a squashed white packet, a pharmacy box that had held tablets, still intact, still dry and bearing a name on the front that both Martin and Karen recognised – Ms Susan Hunter. The box had immediately been placed inside an evidence bag to be transported back to the lab for further forensic examination, and Karen's team searched for any more of the same in the area. They found two other screwed-up boxes, sodden with rain, and placed them in individual evidence bags to give them as much protection as possible.

* * *

With the body on its way to be further examined under drier conditions, the forensics team began to search the grounds. Karen and her group headed back to the station – without a name, there was nothing they could do. By eleven o'clock, Matt and Steve had arrived back in the office, and Karen and her unit had returned to the briefing room.

* * *

Also by eleven o'clock Lynn Earnshaw had pretty much cleared her head of the slight overdose she had wallowed in on the previous day. Once again she vowed to knock it off altogether, promised herself she would say no next time Freddie offered her something new to try. Whatever it had been that he gave her, she could remember very little of the previous day, other than a teacher bringing Josh home because he'd had a severe asthma attack.

Her morning shower had done much to revive her, and she popped a slice of bread in the toaster, before switching on the kettle. A strong coffee and toast and marmalade might just get her back onto the right track to get through a miserable-looking Wednesday, she figured.

It was quiet in the house. She had no idea where Freddie was, never knew where Freddie was, but her lovely Josh was at school. He'd be home around half past three and she could have a chat with him, make sure he was okay. He perhaps needed an assessment appointment at the doctors; they could sort that out later.

She placed the toast and her cup of coffee on the table and sat down. That was when she spotted Josh's inhaler.

'Shit,' she muttered under her breath. Could he have taken another one? She went to check in the drawer where his medication was stored, but he still had two in there.

She felt panic begin to build in her. He had been brought home the day before, the attack had been so bad, and now it seemed he'd forgotten to pick up his inhaler, something that was normally stuck like glue to him.

She picked up her phone and rang school. She began by thanking them for making sure Josh had got home safely after his asthma attack, then explained she'd just spotted his inhaler. She was concerned he hadn't got one, in view of the previous day's attack. Lynn could feel the panic rising in her.

'But we assumed you'd kept him at home, possibly to see a doctor?'

'What do you mean?'

'Josh isn't in school, Mrs Earnshaw.'

'Are you sure?' Panic was now threatening to engulf her. 'I'll check his bedroom.'

'I'll wait here. You go and look, then you can let me know he's okay.'

Lynn threw her phone onto the table and ran upstairs as fast as she could. She checked Freddie's room first as it was the first one on the landing, then opened the door of Josh's room.

Empty.

She checked her own room, the bathroom, even, stupidly, the airing cupboard, then careered back downstairs, stumbling as she reached the bottom.

'He's not here,' she gasped into her phone. 'You're sure he didn't arrive for registration this morning?'

'No, definitely not,' the voice at the other end of the phone said.

Lynn thanked her, said she'd be in touch when she found him, and disconnected. Her first thought was to ring Freddie. Maybe he'd know where his brother was, but her call went straight to voicemail. She simply said, 'Ring me,' and switched off.

She didn't know what to do. Yes, she could ring the police, but the repercussions from Freddie would be bad. She knew he had much to keep hidden from the eyes of the law.

She tried calling Freddie again, but still no response. A flare of anger engulfed her – this most precious of her boys was missing, and she had no idea where he could be. She could barely remember the previous day at all, yet tried forcing her brain into some sort of normality. Had Josh said he was staying over somewhere? She knew she was grasping at straws. He wouldn't stay anywhere but at home if he was having an asthmatic episode.

She opened the back door, needing air. Stepping outside, she headed across the back lawn, and stood, taking in deep breaths as she wondered where to turn next.

'Ey up, Lynn.'

She jumped, then realised it was the voice of Phil Overend, her neighbour who lived in the house attached to her own. She hadn't realised he was in his garden. She quickly dried her tears, not wanting him to ask questions.

'Bad do across the road, isn't it?'

'What?'

'Police cars all over the place, everything down at the Bath House taped off. Summat must have 'appened, like. You not heard owt?'

She shook her head, feeling a deep sense of unease settle somewhere between her stomach and her feet.

'No,' she said. 'I've not been up very long. Brain not in gear yet.'

'There's talk on that Facebook thing that they've found a body. Perhaps somebody's fell in one of t'ponds. Can't trust owt that's said on there, though, can you? I'll let you know if I hear owt else.'

She said a muffled thank you and headed back into the kitchen, down the hallway and out of the front door. Almost immediately opposite two squad cars were parked, then a large black van, with another squad car in front of it.

The unease began to overwhelm her, but she tried to shrug it away. Of course it couldn't be connected to her Josh, there would have been no reason at all for him to be down at the Bath House, and definitely he wouldn't have been anywhere near the ponds.

She stood watching the general activity, along with most of her neighbours. This was normally a very quiet part of the estate, their houses being so close to the Victorian building, and also on the main road.

It suddenly dawned on her that the worry about Josh should also be extended to a worry about Freddie. Neither of them had been contactable and she had no idea where the hell either of them was.

Could they be together? If they were it would be a first-time activity. Freddie was a good six years older than his younger brother, and so far in life they had managed to avoid having to be with each other.

She stood for half an hour then began to shiver. The rain that had stopped for a short space of time was starting again, and she headed back indoors. She leaned against the front door to close it, and remained there, allowing her thoughts to run riot. Should she go across the road, find a policeman and say her sons were missing?

She decided to give it another half hour, and if she hadn't heard from at least one of them, she would venture across the road and mention her problem. That would give them the chance to say they had found a body, but it was a pensioner with dementia who had wandered out into the rain and couldn't find their way back home. Not one of her boys. Or even both of her boys.

Lynn sat at the kitchen table once more, and dropped her head until it rested on her crossed arms. The prayer for help came into her mind, and she asked the God she truly believed in if he could see his way to sending her sons home. 'I ask this in Jesus' name, amen.' She finished her prayer, then added a further amen, as if to emphasise how important it was.

She stood and crossed to the sink to get a glass of water, then whirled around, spilling half of it, as she heard the click of the front door opening, then closing. She almost threw herself into the hall, and saw Freddie.

Wrong one, was her first thought. Guilt washed over her.

'Freddie, where the fuckin' 'ell have you been,' she screeched at him.

'Whoa, calm down, woman,' he said. 'What's going on over the road?'

'I've no idea. It's been on Facebook that a body's been found, and I was scared...'

'That it was me? Nah, I was at a party over at Middlewood last night.'

'So why didn't you answer your phone?'

He took the iPhone out of his pocket and clicked the sound back on. 'Sorry, I turned off the sound, didn't want it ringing out when I was... well... you know...'

She hit him across the face with a blow that sent him reeling backwards. He immediately raised his own hand and she stared at him. 'I fucking dare you, smart arse. I fucking dare you.'

He dropped his arm and stared at her. 'Sorry,' he said.

'You will be,' she retorted. 'Just because I've kept quiet about what goes on in this house, and in that locked shed in the back garden, doesn't mean I'll always stay quiet. Before your father died, he made sure I knew everything, and knew how to look after myself. For some reason you wanted me out of it yesterday. I don't know what you gave me, or when you gave it to me, but you can now start to look for somewhere else to live. Yesterday your brother needed me, and I slept the entire day away and he looked after me, instead of the other way round. Do you know where he is?'

'School, I should think.' Freddie sounded subdued, aware of all he was losing unless he could sweet talk his mother around.

'He's not at school, according to them. He's also not got his inhaler with him, and he had a bad asthma attack yesterday, as you would have known if you'd spoken to him.'

'I did speak to him,' Freddie admitted, then wished he'd kept his mouth shut.

'So you saw him last night?'

He nodded, knowing she was putting two and two together. She'd always been good at maths.

'Did you send him out to deliver something?'

And he very deliberately lied. 'No, of course I didn't. He told me he'd had a rough day, and was going to have an early night. Tell you what, I'll head up to school, see if he's anywhere on his usual route. He might have had another attack. I'll handle whatever needs to be done if I find him. That okay?'

'You ring me straight away if you find him,' she said. There was a threat behind her words, and he nodded before heading back out the front door.

Lynn felt tears slide down her cheeks. She walked to the kitchen window and looked out across the main road towards the increased police presence. What the hell was going on? She watched Freddie drive up the hill, and wondered if he would find Josh. Somehow, she thought not. Where was he, this younger son, who was so different to his older brother? She again offered up another prayer that he hadn't suffered another asthma attack, one that couldn't respond to medication, because that medication was on her kitchen table. 'Amen,' she said, 'amen.'

12

Karen couldn't settle. The deceased was clearly a young lad, and somebody somewhere must be missing him. There had been no reports of a missing teenager and that fact was causing her considerable concern.

'Jaime,' she called, before remembering that Jaime was taking time out from work. 'Sorry, I mean Kevin. Can you do a ring round the local schools, find out if they've got anybody who's absent without explanation?'

'Can do, boss,' Kevin responded, and pulled up the phone numbers on screen. He was fortunate that on his first call he got the same member of staff contacted by Lynn Earnshaw. He spoke to her explaining the issue, and she gave him details of Josh Earnshaw, beginning with the asthma attack the day before. She explained that his mother had rung in to say he'd forgotten his inhaler, and they had had to say Josh hadn't arrived at school. She gave details of the address to Kevin, before they disconnected.

'Could have an ID here, boss,' he said.

He told Karen the full story, and the two of them drove back to the road still busy with police vehicles.

She stared up at the houses that faced the old building, and knew this was where the boy had lived. She felt sick.

She hesitated for a moment, taking deep breaths, then opened the car door. 'Come on, Kevin, let's hope this young lad has turned up, and we're barking up the wrong tree.'

They headed up the incline of the small, grassed area, crossed the pavement and walked up the shared path. The house on the left was their destination.

The door was opened immediately and a woman stood there.

'Mrs Earnshaw?' Karen asked. She held out her warrant card. 'DI Karen Nelson, and this is DC Kevin Potter.' Kevin produced his warrant card in confirmation. 'May we come in for a moment?'

They watched in horror as Lynn crumpled to the floor. Karen manoeuvred around her, and between them they managed to get her upright, and staring vacantly around her as her senses began to return to normal.

'It's Josh, isn't it?'

'We don't know,' Karen said gently. 'Let's get you sitting in a chair with a glass of water, and we can talk.'

With one each side of her, Lynn was led gently into her lounge and lowered to an armchair. Kevin went to get her a glass of water, and Karen leaned forward to take her hands. 'You'll feel better in a minute,' she said, 'once you have fluid inside you.'

Lynn nodded, and drew in a deep breath. 'I'm sorry,' she said. 'I'm just feeling so worried...' and she began to explain her son's disappearance, stressing how unusual it was for him not to tell her where he was.

'My other son has headed off up towards his school to see if he can find him. It's the asthma, see, and we know he hasn't got an inhaler with him.'

'Is that Josh?' Karen asked, and stood to head towards the fireplace, where there was a photograph of Lynn and her younger son.

She nodded. 'It is, taken about six months ago.'

Karen picked up the photograph, and closed her eyes for a moment, recalling the face she had seen on the body a couple of hours earlier. She replaced the picture and turned around.

'Mrs Earnshaw – can I call you Lynn?'

Lynn nodded. 'Of course.'

'You've seen all the police activity across the road?'

'Yes.'

'That's because we were notified of a body, found lying outside the Bath House. We have now removed the body for forensic examination, as there was no ID on him.'

'Him?'

'Yes, and I'm so sorry, Lynn, but I believe it to be your son, Josh.'

* * *

Lynn drained the last of the water from the glass, and Karen gently removed it from her hands, heading into the kitchen to refill it for her. The woman had been distraught, and Karen couldn't help but compare it to how she herself had reacted when Harry had been missing for three days. She glanced out of the window as she was running the water to get it really cold, and saw a car, a red Astra, pull up outside. Instinct told her to take a photograph, but instinct changed the photograph to a video. She watched the young man lock his car door, then walk around the front of the car before unknowingly retracing their own footsteps as they had approached the house.

He walked in the front door and Karen timed it perfectly as she carried the glass of water through to Lynn.

'Who the fuck are you?' His sneering tone almost caused him to have a glass of water poured over his head, but Karen resisted the thought.

'DI Karen Nelson,' she said. 'And you are?'

'I live here.'

'I didn't ask where you lived, I asked your name.'

'Freddie, Freddie Earnshaw,' he muttered.

'Thank you, Freddie. Can you wait in the kitchen for me, please? I'll just take this water through to your mum. I'll let her know you're here, she's told us you were out looking for Josh.'

He glared at her but said nothing further, sitting at the kitchen table to wait for her to return.

Karen handed the glass to Lynn, who was struggling to get her sobs under control. 'I'm sorry,' she said, 'I can't stop crying.'

'You don't need to stop,' Karen said gently. 'I am going to have to ask you to identify him, but that can wait until tomorrow. He's in safe hands now, and being looked after.'

'Is Freddie here? I thought I heard the door open.'

Karen nodded. 'He's in the kitchen. I'm going to have a word with him, then I'll send him through to you. Kevin will look after you for a few minutes.'

Kevin moved to sit opposite Lynn, and Karen left the lounge to return to the kitchen.

Freddie glared at her as she entered the kitchen.

'What's going on? Why are you here, hassling my mum?'

'Freddie, shut up.'

He opened his mouth, then closed it again.

Karen ran a hand through her hair, focusing her mind. 'You've been out looking for your brother?'

'Yes.'

'And can you tell me where you were last night?'

'I was at a party at Middlewood. One of the lasses I know lives there, and her parents are away so we had a party. I stayed over, arrived back here about an hour or so ago. Then I went out to look for Josh in case he'd had an attack on the way to school. I couldn't find him though.'

'Address of party, and names of people who attended.'

He took out his phone, opened up his notes app

and showed her an address. 'That's it. She's called Tanya Sutherland. About eight of us stayed the night, so she could probably give you the names. What's going on?'

'We believe we have found your brother. A body has been discovered down at the Bath House, and I'm sure it is him. I've seen the photograph in the lounge. Your mum will be attending tomorrow probably, to formally identify him.'

Freddie was struggling to speak. He opened his mouth and initially nothing came out. He tried again, and croaked, 'Josh is dead?'

'We believe so. Do you know what he was wearing when you left to go to your party last night?'

'Jeans, Nike hoodie, Adidas trainers. He'd changed out of his school uniform when they brought him home from school. Did he have an asthma do?'

'We'll know more after the post-mortem,' she said, unwilling to add anything else.

'Can I go with my mum tomorrow?'

'Of course you can.'

Karen was warming slightly to the abrasive young man who had first walked through the door. 'I'll contact one or two of the people at the party to confirm your alibi, but if you can think of any reason why Josh would be down at the Bath House, please call me.' She handed him her card, and he slipped it into his jeans pocket.

'Can I go to my mum now?'

'You can. And Freddie, I'm truly sorry for your loss. Look after Mum, she's in a bit of a state, as I'm sure you probably realise.'

He stood. 'Thanks.'

'Just one more thing – do you have any idea why Josh would have been down there on such a miserable night? It was pouring with rain, he was having asthma issues and he knew of the dangers of that, and yet he was down that dark lane.'

'I have no idea. I thought he was going to stay in his room and watch TV, he said he was tired. It affects him like that, when he has an attack.'

She paused a moment, then nodded. 'Okay, Freddie, let's go through to your mum.'

* * *

Karen watched as Freddie pulled his mother into his arms, and they just hugged each other without speaking.

'Lynn, I'll arrange for a car to collect you tomorrow. I believe Freddie wants to attend with you, and that's absolutely fine. I'll ring you in the morning and tell you what time, we should have more news to give you by midday, when the post-mortem and test results are all done. Is that okay?'

Lynn nodded, still wrapped in Freddie's arms, and allowing her tears to fall like the raindrops still running down the windows.

'We'll leave you to be together now,' she continued, 'and if you need to ask me or tell me anything, I've given my card to Freddie. We're deeply sorry for your loss, both of you, but I promise you we'll find out who did this.'

Lynn's head slowly moved to stare at Karen. 'So it wasn't just an asthma attack?'

'We'll know more tomorrow,' Karen responded. 'It may well be that asthma is the issue, but we have to check everything when it is an unexplained death.'

But Karen had seen the bruises around the neck, had seen the blood pooled under Josh Earnshaw's head and the damage to the back of his skull where it had hit the iron railings surrounding the building.

And she had seen three small white medication boxes from a pharmacy with the name Susan Hunter on them. Somehow she had managed to acquire two major crimes that were inextricably linked – it was the job of her team to discover why they were linked, and who now had the serious medication that Susan Hunter should have been taking.

Karen and Kevin returned to the car, and they both sat without speaking for a couple of minutes. The last hour or so had been harrowing, especially the situation once they had both seen the photograph and knew they were in the right home. Josh had been a young-looking fifteen-year-old, with a wide grin, sparkling brown eyes and dark hair, bearing little resemblance to his older brother who had blue eyes and blond hair, although the blond hair wasn't natural, but almost white.

Karen somehow felt the two brothers were unalike in most ways, not just in looks, and she knew she needed to dig further into the life of Freddie Earnshaw. If he was on the police radar, it hadn't reached her specialist unit, but she sensed something was out of kilter with Freddie. His attitude had become aggressive when he realised who she was, and yet it hadn't been necessary, the aggression. Was it fear on his part?

'Kevin,' she said, slipping the car into gear finally and preparing to drive away, 'take Freddie Earnshaw apart. I want to know everything about him. Who he hangs around with, confirm his alibi for last night, everything. Something's not sitting right, and at the moment I'm torn between arresting him for murder and giving him a hug because he's lost his brother. That's not a good place for my head or my heart to be in, so let's find out who he is, and where he stands in all this, okay?'

'On it, boss,' Kevin confirmed, and sat back for the two-minute journey to the station.

13

Karen sat at her desk and leaned back, closing her eyes. It had been a harrowing morning, and she needed a little time out. Her phone pinged, and she reluctantly pulled it towards her.

It was a message from Jaime, and she opened it.

> It's done. They offered to keep a sample from the foetus in case I needed DNA evidence. I agreed. Just in case. xxx

Karen responded with:

Ring me later, hope everything went well. Sensible thing to do, the DNA sample. xxx

She stared into space for some time, her thoughts with Jaime and what she must be feeling. Murderous thoughts, probably. She couldn't imagine having to make such a horrendous decision as Jaime had just had to make, and she knew that for the rest of Jamie's life it would be cemented into her brain cells, this action she had undertaken. She realised Jaime must have been acting on instinct when she agreed to a sample of the foetus being retained – sometimes you just knew when an action was needed, and she suspected Jaime had been at that point.

Maybe, just maybe, she needed to protect her DC. Remove the temptation for revenge that must be within her, albeit temporarily buried. Karen stood and left the office, heading downstairs to where the uniformed officers were based, led by Sergeant Alan Chantry.

She poked her head around the door and spotted him immediately. He waved, his face immediately creasing into a smile.

'If it isn't my favourite DI,' he said. 'You time for a coffee?'

'If it's a quick one, Alan,' she said, and sat in the chair facing him.

He stood and went to get them drinks, handed the cardboard cup to her and sat. 'You okay?'

'I am.' Karen dipped her head. 'But I've an issue I need to discuss with you. We can keep it between the two of us, or...'

Alan frowned. 'Somebody's in trouble?'

'Possibly. If not now, I would say for sure in the future, and I'm trying to prevent that trouble being on our patch.'

Chantry stood and went to close the office door, making his tiny room feel even more claustrophobic than it had earlier. 'I'm assuming it has to stay between us?'

Karen nodded. 'Preferably, but I'm prepared to take it further if I have to.'

'And that's why you're a DI and I'm a sergeant.' He smiled, staring at her face. She looked so stressed, he thought. 'Come on, Karen, what's it about?'

'You have a PC works in here called Leo Hampton?'

She saw Alan stiffen. 'I do.'

'Would you miss him?'

'A bit. Why?'

'I'm going to suggest you have him transferred.

Preferably either to the northernmost tip of Scotland, or Land's End.'

There was a brief lull in the conversation, then Alan continued. 'What's he done this time?'

'This time?'

'About eighteen months ago he had a complaint made against him by one of our female officers. Couldn't keep his hands to himself, and he took no notice of her telling him to back off. So she came to me, asked for a transfer, then told me the reason why. I couldn't talk her out of it, not even by offering to transfer him, so I had him in on a disciplinary. But as far as I'm aware there's been nothing since. The lassie is now on the Major Crimes unit in Newcastle, and is as happy as Larry.'

Karen sighed. 'Then pin back your ears, I've something to tell you.'

* * *

Alan listened to everything that Karen had to say, then pushed his chair away from his desk. He stood and walked towards the window. She didn't speak, simply waited for him to digest everything he'd just heard.

Finally he turned to face her. 'He'll be gone by the time your Jaime returns to work. These lassies make it so difficult to simply sack him outright because neither of them have made an official complaint, but I can make an unofficial one and it will follow him to wherever he ends up. He'll never be anything other than a PC, I'll make damn sure of that. God, Karen, I really don't know what to say. You really think he put something in her glass of water?'

'Jaime thinks so. She says the walk home had helped sober her up, and although she still felt good, she was over feeling drunk. Then she remembers nothing else.'

Alan gave a slight nod. 'Do you trust me to handle this?'

'Of course I do. Just send him to Outer Mongolia if you can. Nobody else knows about this other than Jaime and her mum – and me, of course. We need to keep it that way, so you can't even tell him why he has to transfer.' She stood. 'Good luck with it, Alan. Can you let me know when he's gone, please? I'd like to be able to give Jaime the good news.'

'He'll be gone by the weekend, I promise.'

* * *

Karen took a long drink from her bottle of water, then allowed a small smile to appear. She hoped she had done the right thing for Jaime – she didn't want to take the chance of Jaime handing in her notice, so a little interference on behalf of her DC had felt necessary.

To discover that Hampton had an unofficial report already against him hadn't really surprised her, so she had felt better about raising the problem on behalf of Jaime. It would be over quickly, and once Jaime had recovered physically, even if she hadn't mentally, things could return to normality. She hoped.

She leaned back in her chair, and thought through everything that had happened at the Bath House; her mind gave her the picture of the young boy lying there, sodden after the heavy rain, and wondered at the connection that was obviously there with the Susan Hunter case. The immediate issue of identifying Josh Earnshaw had been dealt with, and the notification to his next of kin.

Lynn Earnshaw's face had been ashen; Freddie Earnshaw's face had been... guilty. She took out her phone and opened up the small video she had taken as Freddie Earnshaw had arrived, parking his car on the main road outside his mother's house. She watched as he opened his door, climbed out, then walked around the front of the car, trailing his left hand along the bonnet as he did so.

He walked up the slight incline of the grass verge,

then the video stopped as she lost sight of him around the side of the house.

She rewatched it, then sent the video to Ray's email. She didn't want to give him any clues in case she was seeing something she wanted to see, so simply put *Watch this* as the message.

She waited two minutes and he appeared in her doorway.

'You reckon he runs his hand along all car bonnets?'

'Maybe,' she said. 'I knew I wasn't imagining it. I'm not bringing him in yet, he's not the sort to collapse in a blubbering heap and confess to everything, so we need something a bit more concrete than running his hand along car bonnets. If he thinks we suspect him, he'll disappear. I don't think he had anything to do with his brother's death, his alibi definitely stands up. He wasn't even this side of the city. Four people have confirmed it, one rather scathingly because he apparently spent the night in bed with somebody one of the other lads had been fancying. No love lost between Freddie and this lad, so no cover-up either. I'll be glad when we get the autopsy report. I could almost believe the asthma attack killed him, if it wasn't for the head injury. That was caused partly, I believe, by a brutal push against those iron railings. There was such a lot of blood. If the asthma kicked in at that point, he wouldn't survive.' She hesitated for a moment at the overwhelming sense of sorrow that suddenly overwhelmed her. 'Didn't survive.'

'But we didn't ask him for an alibi for Sunday night...'

'I know. That will come when we bring him in, just for a chat, after he's been with his mum to identify Josh.'

'You're thinking what I'm thinking?' Ray asked.

Karen nodded. 'He was somehow on the periphery of his brother's death, but Josh definitely didn't die by Freddie's hand. However, Susan Hunter's empty medication packets were at the scene, and I think Freddie Earnshaw probably had quite a lot to do with Susan's death. We just have to work out who the second killer was, the one who battered a child's head against iron railings, who left him to die gasping for breath with no inhaler to help him breathe, and I suspect Freddie may be able to help with that, don't you? Fortunately he doesn't know about the packets we found, so is probably feeling unconcerned about the body discovered at the retail park. He's got a shock coming very shortly, has our Freddie.'

* * *

The Freddie in question was concerned at the reaction of his mother to the tablets he held in his left hand.

'I don't want your fucking muck,' she screamed at him, and he slid the contents of his hand into his jacket pocket.

'Well, they're there when you do,' he said.

'No more, Freddie. Get all your stuff out of this house, and anything that's in your shed. I'm burning it down tomorrow, and I swear if you're in it when I light the match, you'd better be able to run fast.'

He stared at her. 'You're throwing me out?'

'No, I've thrown you out. I don't need you with me tomorrow, I'll identify my best son on my own, without the criminal son with me. And I swear, Freddie, if I find out you're in any way connected to Josh's death...' she sucked in a breath and gasped aloud as the words left her mouth, 'I'll be burying two sons.'

Freddie stared at her. She needed to calm down. He could make her a cup of tea and drop a couple of pills in it. 'Mum, you know I had nothing to do with it. I wasn't even here. I loved our Josh, he was my mate.'

'He was your mule,' Lynn spat out. 'I know you paid him to run errands. Is that what he was doing?'

'No, he probably just went out for a walk to help clear his lungs.'

'That had better be the answer the police come up

with, I'm warning you, Freddie. You've until tomorrow night to get out of here, then I never want to see you again. And the shed is going up in flames tomorrow afternoon, whether you're inside it or not.'

Shock was etched on Freddie Earnshaw's face as he realised the consequences of his brother dying. He'd always thought she preferred Josh, but by God, it was very evident now. How the hell could he talk her round from what she was intending doing? And where could he go? This had been a cheap gaff, with a more than pliable landlady when she had some pills inside her, whether or not she knew they'd been imbibed.

'Mum,' he said, with what he hoped was a genuine-looking smile on his face. 'I'm going to miss Josh as well, you know. He was my kid brother. Let's calm down, and I'll go make us a cup of tea. Open the ginger biscuits? Come on, we'll go in the lounge.'

He held out a hand towards her, and she reached towards the work surface. When her hand came forward, it held a long, pointed knife. 'One more step, Freddie, and I'll use this. Let's see how you can pack up your car with only one hand, shall we? A cup of tea? And how many tablets would you put in it? Trust me, lad, you haven't got enough to calm me down.'

14

Rachel Quixley sank into the squad car on that overcast Thursday morning, and wrinkled her nose. Whoever had been in it the previous night had eaten fish and chips. The vinegar odour was lingering, and she opened the windows wide, sitting for five minutes as she waited for the smell to disperse. It wouldn't look good turning up to collect grieving relatives being transported to the morgue, with this fragrance to greet them.

She had time to spare so she opened all the windows, drove up Sheffield Road, then Occupation Lane, before turning right at the top to lead her back down Birley Spa Lane. She carefully swung the car around at the end of Springwater Drive and drove back up the main road, parking outside the Earnshaw home. She hoped the vinegar had now dispersed; she sniffed as she exited the vehicle, but could no longer smell it.

She rang the doorbell and heard a tinny female voice say she would only be a minute; it always made her smile when doorbells spoke to her. So many people had them now, they must be a real problem to the criminals of the world.

When the door was eventually opened, Lynn was dressed in a black trouser suit. 'Am I okay?' she asked. 'I couldn't wear anything with colour in it, so I settled for black and white. It feels as though the colour has gone out of my world.'

'Mrs Earnshaw, you're fine. Is Freddie coming with you?' Rachel had instructions to collect Lynn and Freddie.

'No, he's gone. I don't know where he is, and I care even less. I heard his exhaust about six this morning. This has been brewing for some time, and yesterday afternoon I asked him to leave. You only need one person to identify my son, don't you?'

Rachel felt a little flustered, but hid it from Lynn. 'Yes, of course.' She was concerned – at the morning briefing the talk had been of suspicions around Freddie Earnshaw, and now it seemed matters had escalated as far as he was concerned, because he'd disappeared.

'Do I have to sit behind you?'

Rachel smiled at the woman who was as tense as a coiled snake. 'No, sit by me. And don't worry, I'll be with you every step of the way. You're not going through this alone.'

Lynn fastened her seat belt, and sighed as she leaned back. 'My husband died,' she said. 'He would have been at my side through all of this, he was a lovely caring man. Josh takes... took after him. Freddie is like my father's side of the family. It's probably where he is right now, but he can't come back to me. We were once a family of four, but now, as far as I'm concerned, there's only me.'

Rachel squeezed Lynn's hand and started the engine. 'Come on, let's go see your boy. Then we'll have a cup of tea, and dry some tears. Yes?'

Lynn nodded, and closed her eyes. 'It's been a long night,' she said. 'I need the crime scene tape to come down, so I can go and be where my boy drew his last breath. Does that sound weird?'

'Not at all. When it's possible, you do whatever you need to do. You have good neighbours?'

'I do. The one I share a path with is especially close, they knocked twice last night to check on me. I think they must have seen Freddie packing up his car and emptying his shed, all unusual stuff, so kept popping across. I didn't see Freddie go, but I no longer need to burn down his shed because it's empty.' The thought finally brought a genuine smile to her face. 'He's taken everything from his bedroom as well, so I'm finally a Freddie-free zone. You know, I always thought I needed him, especially after his dad died, but I don't. I'm going to keep Josh's room exactly as it is, because I can go and sit in there and be with him, but I'm chucking all the furniture out of Freddie's room and turning it into a craft room. As you can tell, I didn't sleep much last night. My brain was in overdrive.'

Rachel was frantically trying to remember everything of the conversation, knowing she would have to repeat it in the briefing room. Lynn clearly had no idea Freddie was a person of interest to them, and was speaking freely about the son she had barred from her home.

* * *

It was almost one o'clock by the time Rachel arrived back at the station. She had spent half an hour with Lynn after the formal identification. They had sipped

slowly at a cup of tea, and Lynn had cried inter-
mittently.

'He didn't look any different,' she kept saying. 'As if
he was asleep. You will let me know why he died?' she
asked repeatedly.

'Of course,' Rachel had confirmed. 'As soon as we
know, someone will be in touch. The post-mortem has
been done, but we have to wait for the official report.'

Rachel was unsure if the information was correct,
but she was desperately trying to soothe the distraught
woman. She dropped Lynn back at her home, took her
inside and made her sit in the lounge. She filled a glass
with water, and left it on the coffee table.

As she left Lynn's home, the neighbour, a woman
in her fifties, popped her head around her own door,
and whispered, 'Is Lynn okay? I'm Netta.'

'She's as well as can be expected,' Rachel confirmed. 'Just do what you're doing, she'll appreciate
that someone cares.'

'He's gone, you know.'

'Her son?'

'Yes, Freddie. Good riddance to bad rubbish. Igno-
rant sod. She'll be better off without him. Drove off
with a car full of stuff early this morning. I'll look after
her, we've known each other years.'

Rachel nodded and thanked her, heading down the grass verge to get into the squad car. No smell of vinegar now, just a faint reminder of Marc Jacobs' *Daisy* perfume that she had detected on Lynn.

* * *

It didn't take long to relate everything she had learned from Lynn, and Rachel was pleased when one or two members of the team held up a thumb in acknowledgement of her remembering the information she had gleaned from the grieving mum.

'Okay, we need to know who the father of Lynn Earnshaw is. We need to do it without asking her if possible, so I'll leave that with you, Kevin. Well done, Rachel, for everything you've done this morning. It's not a pleasant task, taking someone to ID their loved one, and this one is particularly harrowing. She was okay to leave?'

'I'm hoping so. I made sure she was sitting in the lounge with a glass of water, and I also spoke to the neighbour as I left. They're long-time friends, so she's going to look after her. You know... Lynn knows a lot about Freddie. It's why she's kicked him out. She knows he didn't kill Josh, but she knows he's connected in some way. She obviously never mentioned anything about the Susan Hunter situation, and what we suspect, but it's not going to come as a shock to her.'

* * *

Freddie Earnshaw was feeling pretty pissed off. His grandmother hadn't been that pleased to see him turn up with a carload of stuff, making some comment about it suddenly becoming a shitty Thursday. But his grandfather had smiled, with that look that the two of them always shared, grandfather to firstborn grandson.

At first it had been an instant 'No, we don't have a spare room for you,' but Liam Marshall had quelled his wife's protestations with one look.

However, the bedroom was tiny. It seemed the room he used to sleep in as a child had now been turned into an office, and the third bedroom was already occupied by Diana's sister, there on an extended visit. Freddie got the tiny box room, and he struggled to get in the door once all his possessions had been unloaded from his car.

His grandfather stood in the doorway and watched him as he tried to unpack.

'Your mother doesn't want you then?'

Freddie shrugged. 'Seems not.'

'You have anything to do with Josh's death?'

'Course not,' Freddie was quick to respond. 'As if.'

'How much gear you brought?'

'Not a lot. Just had a big delivery, but I had to bring everything. You got a spare outbuilding?'

'There's a caravan in the back field. Any good to you?'

'Does it lock?'

Liam Marshall nodded. 'It does. It looks as though it's falling apart, but that's deliberate. There's a camera in a nearby tree trained on it, and two cameras inside. It's also connected to an alarm I'll show you. Anybody gets in, they'll wish they hadn't.' Liam held out his hand. 'Guessed you might need this,' and he passed the caravan key over to his grandson.

* * *

The post-mortem result arrived in Karen's inbox just before two o'clock. She opened it, read it quickly, and sat back with a sigh. She had half hoped that it wouldn't show murder, but death following an asthma attack. Hope disappeared when she saw that the hyoid bone was broken, and therefore manual strangulation was the cause of death. The bruises now showing clearly on Joshua Earnshaw's neck were further proof that it was a homicide. There was significant blood loss from the head injury where the head had been pushed against the fence, probably while Josh was being strangled and fighting for his life, but the blood loss wasn't a contributory factor. Someone with large hands had killed Josh by squeezing very tightly on a neck that was already under pressure to allow the boy to breathe.

She would call at Lynn Earnshaw's home on her way to her own home and reveal the post-mortem results, not an easy job but a necessary one. There was a hush as she walked from her own office into the main space. It was busy as people worked on the various jobs she had handed out, and she clapped her hands to get their attention.

Going through the details made Karen feel slightly sick, and she finished by telling them she would be calling at Lynn's later to tell her what had happened to Josh.

'Boss, I can go with you if you need me to,' Rachel said quietly, through Karen's open door.

'No, you get off home, Rachel. You've had a hard day. I'll take care of her for as long as it takes. Thanks for offering though. Was that your first accompanied ID this morning?'

Rachel nodded. 'It was, and I don't want another one for quite some time. I've never felt drained like that before. Heaven only knows how Lynn Earnshaw is feeling right now.'

'Unfortunately it's a large part of the Major Crimes Unit. We get all the murders, and although Josh was murdered, I've seen dozens of the more gruesome deaths. Lynn was spared that. We need to find Freddie, though. I want a serious talk with that young man.'

She watched as one by one her colleagues closed down laptops, filed away paperwork they had been studying, and generally attempted a bit of a tidy up before cleaners came in later. They were a good crowd, she mused, not afraid of a bit of hard work and handy with creative thinking. She always felt she could suggest an avenue to explore, and somebody would come up with answers of how to effectively explore it.

Several called goodnight as they left and she responded in kind. Ray asked if she needed anything but she declined his offer, saying unless he had a spare gin and tonic about his person, she needed nothing else. She was just about to close down her own laptop when an email pinged through. From Alan Chantry.

LH transferred to Dover. Is that far enough? Short of chucking him in the English Channel, couldn't get him any further away. Effective next Monday. Tell your lassie I'm sorry. And I gave him no choice. What he's done has been discussed by me and his sergeant in Dover. She'll watch out for anything going on.

15

Freddie stared around at the interior of the caravan. It had looked a proper wreck from the outside as he had approached it, but the interior was pretty smart. Locked steel cabinets covered most of the left-hand side, and he guessed the bunch of keys given to him by his grandfather would unlock them. It was only a small caravan with one bedroom that held a double bed. The bedding was neatly stacked at the end of it, and it suddenly dawned on him that he could actually move in here and have more room than he had in the bedroom reluctantly given to him by his grandmother.

And he could be near everything he had to protect. He took out his phone, spoke briefly to his grandfather, and then moved into the bedroom to put the bedding on the bed. This was a much better arrangement, and it seemed the security on the caravan was linked directly to his grandfather, with alerts on his Apple watch telling him if there was an issue. It also seemed he didn't have a key to one of the locked steel units, but Liam Marshall had made it very clear he wouldn't need that key.

'In other words,' Liam had said, 'It's mine. Keep out. Oh, and you'll need to turn on the gas canister outside the caravan when you want to do anything in the kitchen.'

With the bed made, the gas connected, and everything smelling a little fresher for having had some windows and the door open, Freddie headed back across the field towards the main house. He reckoned he could reload his car, and if he was careful could squeeze it down the side of the house and across the somewhat bumpy terrain of the back field. It would certainly be easier than carrying everything.

* * *

An hour later he had fully moved in. After a brief thank you to his grandmother, Diana, who seemed much happier once she found out he was moving into the tatty caravan, he took the carrier bag she offered him. It contained biscuits, tea bags and coffee, a tub of margarine and a small, sliced loaf, enough to get him through until he could get his own supplies. It also contained two mouse traps.

Liam walked outside with him. 'Don't let Diana know that the inside of the caravan is pretty much spotless and in good nick. She thinks it's got mice in it, so won't set foot in it. I keep it smart because you never know when somebody might want a bed for the night. And there's decent access to it from the bottom of the field to save the dog-leg bit round the side of the house. I've had a gate made, which is also something Diana doesn't know about. The key to the gate padlock's on the bunch but nobody bothers to padlock it anyway, because if anybody opens the gate, or climbs over it, it triggers an alarm on my watch and an alarm in the caravan. Your grandmother doesn't need to know your comings and goings, so just keep yourself to yourself, okay? Don't bother checking out the old shack by the side of it, it's where I dumped the stuff that didn't work in the caravan, so it's only rubbish in there. It's yet another thing to keep my wife away from this field.' He gave a slight laugh. 'The whole thing would probably collapse around you if you even attempted to open the door.'

Freddie grinned. He was definitely seeing a new

aspect of Liam Marshall. 'Seems a good way of stopping her from knowing your comings and goings as well?'

Liam playfully cuffed the back of Freddie's head. 'Cheeky blighter. Go and get moved in.'

* * *

With the gas sorted, he made himself a coffee. Then he allowed himself some thinking time.

His young brother was dead, and although he'd not heard it officially, he knew it wasn't asthma that had killed him. There was only one person to be blamed for this, Gordon fucking King.

And Gordon fucking King would pay for it.

* * *

Over at the other side of the city, completely unaware of any shenanigans going on regarding the family of the boy whose death had so upset his partner, Matt Forrester was quietly watching the person sitting across from him.

Carol had spoken to the lady that morning, and after saying her name was Annabel Beecham she had explained she needed to speak with a private investigator. 'Matthew Forrester comes highly recommended,' she said.

As a result of that short conversation, Annabel was now facing Matt, wondering how the hell she was going to explain her predicament.

'So where do you want to start?'

Matt could sense her unease, and was trying to gently coax the story from her. Her eyes kept going out of focus as she was speaking, and he knew whatever the story would prove to be, it was currently not escaping her brain and her mouth at any speed. He judged her to be around thirty, maybe a little older, very attractive, slim with long blonde hair that curled softly around her gamine face.

'Hang on,' he said, when she gulped. 'Shall we have a cup of tea before we talk? Let's get to know each other a little, and then you can tell me your story. I have no other appointments this afternoon, just a pile of paperwork that's nothing essential, so let's relax a little first.'

She heaved a sigh of relief. 'Oh, thank you. Your secretary offered me a drink but I was so wound up I said no. Now I think it will calm me down.'

Matt stood. 'Give me two minutes, I'll go and ask her to get one for both of us.'

* * *

Carol looked up as her door opened and she smiled at Matt. 'Matt, we do have an intercom.'

He waved a hand in dismissal. One day he would remember that small point. 'Would you mind making two cups of tea, please? Mrs Beecham is a little on edge, and I think we just need to chat about anything other than why she is here.'

'On it,' she said, and pushed back her chair. 'Biscuits?'

He nodded. 'Thanks, Carol, you're a star.'

'I know,' she said, and ushered him back into his own office.

* * *

Annabel laughed, and sipped at her tea. 'Absolutely love Bourbon biscuits. You think it's apparent? How did Carol know?'

Matt smiled. 'You want a tip? Never underestimate what Carol knows. She will be adding you into our files, even if you don't use our services at this time. You've been in this office, so you will be logged in, but it will be noted that you like tea and Bourbon biscuits. The woman is a miracle worker. She rules my work partner and me with an absolute rod of iron, all while handing us scones served up on posh little china plates she got from the charity shop across the road. She arrived here the day we officially opened and she decided we needed her. She's never left since, I'm convinced. When I arrive in a morning, she's here. When I go home in the afternoon, she's here. So she knows everything from your shoe size to biscuit preferences.'

Annabel's smile grew as she relaxed in Matt's company, and he felt relieved. Eventually she would start to talk. He still didn't have a clue why she was there, but he could see the difference between the uncomfortable woman of twenty minutes earlier, and now.

'Are you married, Mr Forrester?'

'Please call me Matt. No, I'm not but I do have a life partner. And a son, Harry.'

'Harry is your child who disappeared?'

'He is. You knew about that?'

'I was part of one of the search teams for a few hours. I couldn't give long, but I knew I needed to help.'

'Then for that I sincerely thank you. When we got him back he was seriously ill, and he had a longish stay in the Children's Hospital with pneumonia. But he's fine now, back at school thankfully, and totally immersed in football rather than maths and English. Do you have children?'

'Not yet, no. It's partly why I'm here.'

Matt waited without speaking. Finally she was starting to trust him enough to tentatively begin her story.

'I have a husband, Dominic. We met two years ago in a gym, and grew very close, very quickly. Three months later he proposed and we were married three months after that. I do love him, but...'

'But?'

'Look, Matt, I'm quite wealthy. I thought I'd kept just how wealthy from him, but now I'm not so sure. We'd said we would do a lot of travelling, but the furthest we've been since we met is Bridlington, and that was only for a couple of days. But that's not the issue. What he really wants to do is have a baby. He's pushing for it, seems to be the main topic of conversation between us, but I thought maybe in three or four years. I want to spend time with him first, before we commit to a family. He does know that's how I feel, I told him right from the start, so maybe he doesn't really want a baby, it's just being said to fool me. To stop me from seeing what he's really up to. And I need to trust him, but honestly, I can't.'

'Let's start at the beginning. Your first comment

was really about you being wealthy. Shall we talk about that, and why it's an issue.'

'I'm wealthy because I'm an only child. When my uber-rich grandparents died within a year of each other, I inherited all their wealth. I was eighteen, so Mum and Dad helped me invest wisely, but left me a million or so as spending money, if you like. They inherited Nan and Granddad's house, but they didn't need the money, they were mega-rich anyway. It was a strange world I lived in. Then five years ago Mum and Dad were flying over to France in their private plane and it came down in the Channel. I then inherited everything, although I don't think I'll ever get over losing them. So I now have millions stashed in various places. I have no idea of my true worth, that's for my accountant to worry about, but I thought Dom knew I was okay for money, just not the extent of it.'

'Is he helping himself?'

She nodded, with such a look of misery on her face. 'Maybe it's my fault for not being totally honest about everything, but how can I have a baby with a man I can't trust? I know this is all down to me, I need to make decisions on my own, but I feel as if I don't know him any more. I want you to find everything out about him that you can, so I can make the right decisions. I made my current account into a joint account when we married, but there are large amounts disappearing from it. The bank has alerted me, but I haven't taken any action like removing him from the account, I've let it go until I get some answers. He doesn't seem to be buying anything, doesn't actually need anything. I bought him a brand-new Audi for a wedding present, and I keep suggesting we go on holiday, but really neither of us need money.'

Matt pulled his notepad towards him. 'Is there a time limit for this research?'

She shook her head. 'No, I need you to be thorough. This folder contains my bank statements for my current account for the past two years.' She pushed a black loose leaf folder towards him.

'Thank you. So he's Dominic Beecham? Middle name?'

'Michael. As far as I'm aware he was born in Sheffield, doesn't seem to know much about the rest of the country, or the world, because his parents weren't big earners. His mum couldn't work because of illness, so the only income when he was growing up was from his dad. He was a lorry driver. When Dom left school he went to work in tech sales in Meadowhall, and that's where he is now, albeit as a manager.'

'Do you work, Annabel?'

'Kind of. Just a couple of days a week. I own a plant

nursery with a small garden centre attached to it. It was failing miserably, so I bought it. I've always loved gardening, and this seemed like a perfect opportunity for me. It was really starting to take off when I met Dom. I'm on the lookout for a second one now, I'd really like to build up a chain. But if I do follow through on this plan, Dom will learn about my wealth, and that fact scares me more than a little bit. Tell me who he is, Matt, just tell me who he is.'

16

Matt walked Annabel to her car, and held the door open while she settled herself inside.

'Nice car,' he said, and she smiled.

'Had it about eighteen months now, love it. Thank you for taking on my case, Matt, and as I said, there's no rush. I'd rather it was in depth and accurate, than only a partial overview.'

She pulled away with a brief wave of her hand through the open window, and Matt headed back inside.

'Can you do a quick scan of WATSON, please, Carol? I need to find everything out about a Dominic Michael Beecham, and he works at one of the tech stores in Meadowhall, as a manager. I don't recall his name at all, so I don't expect we'll have anything, but I suppose he could be in there as one of Dad's old connections. Worth a shot anyway, and I can rule it out if there's nothing in our files. I suspect this one is going to be an internet case, lots of searches and stuff.'

'Her husband?'

Matt nodded. 'He is, and unfortunately she has doubts about him. He also seems to be helping himself to money that he's not spending.'

'Stashing it away? Ready for the great escape?'

'She hasn't said that, but reading between the lines I think she's worrying that's the case. However, he's also pushing for a baby that he knows she doesn't want yet, so maybe she's getting it wrong. Why would he want a baby if the money is the prime objective? This is what's making me think he's deflecting her thoughts in a different direction. Sort of, look how happy we are, let's have a baby and you won't notice I've got somebody else on the side.'

'I'm getting a definite feeling he has some plan going on. I'll start now, see what I can find. You'll follow the money?'

He laughed at her words. 'That seems to be my role in most of our jobs these days. It's good that the police trained me in forensic accountancy, but once I moved to Major Crimes I thought I'd left the money behind. Seems not.'

'Okay, I'll check if he's in WATSON first, then maybe widen the parameters. You write up the report then I'll log it that so all three of us are aware of the details.'

'I think Steve will be interested – our new client owns a garden centre, and is looking for something suitable to open a second one. He's in later, after Hermia's midwife check-up.'

'How's she doing?'

'Been up most of last night according to Steve, uncomfortable aches and pains. This baby is definitely on the way, so we'll see what they say after today's visit.'

Matt's phone pinged and he glanced at it. 'Speak of the devil. It's Steve.'

He opened the text, then glanced at Carol and read it aloud. 'Herms admitted. Five centimetres dilated. You're about to become an uncle.'

Carol clapped her hands. 'Wonderful.'

'Well, it certainly explains their uncomfortable night. I feel as if I should be pacing up and down now. The expectant uncle. And we need to check Steve's diary, because he's not going to be in for at least three weeks. Transfer stuff to mine, but not his own landscape business stuff. He's pretty much not taken anything on with that, passed it all to Rob who's been in charge of most stuff. In fact, he seems to do the complete job these days, for Steve. We've built this business up so much, Steve's landscape business is well and truly in the capable hands of Rob and the workforce.'

'So, we need to prioritise.' Carol glanced up at Matt. 'I can handle all the smaller bits and bobs that can remain inside the office, and it seems to me the two big cases at the moment are the work we need to do at the Birley Spa Bath House, which is still a crime scene until Karen releases it, and this new one with Annabel Beecham. Now I realise she'll have said be thorough, not fast, but that's her way of putting off finding out the truth, because she doesn't really want her suspicions confirmed. Am I right?'

'You are. Dead right.'

'If he's squirrelling away money, he could disappear at any time. This is probably more urgent than anything, and I think we should prioritise this one in the short time we have before Karen says we can go back to the Bath House. I can take over anything Steve has ongoing, because I can transfer our telephone to my mobile number, and if poor reception stops that being effective, that's what answer machines are for.'

'Am I being organised?'

'As always,' she said. 'Now message Karen and tell her she's well on the way to becoming Aunty Karen.'

He shook his head as he walked back into his own office. This woman could organise NATO given a mobile phone and an answerphone, and for the millionth time he wondered what they would do without her, if she ever decided retirement was on the cards. Note to self, he thought, never mention the R word in front of Carol, just in case it put the thought into her head.

He sent a text to Karen and the return text was a huge YES followed by three big red hearts. His next text was to Steve, asking that he pass on his love to his sister, and sent love and happy thoughts from both him and Karen.

Carol opened up WATSON, the system she had invented, installed and updated daily since the start of her new career with the Forrester Detective Agency, and typed in the name Dominic Michael Beecham.

The hit was instant. The blue lettering indicated it was connected to the days of Dave Forrester, not the new days of Matt and Steve. She clicked on the link, and it took her to... nothing really.

It was simply a name that had been mentioned in a report typed by Dave Forrester after the completion of one of his cases. A financial case that had resulted in an eventual prosecution and a five-year prison sentence. Dominic Beecham had been someone questioned by Dave but nothing further appeared in any report. She printed out the report to show Matt.

She then typed in Beecham on its own, followed by Dominic on its own, but nothing further was forthcoming.

Carol closed down WATSON, a thoughtful expression on her face. The fact that only his name had showed up was somewhat irrelevant; the fact that it was as an add-on to a financial case that had been proven was of more concern. Their issue with him was definitely money, and his acquisition of his wife's wealth.

She knocked quietly on Matt's door, and opened it a fraction. 'You busy?'

'No, just planning what I can buy my new nephew.'

'I thought you said they had chosen not to know the sex until the birth!'

He waved a hand. 'I'm going to win this bet. I've said a boy.'

'What did Karen say?'

'She, of course, said a girl. So did Harry. Steve was non-committal, kind of. He said it needed to be a boy so he could train him to take over the landscaping business by the time he was five. I had to point out girls can be gardeners as well. But it's a boy, I just feel it in my bones.'

'Well, I'd definitely hold off planning what you can buy your nephew, until we get the real news,' she said, easing into the room. 'I've printed off one thing, and that's all we've got in WATSON. I haven't looked anywhere else yet, but this made me a little uncomfortable. It's one of Dave's reports and basically tells us nothing. It's just a mention of his name, but... No, you look, and see if it makes your toes tingle a little bit.'

'Tingling toes? I don't think I've ever had that with a case before.' He pulled the printout towards him and read it swiftly, then re-read it. 'I remember this. It was passed to us in forensic accounting after Dad had taken it on via a private client. He discovered how the scam was being worked, and the client asked that it be passed to the police for prosecution decisions. I was in the process of moving to Major Crimes a week later, so I didn't do any work on this, murder always trumps money and I was keen to move onto the murders. So our Dominic spoke to Dad at some point, or he wouldn't have been mentioned. I'll get Karen to check if he has any previous at all, even if it's just an unpaid parking fine.'

'See! Are the toes tingling just a little bit?'

He wriggled his feet. 'Nope. Maybe they will if we find out he's got form though.'

She laughed at him, and left him rereading the report his father had written several years earlier. She knew just how much he had loved his dad, and he was probably feeling the connection strongly, as he read something written by Dave.

He opened up his computer, pushed the report to one side, and typed Dominic's full name into Google. Nothing.

He changed tack slightly and typed in Annabel's name but again there was nothing. However, he realised that Annabel hadn't been Annabel Beecham for very long, and he pursued the route of news surrounding a private plane crashing into the English Channel. That report told him Annabel's maiden name was Lebrun, and further investigation revealed she had been born to a French father and an English mother, so he then checked out Annabel Lebrun.

This revealed she was the proprietor of the Summertime Garden Centre, and he spent a pleasant time looking at the website, admiring the pictures, and slowly coming to realise it wasn't quite the 'small' outfit she had spoken of – it was quite substantial with its own plant nursery as well as the large premises for selling everything garden-related to the general public.

It was located on the outskirts of Sheffield, almost in Barnsley, and he thought he might suggest going there to Karen and Harry just to enjoy the place. He felt it wouldn't offer any help to his investigation, but it certainly looked like a place that was well worth visiting.

It was as he was closing down the website he spotted a second mention of Annabel Lebrun, stating that she had married Dominic Beecham, but with no further information he finally closed the screen. He stared out of the window, lost in his thoughts. His earlier visitor had been full of stress, and it had been a primary concern to settle her down, and get her to talk to him. He felt she had been scared, rather than worried.

Scared of what? Her husband? At a push, she could simply throw him out. Her house was her house, not his.

He glanced at his watch, decided enough was enough for today, and waved his car keys at Carol. 'We're done,' he said. 'Let's have an early finish. I'll go and get Harry, then he doesn't have to catch the bus.'

She smiled. 'Okay, I need to cut my lawn. I'll lock up. You get off, and let me know when your nephew or niece is born.'

He grinned. 'It's a nephew, you wait and see.'

* * *

Thursday, 23 March 2023 drew to a close with the news that Steve and Hermia had taken delivery of a beautiful baby girl weighing a little over seven pounds, and already suckling happily at her mother's breast. Her name was still under discussion, and would continue to be Peanut until agreement could be reached.

Uncle Matt removed thoughts of trains and cars from his brain, and replaced them with dolls, doll houses, and prams.

Aunty Karen simply gloated that she had been right, and cousin Harry punched the air and said he had been right to follow Karen's lead, and not his numpty of a father.

It was a good Thursday.

17

'Hermia's had the baby, a little girl called Peanut.'

Ray smiled. 'Not sure about the name, but glad it's over for her. I'll tell Angela, she's been itching to get something for it but wanted to wait until she knew the sex.'

'Fortunately the name is temporary until they can agree on one,' said Karen. 'I think they have several ideas, but they wanted to see what the baby was, and what it looked like before making any decisions. They can scrap all boys' names now, and hopefully reach a sensible decision soon. It's been Peanut since she found out she was pregnant.'

'If you go to see her, give her our love and congratulations.'

'I will. So, back to work. We found Freddie Earn-shaw yet?'

'No, but we've bits of info filtering in. Just waiting for you to start the briefing, boss. Everybody's here. You want a coffee?'

'Probably might benefit from one. I feel half asleep. We spent half the night talking babies.'

Ray grinned. 'As long as you weren't making them. We need you here, not at home changing nappies.'

'Nope. Harry's enough for me.'

'Thank heavens for that. I'll get us the coffees, you go and pacify the troops. Won't be a minute.'

Karen gathered up anything she might need, along with a couple of notes she had made during the long night, and walked into the briefing room.

There was silence as she moved towards the white-board. She waited for Ray's return before starting, then began with the name Freddie Earnshaw. 'I want this person downstairs in an interview room and the sooner the better. We know he wasn't directly involved in the murder of his brother, but I suspect he may well be indirectly involved. We need to find him. Anybody anything to offer on that?'

She saw Kevin stand and wave a piece of paper. 'I've some facts sorted,' he said. He glanced down at his notes, and lifted his head. 'Basically, Lynn Earnshaw is

the daughter of Liam Marshall. That makes Freddie
the grandson of Marshall, and I think it's possible
that's where he's gone to lick his wounds, so to speak.'

'And the lovely Diana Marshall is presumably his
grandmother then. Okay, well let's get out there asap.
We've certainly been before, I seem to remember we
arrested Niall there. And therefore that would make
Niall the brother of Lynn Earnshaw. Strange how she
didn't mention any connection... and it's strange that
she's living in a council house, when her dad has the
biggest haulage business in Sheffield and lives in a
property the size of Buckingham Palace. Well, maybe
not quite that big, but it's a sizeable piece of real estate.
Wouldn't mind betting she's estranged from the family,
making her own way in the world. And now she's lost
her son, and I suspect the other son will be locked up
before much longer. Okay, Ray – you'll go with me.
Kevin and Rachel, I want you in a second car. I also
want a car with two uniforms in it parked outside the
gates. Do we have anything else from forensics?'

Ian stood, a small piece of paper in his hand.
'Came through a few minutes ago, boss. It seems
they've managed to get a fingerprint off one of the
soggy medication packets, the one that was underneath the victim. His body kept it dryer than the others

they found, it seems. The print belongs to a Gordon King, a name some of us know all too well.'

Karen took a deep breath. 'And one who's never served anything longer than a six-month stretch. Let's get Freddie Earnshaw sorted first, then we'll bring Kingy in.' She used the name she had known him as for so long – Kingy, who ran most of the girls in Sheffield, who looked after them until they broke his rules. Dealer of drugs, including the high-end stuff, that he sold and used to control his girls.

'Okay, I'm going to have a quick read through of the post-mortem report now we have the details, and then I want to get off. Ray, organise the uniform support, will you, please?'

Ray saluted in acknowledgement, and she headed for her office. She knew she didn't have to tell anyone else what to do, they would continue to dig for information, and somebody would be concentrating on Gordon 'Kingy' King.

* * *

They pulled up at the gates of the large Marshall residence, and waited for someone to release the lock from inside the house. It didn't happen. Karen impatiently hit the horn and watched as Liam Marshall walked slowly down his driveway towards them. She held her arm out of the car window, holding her warrant card in it.

'Sorry,' he shouted. 'I tried to release it from the house, but it seems there's something wrong with it. Give me a second.'

He fiddled with the lock, and slowly the gates began to open. Immediately the two police cars containing Karen, Ray, Kevin and Rachel all drove by him without acknowledging him further. The uniforms in the car following them pulled up across the gates, blocking any in or out movement of any vehicles until Karen gave the go ahead for them to move.

'Wonder why he delayed us getting in?' Ray mused.

'Maybe he's got a grandson here he's had to hide first?'

'Maybe.'

'Think it's more probably,' Ray continued to muse. 'I'll ask to use the toilet after a couple of minutes, see what I can find.'

She gave a brief nod, and turned as Liam Marshall sauntered back up the drive and climbed the four steps to his front door.

'Sorry about that,' he said. 'It's been playing up for a couple of days, but they're coming later to sort it out.'

'Make it sooner rather than later,' Karen suggested. 'You never know who might want to visit you next. Armed response would just shoot the gates off their hinges, and it could cost you more than simply a malfunction call-out.'

'Armed response?' Liam raised his eyebrows.

'Murder investigation,' Karen replied. 'You never know what's likely to happen. Get the gates sorted before they have to prove they can get in anywhere.'

He opened the front door and the four officers followed him inside. He led them through to the conservatory, and Diana tagged along at the back. She looked at her husband, but he merely shrugged his shoulders.

'Can my wife get you teas or coffees?'

'No, thank you,' Karen said. 'We're not here to socialise. We've some questions to ask you. We're actually trying to find your grandson, Freddie. We understand you have a particularly close relationship with him, and we can't find him.'

'But he's just lost his brother. He may have gone away for a couple of days to sort out his head.'

'Has he come to you?'

'He called in briefly yesterday.'

Karen glanced at Ray. They both knew he was covering any tracks Freddie may have left.

'And he's not here now?'

'He said he had a mate in Doncaster. Didn't say he was going there, but that was the feeling I got. I told him we're always here if he needs us, and to tell his mother the same thing.'

'You couldn't tell Lynn that yourself?'

'We rarely speak, but she did ring to tell me Josh had had an asthma attack and died.'

'I see. And then Freddie turned up here?'

'Yes, but as I've already said, it was only a flying visit. We fed him, and off he went. I haven't heard from him since, but surely you don't think he had anything to do with his brother's death? I thought it was an asthma attack, going by what Lynn told me. Young Josh has had asthma for years.'

There was a muffled sob from Diana, and she turned and left the room. Karen nodded to Rachel, who followed the upset woman.

'You mind if I use the toilet, mate?' Ray asked, taking advantage of the lull caused by Diana and Rachel walking out.

'Guest bathroom, first right top of the stairs,' Liam answered, without really thinking about it; his mind was focused on the smart copper in front of him. He'd need to keep his wits about him while she was around.

Karen kept him occupied, explaining as far as she

could why they now believed it to be a murder case and not an accidental death.

Ray walked along the corridor containing four bedroom doors and two bathroom doors, checking as quickly as he could into each room, but seeing no evidence of anyone until he reached the last room, where he quickly closed the door. He could hear a woman singing softly to herself while she was in the en suite shower, and he figured they had a guest they hadn't bothered to mention. He did a quick about turn, swiftly used the guest bathroom and flushed the toilet, then headed downstairs to rejoin Karen, Kevin and Liam.

'Okay? You found it?' Liam asked, and Ray nodded.

'I did. Was entertained by somebody singing. "Copacabana", I think.'

'That's the wife's sister. Big fan of Barry Manilow, for heaven's sake. Just left her husband, so she rocked up here.'

'I'd like a word with her before we leave. Did you forget to mention her?'

'To be brutally honest, I forget she's here. Stays in the bedroom all the time, says she's writing her autobiography, so she's tap-tapping away on her laptop all day long. Her name's Paula Robbins. As you can see, I'm cooperating fully. I really have no idea where my grandson is, but sooner or later he'll be in touch and I'll tell him you were looking for him.'

'Thanks, but that's not quick enough. We have further information that I can't reveal to you, but I want him at the station today, so maybe you can pass that bit of information on when you see him.'

'You tried ringing him, or is that too simple?'

Karen seriously wanted to punch him in the nose. 'You think we haven't tried? Don't get cocky, pal, or we'll bring you in. We haven't ruled you out yet.'

The door opened, and Rachel returned from her mission of providing comfort to the upset Diana.

'Rachel,' Karen said, 'there's a lady upstairs in one of the bedrooms. Just pop up and have a word with her, will you? Check she's no idea where her errant nephew is. Her name is Paula Robbins, and she's Diana's sister.'

'Yes, boss,' and Rachel turned and disappeared out of the door she had just entered.

'So let's talk about you. You're not at work?' She was fully aware that Liam owned the largest haulage business in the area.

'Partly retired these days. I go in three days a week, never the same days, but I've got a manager who knows the business inside out and we've got mobile phones that just link the two of us, so if he needs me he can get me anytime. The wife needs looking after.'

'She's ill?'

'Nymphomania.'

Karen had to stifle her laughter. She waited.

'Too many other men, so I've had to implement changes. I'm home at odd times, when she doesn't know what days I'm working and when I'm not, and we go on holiday unexpectedly, things like that. Not easy to have an affair when your husband can't be relied on to be out of the house, or even the country. To be honest, this plan of action seems to have brought us closer, so...'

Karen sensed the man was being genuinely honest for the first time. 'Thank you for your time, Liam.' She stood. 'And don't forget we need to speak to Freddie if he contacts you before we find him. And we will,' she confirmed.

* * *

The four officers got into their respective cars and drove down the drive. Karen pulled up and got out to speak to the uniforms in the squad car waiting patiently for permission to return to base. She thanked them for their time, and asked if by any chance they had a drone in the boot.

They laughed. 'I wish,' one of them said. 'But just say the word and we can get you a drone-trained operative out here.'

'Can I leave it with you? I want a scan of a mile around this property, as close in as they can get without crashing the drone.'

'Consider it done.'

18

Matt stared at his niece in total wonderment. 'She's so beautiful. I mean, truly beautiful. Steve, she's got more hair than you.'

'Thanks, mate. You make me feel so good.' Steve grinned at his best friend. They'd managed to get permission for an early visit for Matt by saying he was catching a plane from Manchester at two o'clock and wouldn't be back for three weeks. All lies, but it had the desired effect and Matt was holding the precious child in his arms by nine, gently stroking the head of dark curly hair.

'She's smiling,' he announced. 'She already knows who the sucker in her life is going to be.'

Hermia grinned, and both parents said in unison, 'It's wind.'

'So,' Steve said, 'she has a name. All the names we've gone through, not knowing whether it would be a boy or a girl, and at three o'clock this morning Herms texted and suggested Rosie.'

'Beautiful name, after your mum, Steve. What a lovely idea, and doesn't it suit her already? Is she having a middle name?'

'She is, but it will be a Shakespearean name. I'm going to research that before we have to register her,' Hermia sleepily explained. 'But I kind of knew in the middle of the night it had to be Rosie, we loved Steve's mum so much. So I texted him because I was awake, just staring at our beautiful daughter. Turns out he was awake as well, so we agreed instantly.'

A nurse appeared at the bedside, and smiled as she saw Matt holding the baby. 'Beautiful, isn't she? She'll need a haircut soon. I'm sorry, but I can only give you another five minutes, Mr Forrester. It is supposed to only be partners.'

Matt stood, carefully laid the baby back in her plastic crib, and straightened his back. 'It's okay, I have a plane to catch. Thank you for allowing this, it means a lot.'

* * *

He drove back through the centre of Sheffield with several photographs of the newest member of their family on his phone, ready to be sent off en masse to Karen. It had been a memorable morning, and Herms had been so sleepily happy. There was a possibility mum and baby would be home later that day and he couldn't wait to start this new chapter in all of their lives.

He walked into the office and Carol grinned at him. 'You blagged your way into that hospital, didn't you?'

'As we speak, I'm on my way to Manchester Airport for the start of a three-week holiday,' he confessed.

'You're wicked, Matt Forrester. Everything okay over at Jessops Hospital?'

'Everything's wonderful.' He took out his phone, opened up the photos app and handed the pictures to Carol.

'Look at the hair,' Carol commented immediately. 'She's got more than her daddy.'

'I said that. Don't think Steve was impressed. They're so happy, Carol. And she has a name, Rosie.'

'Love it. Family name?'

'It is. Steve's mum had MS, ended up in a wheelchair and died when Steve was about sixteen. She was

Rosie. Much loved and much missed. His dad will be over the moon at their choice of name.'

'So are you in work now? Or skiving to go buy some champagne and nappies, possibly a doll's pram?'

'Actually, I thought I might get stuck into those bank statements that Annabel left with me. Then if Steve needs me for anything, I'm available. They only went to hospital for an antenatal visit, but she was well on in labour so they admitted her. They might need some shopping getting in, or something, so I'll keep myself available in the office doing something I can stop and start whenever I want.'

She nodded. 'Sensible idea. And go get Harry from school. He'll want to hear the news, see the pictures. You want me to photocopy the statements so you can write on them?'

Matt looked at Carol and shook his head. 'You amaze me, Carol Flynn. Why didn't I think of that? I'd have just scrawled all over the originals. Hang on, I'll get them.'

* * *

By mid-afternoon Matt was seeing figures everywhere, but he was well aware that Annabel's husband had found a valuable source of income. There was no pattern to the withdrawals and transfers, it all seemed to be very random, but a considerable amount of money had been moved.

He locked both the originals and the copies of the statements into his large desk drawer, and sat back, his thoughts once again drifting to Hermia. His dad would have been so proud to become a grandfather once again, and Dave Forrester dying had been such a massive loss to all of them.

He checked through the notes that he'd taken when Annabel had first approached Forresters, double-checked where Dominic Beecham worked, and decided to pay him a visit at the shop, to get a feel of who he was, how he interacted with customers and staff. He could always pick up Harry and head straight to Meadowhall to get his son a new game for his PlayStation. A little coaching for Harry on how to take his time choosing exactly what he wanted, while leaving his dad to just wander around the store, would be advisable, Matt felt.

This case wasn't just about confirming what Annabel knew, it was about finding justice for her, settling the nerves that were very apparent in his client. And he'd liked her, she didn't deserve a husband who seemed to be using her.

* * *

'I was going to catch the bus with Isaac,' Harry grumbled, as he climbed into the front seat of the Land Rover.

'We're not heading home,' Matt said. 'We've somewhere else to go. I'll tell you all about it when we get there, and it could involve a Big Mac.'

Harry's face lost its disgruntled look, and exploded into a smile. 'But it's Friday. McDonald's is usually Saturday.'

'This is one of the perks of the job. We're actually working, a Big Mac is part of the wages. So sit back, enjoy the M1 on a Friday afternoon, and we should be there hopefully in about twenty minutes.'

They spoke little during the journey to Meadowhall; the motorway was horrifically busy, but that route had become Matt's preferred way to the huge shopping mall. He breathed a sigh of relief as he parked up, and then he carefully explained why they were there, what Harry's role would be, and sealed it all with the guarantee of the Big Mac.

Harry listened carefully, then pushed his luck a little. 'Don't suppose my wages would run to some new football boots as well?'

'Definitely not. We're here for me to observe this

feller if he's there, to get you a new game, to eat food of some description, and to go home.'

'But my boots are a size three, and I've just moved into a size four with my trainers.'

Matt sighed. 'Okay, I give in. We'll add football boots to the list. There's nothing else you want to try for while we're here?'

Harry shook his head. 'No, I'm good, thanks. Wait while I tell Isaac.'

'You won't tell Isaac the real reason we're here though?'

'Nah, that's work. I don't tell him if I do anything that's connected with what you do. I've to think about the reputation of Forresters, it'll be mine one day, you know.'

Matt spluttered as he tried to control his laughter. 'Get out of the car, cheeky monkey. Let's go shopping.'

* * *

Meadowhall was heaving. It seemed to Matt that most people had collected their offspring from school, and taken them to the massive shopping mall. They walked through Next and headed towards the escalators that took them up to the upper level and their destination.

Matt and Harry perused the shop's windows for a

minute or so, although Matt's eyes were scanning the interior.

They entered and Harry immediately wandered over to the games section after briefly touching his father's arm to indicate he understood they were both now in work mode, and all joking was done.

Matt walked over to the more expensive equipment, the computers, and began to pay close attention, wandering between two or three of them, even going so far as to take photographs of the items. He figured he was most likely to be approached by a manager if he was showing real interest in the higher-priced stuff they sold.

It didn't take long.

'Can I be of any assistance, sir?'

The name badge told him this was Dominic, but Matt would have recognised him from the wedding photograph of him and Annabel that she had supplied with the folder of bank statements.

'Possibly,' Matt said. 'My computer is old now, and I'm getting ready for an upgrade to something that moves considerably faster than my current one. I've been looking at these three,' he pointed carefully at the inanimate objects that had become his assistants, 'and I'd like information on them. I'll also be wanting an Ecotank printer, the one I'm currently using only prints when it's in a good mood, and when the wind is blowing in the right direction.'

Dominic laughed. 'That describes most printers, sir, but I highly recommend all models of the Ecotank. Unless you're constantly printing every minute of the day, the ink that comes with it will last you two years easily. I do a lot of printing on A3 paper, and I have one of the larger models. But if you only need it for A4 paper, obviously you won't need to go that large.'

'Thank you, I'll take the printer with me today, but I'll be coming back tomorrow to get the computer. I need to take the info away with me for a discussion with my wife. We can't decide whether to have a new PC each, or manage with one between us. But she really is the one with much more knowledge than me, I'm just the advance party.'

He saw thoughts of commission light up Dominic's eyes. 'Then perhaps we should set up an hour's appointment for tomorrow, so that I can make sure I can give you my full attention.'

'That would be brilliant. I'll be making a couple of purchases today – my son is currently hyperventilating looking at your PlayStation games, and I'll go with an A4 printer, if you can organise that for me.'

'I can.' He looked around and waved towards a female member of his staff. She attended immediately, and stood by Dominic's side. Her name badge informed Matt that she was called Marnie, and he smiled at her. 'Hi,' he said.

She smiled in return and moved closer to her boss. 'You want something, Dom?'

There was an interaction between them that stood out a mile. Matt held his breath. Had he got the answer right in front of his eyes?

'Yes, please,' Dom responded, then shook his head. 'I mean... erm... can you go and collect an Ecotank ET2810 for me please? Mr...?'

'Forrester, Matt Forrester.'

'Mr Forrester would like to take the printer so just put it behind the desk because he's buying a game as well. I want information leaflets on this, this and this,' and he pointed to the three computers in which Matt had expressed an interest.

She lifted her eyes to Dominic's face, and Matt could see tiny beads of sweat on the man's forehead. The sexual tension between the two was palpable, and Matt knew without a shadow of a doubt just what Dominic Beecham's great escape was going to be.

19

Karen received two texts within a few seconds of each other. The first to appear was from Matt saying he was going to collect Harry from school and take him to Meadowhall, and he signed off with a row of pound signs. The second was from someone called Tomaz saying he had emailed her drone footage as requested.

Suddenly she felt a burst of something that felt suspiciously like enthusiasm. It hadn't been a particularly successful day; Freddie Earnshaw hadn't been at his grandfather's home as far as they could tell without actually producing a search warrant, and the two uniforms who had been despatched to bring in Gordon King had reported no sight of him. They'd checked out his home address as well as the address of the house where his girls lived when they weren't out walking the streets looking for clients, but there had been nothing. Nobody, of course, had any idea where Kingy was.

She forwarded the email containing the drone footage to Ray's computer, and he set it up to show on the large screen on the wall.

'Okay,' Karen said, 'for those of you that didn't go out to the Marshall homestead this morning, we asked for drone footage of the property. We don't need a search warrant for that,' she said with a grin.

'We investigated as much as we could. Ray disappeared for a wee and a bit of a quick look round and found some random woman, but it turned out to be Diana's sister who is temporarily living there. The other bedrooms gave us nothing. But our nice back-up lads organised a drone operator to go out and just do a bit of filming around the general area. I've not seen this yet, so we all need to concentrate. You spot something, shout up. Ray?'

Ray gave a thumbs up and started the footage.

From high up it looked like a very large mansion, but as the drone dropped lower it put the size of the property into perspective. It picked up Diana and Paula getting into a taxi and leaving through the gates that now seemed to miraculously work effortlessly, and it picked up Liam Marshall leaving via the kitchen door with a small dog on a lead. He walked it out into the field at the back of the property, and they all saw the ramshackle caravan.

They watched it through to the end, and Karen turned to face them. 'Thoughts?'

There was a moment of silence and then Rachel held up a hand.

'We're not at school, Rachel,' Karen said quietly. 'You can just shout out like the rest of them do.'

Rachel blushed. 'Sorry boss, it's all still a bit scary. Anyway, I'm sure we all saw that caravan kind of tucked away in that little tree area, but there was a sort of path leading from it down to a gate at the bottom. Wonder if that gate is controlled by remote control like the main gates? Or if you just have a simple key to come and go as you please. Just a thought,' she finished.

'And that path isn't a manmade one, it's been created by the coming and going of cars. Looking at the caravan, it definitely looks to be in a state of disrepair on the outside, but...' Ray continued, and tried to zoom in to look more closely at the small mobile home.

'But it could be made to look like that? We need to get a look at it a bit closer. And we need a bloody search warrant, but we're not going to get one on the strength of us saying Freddie might be inside. We have no proof anyone is in it.' Karen frowned as she tried to see something that she knew she couldn't see.

Ray stood. 'I'll take the missus out tomorrow for a drive, might just have an engine malfunction outside that gate. Might have to get out and sort out the car, and inspect the lock.'

'Good lad, Ray,' Karen said. 'Try not to get into bother.'

'As if. I'm taking Angela, she's my protection officer.'

* * *

Karen felt a sense of frustration as her team said goodnight. It seemed nothing was progressing, and now they'd reached the end of Friday, which meant things would die away until Monday morning.

The drive home took longer than usual and she pulled into the driveway a mere minute after Matt and Harry arrived, and was able to help them carry items in. It seemed that her menfolk had spent most of their combined annual salary in the money pit that was Meadowhall, but she felt grateful that they had spent a bit more in McDonald's in the mall, meaning she didn't have to cook.

'We needed a printer?' she asked.

'Herms has been talking new printer words for a long, long time. I had to go to a computer shop as part of an investigation, so I took advantage,' Matt said, a huge smile on his face. 'Came highly recommended, this one, but mainly by Herms.'

'And the football boots?'

'He's grown another size, so needed some.'

'And the game?'

He laughed. 'Okay, hands up, I bribed him with the promise of a game to get us to have a valid reason for going into the shop. I only thought of the printer after we'd gone through the door. I'm going back tomorrow to make a decision on which new computer to buy.'

'What?'

He held up his hands. 'That's what the shop manager thinks. I'll tell him we've decided to have our old one upgraded or something, but it will get me back in there to do a bit more observing.'

He spent some time detailing what little signs he'd already spotted, and the money transfers he'd already annotated, and in the end Karen sat back with a sigh.

'Can I have a glass of wine now, please?'

'You can, my love,' and he stood to go to the fridge.

He poured out two glasses, and grasped her hand as he sat back down. 'Need to talk?'

'I don't know. I find it irritating that the weekend

gets in the way of our investigations sometimes, and I always make sure my team get their weekends off if it's at all possible. Ray is going out on a bit of a surveillance mission tomorrow morning, taking Angela with him. It'll probably turn into a shopping expedition for them, and maybe some lunch out, but even so... we work long enough hours during the week.'

'We can do it instead if you want Ray to have his full weekend off.'

She shook her head. 'No, we have a new niece. She'll be home at some point tomorrow, and I'd rather be here in case they need any help. It's quite possible they'll want some shopping doing, or a baby cuddling, or something like that.'

'Unless it's pouring with rain on Sunday, I'll take Harry for a kickabout in the new boots. And maybe we can go visit a garden centre in the afternoon?'

'Wow! It's ages since we did that. Shall we go to New Leaf?'

'Erm, no. It's a specific garden centre I thought we could visit. Summertime, it's called.'

'Your investigation?'

'My client owns it, just thought I'd like to see it. This husband of hers is definitely playing away, and I'd like to understand the garden centre set-up, in case there's something about that which helps me understand it all better. Sunday is always a nice busy day at any garden centre, and I'll buy you a coffee.'

'I'll hold you to that. I'm just going to make myself a sandwich or something, have a chat with Jaime, then maybe we can set up this printer? I'm assuming Harry doesn't need help setting up the new game or tying the laces on his new boots.'

'I don't think we'll see him at all tomorrow, and he's already playing the game.'

* * *

Karen spent half an hour on the phone with Jaime, who was clearly wanting to return to work sooner rather than later.

'You're definitely well enough to come back Monday?' Even Karen could hear the doubt in her voice as she asked the question.

'Honestly, boss, I'm fine. I felt a bit rough on the first day, but I'm good to go now.'

'Okay, come back Monday, but desk duties only for the first week. Understood?'

'Understood. You want to fill me in on anything?'

'No, I'll go through it all Monday morning, but it's a bit frustrating. We can't find anybody we want to find. We have suspects – can't find them. By the end of next week I want everybody in custody who should be in custody, and if I don't get them I'll go for a walk outside and pick up a couple of locals instead. It's so damn irritating.'

'That's a new way of arresting people, just walk outside and say come here, I'm charging you with first-degree murder.'

'I could make it work.'

'I don't doubt,' Jaime responded with a laugh, 'but it might be frowned upon.'

They disconnected after Jaime once again reassured her boss that she was absolutely fine, and wanted to return to work.

* * *

But Jaime wasn't absolutely fine. Mentally she felt a wreck. One day she hoped to have a baby, but she wanted to have some say in who the father would be, not simply have the father be the sperm donor. She felt dirty, sullied beyond anything she could have imagined.

It seemed that Leo Hampton had been transferred, and Karen had reassured her that it was a long distance – she need never see or hear of him again. But Karen knew there was no guarantee. He could be seconded anywhere in the country, just as she could be, maybe not on a permanent basis but on the basis that they knew the area from a previous point in their career.

On the night that she had returned from the clinic having had the successful procedure to dispose of her unborn foetus – she didn't dare think of it as a child – she had told her mother everything. Sitting side by side on the sofa, having hot chocolate drinks before heading off to bed, Jaime knew she had to talk. She didn't reveal Hampton's name, but she told her mother the details of the night that had brought her to the current place.

Trying hard not to show her anger, Jaime's mum had held her, rocked her as if she was a baby herself, and soothed her head. Slowly the tears stopped, but the words didn't.

They discussed the possibility of Jaime seeking counselling, but she hadn't wanted to even consider it. 'I don't do a nine-to-five job, Mum, where I can disappear for a couple of hours to have a session with a psychiatrist. It doesn't work like that. No, I'm going to have to battle through this, with you and my boss being the ones I can talk to. But first I need to go back to work. I want the others on the team to think I've just had a touch of flu, and I'm better now.'

She watched as her mum's head nodded in reluctant agreement. 'You'll stay with me until the weekend?'

'If that's okay?'

'Of course it's okay, Jaime. You're my daughter, you're welcome here anytime, as you very well know.'

'Then I'm going back to work next Monday. Physically I'm fine, and I don't do much of the running about to crime scenes and stuff, my expertise lies in computer work, tracing people, that sort of stuff, so I reckon I'll be absolutely fine. And gradually this will all seem like a bad dream, as the years move on.'

They held each other tightly, and Jaime stood. 'Thank you, Mum. I love you.'

* * *

Jaime returned home on the Saturday, cleaned her entire home from top to bottom, bought a new suit for work after accidentally popping into Marks and Spencer for some food to replenish a remarkably empty fridge, and spent Sunday reading a new book she had picked up before returning to her car. A crime thriller, just what she needed.

20

Saturday morning was a little overcast, and as Ray switched on his engine, the rain showed as a slight drizzle on his windscreen.

He cleared it, and by the time they had reached the end of their road it had become a little heavier.

Angela looked out of the windscreen and frowned. 'You know your plan to pull up where this gate is at the bottom of that field, and pretend something's wrong with the car? You don't need me as a co-actor, do you? I can continue to be the silly little wife who knows nothing about car mechanics, and stay inside in the shelter?'

'Yes. Although I do need you to show me what I can disconnect to make it look as though we've genuinely broken down. You know that old saying about not keeping a dog and barking yourself? Well, in my case it's something about not having a car mechanic and working under the bonnet yourself. Or whatever it is.'

'But it's raining.'

'It'll have stopped by the time we get there.' Ray sounded full of confidence.

Angela sighed. 'It's a good job my umbrella is in the car, isn't it?'

Ray shot a quick glance at her. 'Ah, we might have a problem with that.'

'You've given it away again, haven't you?'

'Not exactly. I gave one of the young lassies a lift home, because it was pouring with rain, and I handed her your brolly to get to the house. She did bring it back the day after.'

'So where is it now?'

'In my desk.'

Angela sat in silence for the rest of the journey, hoping it would have stopped drizzling by the time they reached their destination. Ray's 'expertise' as a car mechanic meant it would be her looking under the bonnet to disconnect something, that had to look as though it was a genuine sudden fault, in case they were questioned.

Ray's lack of mechanical knowledge had been how they had met – she had worked for her dad in his car repair shop from being about twelve years old, and was fully qualified by the time she was eighteen. Then Ray Ledger had limped his little old mini in, explaining something was wrong with it. He collected it two days later, and asked her out to say thank you.

And now, even though her life had been devoted to bringing up their children, that knowledge was surfacing once more to help her husband. And if she was brutally honest with herself, she was never happier than when her head was underneath a bonnet, or fiddling around with an exhaust pipe trying to extend its life for hopefully another year.

Ray pulled into a layby and took out the sketch he had worked on the previous night. There was a very tiny road that led to the field that held the gate. He needed to be sure he could find his way. He studied it for a couple of minutes, then put it in the glove box before restarting the car.

'Two minutes away,' he said to Angela. 'Keep your eyes peeled for what I suspect is an unmarked road.'

She nodded and peered through the raindrops running down her side window. 'Coming up on the left now,' she said, and she felt Ray touch the brakes.

He turned without indicating, and drove slowly

until he saw what appeared to be a fairly new gate. He pulled the car completely across the length of the gate, effectively stopping anyone from leaving. It was an automatic way of working, it was what they were trained to do, and yet he didn't think for one minute anybody would appear.

He switched off the car and released the bonnet. Both of them exited the vehicle, and Ray raised the bonnet, anchoring it in place. Angela reached in a hand and disconnected a cable. 'Pass me the keys,' she said quietly.

He handed them to her and she got into the driver's seat, inserted the keys into the ignition and tried to start the car. Nothing. A futile attempt at coaxing life into the engine, with nothing to show for it. Angela smiled. She really hadn't lost her touch.

She sat for a while longer, staying out of the rain and smiling to herself as she thought of Ray getting wetter and wetter. Maybe she might mention to him that if he'd returned her umbrella to the car he could have remained dry... She made an ungainly move, clambering over into the passenger seat. She could watch what her husband was doing much better by doing that, and she waited patiently.

Ray moved towards the gate. There was no lock. Just a large metal gate that looked as though it would move smoothly, with no clumpy grass sods to impede its progress. For a fast escape from the big house? Access to a tatty old caravan? He stared hard at the dwelling as if willing the door to open and some nefarious hooligan to step outside. Nefarious hooligans seemed to be on strike, he decided.

He opened the gate a fraction and slid through into the field. He didn't hear the harsh intake of breath made by his wife. He moved a little way up the hill, then stopped about halfway up. He had already worked it out that if someone was in the caravan, they would see him walking towards them, and come out to meet him. He hoped his warrant card was enough protection.

He would tell them he had broken down and was waiting for the arrival of help to get him going again. He could talk himself through most situations, he reckoned.

There was no movement from the dwelling. If someone had been walking around inside it, he felt sure it would have shaken the structure. It really looked as if it was ready to collapse to the ground.

He waited a few minutes then headed back down to where Angela was waiting for him. He knew she would be worrying if he attempted to go near the caravan, and he remembered Karen's words that he wasn't to approach it, merely to observe. If that observation drew somebody out into the open, all well and good, but if it didn't, he wasn't to approach without back-up. He guessed she wouldn't count Angela as back-up, so he reluctantly returned to his car and sat in the driver's seat. He felt wet. An umbrella would have been handy, either as a rain-shield or as a weapon.

'Nobody about?' Angela asked.

'Not a soul. Just using my eyes showed me that track running up the field leads directly to that caravan, but I couldn't see a vehicle from down here. There may be one the other side of the van, but it was like I had Karen in my ear telling me "observation from a distance only", so I came back down. We couldn't see evidence of a car on that drone footage I told you about, so we'll wait another couple of minutes before you work your magic and reconnect our car.'

'What shall we do when we've left here? That's assuming nobody shoots us with a rifle from that caravan.'

'You always this cheerful? What do you want to do?'

'Wentworth Garden Centre for a new chimenea? And some lunch? On you, of course.'

'Why do we need a new chimenea?'

'You broke ours last summer.'

'I didn't.'

'You did. And you took it to the tip.'

'We need a new one then?'

'Yes, and lunch.'

'Think I can put this on expenses?'

'Shouldn't think so for a minute,' she said. Her grin stretched across her face. 'Come on, let's get this car repaired and get over to Wentworth. Love it there.'

He shook his head in disbelief at how much this surveillance job was about to cost him. Easing himself out of the vehicle, he walked to the front and stared at it, before remembering he had to release the catch by the driver's seat for the bonnet to open. Angela was laughing when he walked back.

'Forget, did we?' she asked.

'Shut up, woman, and let's get this thing sorted. Complete waste of time. A gate with no lock, a derelict caravan, something tells me we're barking up the wrong tree here. I bet it's used as a play area for the grandkids or something, and because we don't know where bloody Freddie Earnshaw is, we're reading more into it than we should be.'

Angela reconnected the cable, and Ray started the engine while he waited for her to finish looking at it; he knew she missed the work she had loved so much, but despite his suggesting she might want to return to working with her dad, she had always said her job was to bring up the kids.

He squeezed her hand, put the car into gear and pulled away. 'I've got an idea,' he said. 'Keep your eyes peeled.' She stared at him. This was starting to have some James Bond elements to it, and as usual, her husband was making her smile.

* * *

Freddie Earnshaw exhaled slowly. He knew the feller that had walked up towards the van – he'd seen him at the Bath House, one of the Major Crimes team. How the fuck had they found him? Or had they? If they'd really thought he was living in such a decrepit old thing they'd have been in it anyway. How did they know about the van...? That bloody drone that had been buzzing about. He opened the window and took a deep breath of fresh air. Liam Marshall had done a damn good job of fitting out this van, but the heating was hot and a little overpowering.

He stood at the window for a minute, then went to the bathroom. He'd been wanting to pee, but hadn't dared take his eyes off that copper. He needed to know what he was doing. And what had his missus been doing under the bonnet?

He missed seeing the car drive past the gate on its return journey from where Ray had turned round at the end of the small lane. He missed seeing both Ray and Angela staring up the field, but he did have a very long and satisfying pee.

* * *

'Did you see that?' Ray asked.

'The open window? Certainly did. There's been no open window all the time we've been sat here. We drive away after repairing our poorly car, and suddenly there is an open window.'

'What do we do now?'

'I'll ring the boss when we get to Wentworth. She can be the one to decide whether to let it simmer or not, or whether to send in the troops this afternoon and get him out of there. The problem is, we're acting on a hunch more than having proof of anything here, and no judge will agree to a search warrant, much less an arrest warrant, unless there's some sort of proof. Now, if we'd found something like this with regard to Gordon King, we'd have gone in and got him. We have his fingerprint on a medication box found at a murder scene, but young Freddie – we just know he's involved, without any sort of concrete evidence. Yet...'

'You got this King bloke?'

He shook his head. 'Not yet, but he doesn't know we're looking for him really, so he's probably gone to the Costa del Sol for the week or something. We'll have him as soon as we can find him.'

'Ray Ledger, I love it when you talk dirty. Pull into a layby and kiss me.'

'It will be my pleasure,' he said. He drove for a mile, put on his indicators, and spent a pleasurable five minutes fulfilling his wife's request.

21

Karen listened to Ray's explanation of his morning with a smile on her face. All had seemed to be a waste of time until he had apparently had the smart idea to make it look as though they were leaving. Instead he had simply turned around and driven back down past the place where they had sat for some time repairing their car. The newly opened window told them there was somebody inside, and now it left her with the problem of what to do. If they brought Freddie Earnshaw in for questioning, she would have to spend the weekend in work, because legally they couldn't hang on to him in custody until Monday morning.

'Let me tell you what I plan to do,' she said to Matt,

'and then I want you to tell me if you would have done the same.'

He waited, feeling a little shocked. She rarely consulted with him, but he was aware there was a lack of any sort of evidence at the moment with the case.

'I'm going to let him think he's got away with it, that we have no idea Freddie Earnshaw could be inside that caravan. Then at six on Monday morning we'll go get him. The team will have had their weekend off, Jaime will be back to do what she does best with her computer, and we'll bring Liam Marshall in as well. Aiding and abetting a fugitive. He categorically denied any knowledge of Freddie being there, and yet I'm fairly sure that's who we'll find when we knock on that rickety door on Monday morning.'

Matt thought for a moment. 'I'd probably have done the same. There's nowhere to hide a couple of uniforms to keep an eye on things?'

'Not according to Ray. Open countryside, and as yet we have no proof he's actually done anything.'

'Okay, let's go tell this feller in Meadowhall we've changed our mind about a new computer. We'll drop Harry off at Becky's, and if you can possibly get a photo of Dominic Beecham behaving inappropriately with a member of staff called Marnie, it would be much appreciated.'

* * *

They stopped outside the shop and stood for a couple of minutes looking through to the interior of the shop.

'The bloke with the dark hair and the navy suit is Beecham. The girl he's standing really close to is Marnie. I don't know her surname.'

They watched as Marnie looked into Beecham's face and laughed at something he said. It was an intimate gesture; they were obviously comfortable with each other.

Karen raised her phone and took a picture, keeping her fingers crossed they could see anything on it.

A couple of minutes later they walked into the store and crossed towards a member of staff.

'Is Mr Beecham in?' Matt asked.

The young blond male assistant looked around. 'He was here a minute ago. He may have taken his coffee break.'

An equally young female assistant looked across and smirked. 'He'll not be long. They've gone into the storeroom.'

Greg, as his name tag suggested he was called, glared at his colleague then turned to Matt. 'Is there any help I can give you?'

'I was in yesterday and had quite a long chat with

Mr Beecham about the possibility of purchasing a new PC, so I'd prefer to deal with him, if that's okay. I'll just hang on for a bit until he gets back from his break. We'll have a look in the games section while we wait. Thank you for offering to help, but Mr Beecham has the information of what we're looking for, already.'

Both Beecham and Marnie had definitely disappeared so Matt and Karen moved towards the games section situated nearer the back of the shop, and only steps away from the door through which their new printer had arrived the previous day. Presumably the storeroom, where the young girl had suggested Beecham might be.

Ten minutes of patience was rewarded when Karen got a video of them returning to the shop floor, Marnie doing remedial work on her ponytail, and Beecham checking with her that he looked okay.

He spotted Matt straight away, so switched on a smile and walked towards him. 'Mr Forrester. Can I help?'

'Well,' Matt said, 'I'm not so sure now. We've had a look at the PC I was most interested in yesterday, but now we're undecided, wondering if we might be better getting two laptops. Coming here today has helped us to partially clarify it in our minds, but we don't want to make too hasty a decision. We've taken photos of two or three different ones, so now we're going home again to have a glass of wine and a laptop discussion.'

Beecham looked disappointed but forced a smile. 'Well, thank you for returning to let me know.'

'We actually came to buy one, but my partner thinks we need to discuss it a little more now, since she's had time to look around while you were on your coffee break.'

'Coffee break? Oh... no, we were tidying up in the storeroom, it was becoming a bit of a hazard in there. We've a big delivery arriving tomorrow, so they can fit it in now.'

'Well, thank you for your help. I'm sure we'll be back in the very near future.'

They left Beecham looking quite disgruntled and out of sorts, and walked out of the shop.

'Now what?' Karen asked.

'Garden centre?'

'You're going to tell her?'

'I'm going to advise her to get him removed from the joint account as a starting point. There's clearly something going on with him and Marnie and I suspect he's filling up his coffers with Annabel's money before leaving for pastures new. What did you think?'

'Without a doubt. You could see it in their faces when they came out of that storeroom. You want a coffee while we're here, or shall we wait until we get to Summertime?'

'We'll wait. I've had more than my fair share of Meadowhall, thanks.'

* * *

Summertime Garden Centre had a large parking area that was three-quarters full by the time Matt and Karen drove through the gates. They parked and headed through the entrance, straight into a gift section.

'This is pretty,' Karen said, stopping and taking in the large welcoming area. 'I didn't imagine it would be as big as this.'

'Neither did I. When she spoke about it, I imagined it to be quite small. I suspect she's put a tremendous amount of work into it since she first acquired it. She's obviously got a flair for it, so no wonder she's looking for a second property to develop. Let's see if we can find her, and maybe treat her to a bun and a coffee in her own coffee shop.'

They were directed to Annabel's office, where they found her staring out of a large window at the comings and goings in her outdoor plant area. She smiled as she recognised Matt.

'Lovely to see you again, Matt.'

'Thank you, Annabel. And this is my partner, Karen. We've been working on your behalf this morning, so thought we'd invite you for a drink in your café before telling you what we know.'

Annabel laughed. 'Let's hope it's not too busy. I had a meeting yesterday afternoon to discuss the possibility of extending it, as I seem to sell more tea and coffee than I do plants! It's become a really popular eating place.'

They followed her outside and then into the door of the eatery. It was busy, but Karen and Annabel commandeered a table while Matt went to the counter to order drinks and an assortment of buns.

The two women seemed to be getting on very well, and after paying he returned to the table to wait for their order to be delivered.

'Good staff,' he remarked.

'I think so,' she said. 'It's something I insist on, the rapport with my customers. And I don't just mean in here. Throughout the plant sections my staff are trained to have knowledge of the plants, not to just be salespeople. And as a result, the coffee shop now needs to expand,' she said with a laugh.

They waited for the order to arrive before beginning to talk about why they were really there. Matt opened the discussion by telling Annabel he had been twice to Meadowhall over the previous two days.

'I'm taking it it's not because you like Meadowhall?'

'Definitely not, I went specifically to meet your husband.'

Annabel waited expectantly.

'Annabel, I think the first thing you have to do is go to your bank and explain the situation, telling them you want him removed from the joint account. They will be able to see how much he is transferring, and understand your concerns. I think you need to do this sooner rather than later.'

'You think it was all a scam from the start?'

Matt spoke carefully. Presumably she had married Dominic because she loved him.

'I don't know yet, and believe me, this case isn't closed. I did feel there was reason for the urgency in stopping him having further access to your money. Presumably his own salary goes into his own account and not into your joint account? When I checked the statements there was no evidence of money going into your account from him, just out of it to him.'

'That's right. I told him to leave his own arrangements as they were. I just continued to pay for utilities and such mundane stuff, which is why I couldn't understand his need to withdraw such large amounts.'

'Annabel,' he said, biting into a large strawberry tart, 'you have to do this first thing Monday morning.' He hesitated before continuing. 'I also think there is some evidence to suggest he has another woman, somebody he works with.'

He watched as the colour drained from Annabel's face.

'You're sure?' she asked quietly.

'Reasonably sure. I will put surveillance on him, and we will get definite proof, but I'm simply speaking from observation of his behaviour over the past two visits to the shop. We also have a video of the two of them coming out of the storeroom. I believe the other staff members are aware of what's going on.'

Karen opened up the video and passed it to Annabel. The white-faced woman watched it in silence and then clicked on it to re-watch it. She opened up her fingers to enlarge the picture.

'She needed to adjust her bra. Is her name Marnie? That's what it looks like on her name tag.'

Karen nodded. 'It is, and she did. And his trousers seemed to be a little uncomfortable as well. I will run a check on him and pass the results onto Matt if there is any previous evidence of him scamming anybody, and I'll do it as soon as I get into work on Monday. If there is evidence, you need to bring the Fraud Squad into it.'

Annabel looked puzzled. 'You're with the police?'

Karen nodded. 'DI Karen Nelson, Major Crimes Unit, during working hours, today I'm Karen, Matt's life partner. Matt will produce a report for you, but if I do find any trace of anything he's done before, you have to stop him doing it to anyone else. The case won't come to me, I tend to deal in murders, but when Matt was in the police he was in the Fraud Squad before he became DI in Major Crimes, so he knows exactly what they will want. Do what he tells you to do, and maybe the courts will get back anything he has already taken. But if he is a con artist, they'll put him away. Other women will be safe from him then.'

Annabel leaned back on her chair. 'I thought he loved me.'

'Maybe he did at the start. We don't know if he's done this before. I suspect it was an added bonus when he realised how wealthy you are. I'd guess he's been steadily filling his coffers, and I'm not saying it's because he's going to plan an escape with Marnie, I'm of the impression he's building up a fund in case you find out. You'd pack his bags, wouldn't you?'

'Too damn right I would,' Annabel said, smacking her hand down hard onto the table. 'Too damn right I would.'

22

They loaded up the car with two Salix trees, a gnome in a policeman's uniform who looked remarkably like Ray Ledger, and a pink Kalanchoe plant in a pretty, cerise porcelain pot that Karen intended taking into work on Monday morning and placing on Jaime's desk.

'A successful trip?' Karen asked.

'It was if we've convinced Annabel to do nothing over the weekend. She's a sensible lady though, I don't think she'll jeopardise anything for the sake of waiting till she can be in full control on Monday. You seemed to get on well with her.'

'I liked her. Certainly admired her for what she's

done with her business. I hadn't realised it was just a plant nursery at the beginning, and she's expanded it into a full-blown garden centre. We must tell Herms and Steve about it, it's the sort of thing I can imagine Steve wanting to do in future years. I know his land-scaping business is his, but he's handed over control to a manager almost fully now. This might be a next log-ical step for him.'

'There's always a demand for garden centres, even in the winter, because Christmas is a big thing for sales then. And straight after Christmas we're preparing for spring. It's certainly a year-round thing.'

Karen smiled. 'And we didn't go into the place to buy anything other than a coffee, and we've spent a small fortune. I'm going to send a picture of our new gnome to Ray, tell him we've named it after him. Let's head home now, check that the new family are okay and don't need anything.'

'Just give me a minute.' He indicated and pulled into a layby. They sat for a moment enjoying the newly emerged greenness of the trees surrounding them, and the sunshine filtering through the windscreen.

'Rosie's a beautiful baby,' Matt said.

'Certainly is,' Karen agreed.

'Should we think about it? Having a baby, I mean.'

Karen was clearly startled. 'We've got Harry.'

'Is Harry enough for you? I don't want to presume you don't want a child of your own. That would be wrong of me.'

'It would,' she laughed, 'but my career is pretty important to me, and although I love Harry as if he's my own, he's definitely enough for me. So no, you don't have to panic about making me happy, I've never felt so settled and fulfilled.'

He breathed a sigh of relief. 'Okay, on to part two. I love you.'

'I know. I love you too.'

He reached over to the glove box and dropped it open. A small box lay just inside, and he took it out.

'So will you marry me?' he asked, and opened the box.

The solitaire diamond flashed in the sunlight, and Karen drew in a sharp breath.

'Oh, my God. Oh, my God!'

'Is that yes or no? Would you like to spend the rest of your life with me?' Matt sounded worried.

'It's a yes, you muppet.' She pulled him towards her and kissed him very firmly. 'I'm just a bit shocked, that's all. We've just never mentioned that sort of commitment...'

'I waited till I thought you were ready. Your first marriage wasn't a good one, and I needed to be sure that mentally you'd recovered from that.'

'Oh, I have,' she laughed. 'You make me happy, Matt. So, are you going to put it on my finger, or is it just for show?'

He removed it from the box, and slid it carefully onto her third finger. It fit perfectly. He didn't admit to taking her old wedding ring to the jewellers for the sizing of the engagement ring, he thought it might rather take away from the romance of the occasion. Better that she thought he was pretty damn clever to have guessed the right size.

* * *

Steve and Hermia looked tired. 'She's such a good baby,' Steve said. 'Sleeps all day. Wakes up as we go to bed.'

'Then sleep when she sleeps,' Matt said. 'I remember having the same issue with Harry, so we changed our sleep patterns to fit in with him until we got over the first part. It will pass, and if we can do anything to help, you only have to ask. Do you need anything at the moment?'

'Shopping.' Hermia waved a list.

'We'll go, you two get your heads down for a couple of hours until Rosie wakes up again. And come for a meal tonight? We've all got some celebrating to do. Sorry you can't have much champagne, Herms, but we can.'

Matt lifted Karen's left hand, and Hermia burst into tears. 'That's so freakin' wonderful,' she sobbed. 'And a shot glass of champagne won't hurt, I'm sure. Of course we'll come.'

'It'll just be the four of us, Harry's at his mum's. We sent him a picture of Karen's left hand, and he's over the moon. Wants to call her Mum Two now instead of Karen.' Matt picked up the shopping list and they left the two baby parents to attempt some sleep.

* * *

'Does that look like me?' Ray held his phone out to his wife.

She spluttered with laughter. 'Too right it does.'

'Karen and Matt have just bought it from a garden centre. She bought it because it looked like me, and now they've called it Ray.'

'We need one for our garden. Find out where they got it from.'

'Angela, we are not having a policeman gnome in our garden, especially one that resembles me.'

'You're mardy, Ray Ledger.' Angela made a mental note to ring Matt when Ray wasn't around to find out where they'd bought it from.

Ray continued to stare out of the lounge window, and she knew he was lost in his thoughts.

'What's wrong?'

'He was there, that little toerag was there in that caravan. And I had no authority to go and yank him out of it. He thought he had fooled us by remaining perfectly still, didn't he?'

'You'll get your chance to explain to him just what he did wrong when he opened that window, and one day you'll be able to tell him he should never underestimate DS Ray Ledger.'

She put her arms around her husband and hugged him. He was definitely out of sorts, and she hoped Karen would ask him to go to the caravan in the early hours of Monday morning. He certainly should be the one to bring in Freddie Earnshaw.

* * *

Lynn Earnshaw was lying on Josh's bed, cuddling his Sheffield Wednesday shirt. She couldn't stop her tears;

every time anything happened it brought it all back, and she seemed to be permanently crying. The bunches of flowers leaning against the green railings across the road from her kitchen window almost matched the small mountain of flowers that had been left in her front garden. Every bunch had a message for Josh.

There was no longer a police presence at the top of the incline leading down to the Bath House, but crime scene tape was still in place. She wanted to walk down and be where it had happened, where Josh had breathed his last breath, and DI Nelson had promised her she could do that once they were completely sure there was nothing left for them to find.

What could they possibly find now? Wasn't it enough that they had found her Josh? She watched two young girls who looked to be around Josh's age as they walked across the road and towards her garden. They were carrying flowers, and they came on to her path and leaned over to place their offering. They looked at some of the other names, and both of them were visibly upset.

They jumped as she exited her side door, and began to approach them.

'Thank you,' Lynn said. 'Thank you for caring enough about Josh that you brought him some flowers.'

'We would have brought them before this,' the blonde-haired girl said, 'but we had to wait to get our spending money first.'

Lynn couldn't speak. That these two girls should choose to spend their own money on flowers for her boy was almost unbelievable.

She took a deep breath and tried to smile. 'Thank you,' she said. 'Josh would have appreciated the thought so very much.'

'We really liked Josh,' the blonde girl spoke again. The other girl was visibly upset, and Lynn suspected she wasn't capable of speech.

'I think Josh was very well liked. Look at all these flowers, and all those over the road.'

'Have they caught anybody yet?' This time the second girl spoke.

Lynn shook her head. 'Not yet, but they will.'

'I hope so,' they said in unison, and then turned to walk down the path.

Lynn bent down to look at the flowers they had left, and their card said:

We'll miss you so much, Josh. Love Carrie and Megan. xxx

She was violently sobbing as she returned to her

lounge. Every day was a little bit harder, and it didn't help that the police weren't saying anything. She picked up her phone and almost rang Freddie, but then threw it onto the sofa. No more Freddie in her life, he was bad news.

She had no doubt he had descended on her mum and dad, but she wasn't sure her mum would have welcomed him with open arms. Her dad would have done, though. Whatever Freddie wanted, Freddie got.

Maybe she should come clean and tell that policewoman what she suspected as to her son's whereabouts. Maybe a short sharp shock of a police visit would be the thing that could steer Freddie away from the drugs.

A short sharp shock...

* * *

Freddie was planning his own short sharp shock, without any idea of his mother's thoughts. He'd had word that Kingy had returned to Sheffield, and Kingy now had to be dealt with.

The police might not have any idea of who had killed Josh, but he had more than an idea. He knew.

And he had no intentions of dobbing Kingy in to them, because that would inevitably see him ending up inside as well. But he could deal with him. And it would be terminal. An eye for an eye and all that stuff. The bastard hadn't realised how much he cared about Josh, how as little kids they'd been there for each other, and Kingy had stopped any chance of that carrying on.

Kingy's girls would have to source their own drugs in future – and he, of course, could let them know he could keep them well supplied. But the main objective was to do to Kingy what Kingy had done to Josh.

Josh had hated being asked to deliver stuff, and if he hadn't been going to that blasted party, he would have dropped the stuff off himself. And Kingy wouldn't have gone for him, he was too valuable, made life easy for the pimp.

So now it was payback time. Freddie didn't suppose he would ever find out why Kingy had killed Josh, but he damn well knew he had. And there was also no way the police could have worked out Kingy was there that night, so it was down to him to get justice for Josh.

Justice for Josh. It had a nice ring to it, and he stared out of the caravan window and looked down to the bottom of the field. That bloody car hadn't come back, so his worries were over about that. He guessed the bonnet being up meant they had really had a problem, but they'd obviously sorted it and gone.

Nobody but his grandparents knew where he was, and right at this point in time that suited him. With his car hidden inside the small coppice of trees, he was invisible to the world, until he decided it was time to become visible.

23

Freddie Earnshaw chose Sunday evening to kill Gordon King. It would be a momentous thing, and maybe he could always stick to Sundays for killing people, he thought. The biddy who wouldn't give up her drugs the previous week had paid for being stroppy, although in all fairness he hadn't expected her to die. He thought he'd only knifed her a little bit, but her dying had seemed to be the start of all this shit that had dropped on his world.

His grandfather had taken him along to the shooting range from an early age, alongside Niall, his son. Freddie spared a brief thought for Niall, now locked up for murder, and took out the gun he had found in one of the filing cabinets.

Liam had said, as he left the caravan, that he might find something useful in the bottom drawer, and sure enough there was a loaded gun. He had taken it out a couple of times, and knew that this was how Kingy would die.

Justice for Josh.

* * *

He spent Sunday mainly dozing or listening to his music, then around six he began to prepare for his evening. He wasn't hungry, so settled for a couple of slices of toast, having not been bothered about food all day.

He locked up and headed towards his car, his eyes scanning the vista laid out before him. It was really all fields and trees, and he knew it had helped with his coming to terms with losing Josh, and had helped just as much with deciding how to kill the bastard who had caused Josh's death.

The track down to the gate was quite steep and he drove carefully, pulling up at the bottom to open the gate. He felt sure his grandfather had said the padlock wouldn't be locked, but it appeared to be missing altogether. He pulled the car through, then went back to close the gate.

He knew exactly where the pimp and his girls would be on that night – they went every Sunday to a nightclub called The SteelTrap, where Kingy's girls were always appreciated.

He drove into the city centre and parked on a side street, being careful to pay for the parking. Then he walked the mile or so to where The SteelTrap was located, the gun concealed in the bottom of his backpack.

He calculated the distance he would need for the shot to be accurate, and sat on a small stone wall to wait until taxis arrived bringing Kingy's crowd. Darkness would have fallen by then, and he pulled up his hood to wait out the time.

* * *

Taxi number one carried Kingy and three girls. Taxi number two pulled up behind it, and everyone began to spill out.

Freddie aimed carefully – he had one chance. He knew the girls would scream and scatter, so Gordon King had to become the late Gordon King with one shot.

Kingy went down and there was a stunned silence for a moment before everyone started screaming and diving for cover back inside the taxis, where the drivers were trying to push them back out. They didn't want to be called in for questioning. They had a living to earn and they couldn't do that sitting in interrogation rooms all night.

There was a pool of blood growing under Kingy's head, although Freddie didn't see that, he was already running down backstreets and heading for the city centre. It would be on Facebook quick enough to tell him if he'd been successful, but his heart was telling him he had. The shot was good, it was clean, and it took Kingy down instantly.

He crossed over the River Don that ran through Sheffield city centre and was tempted to throw in the gun, but it was a good tool, and one he thought he might regret tossing. He paused for a moment staring into the river, mainly to get his breath back, then continued on to collect his car.

* * *

Once back in the caravan, he poured himself a whisky. Then he poured a second one. He tried not to think about potential ramifications of the night's events if Kingy survived, but he knew he had to believe in himself. He'd always been a good shot, the bullet trajectory had been clear and straight, and Kingy had gone down instantly. He had to be dead. Didn't he?

Justice for Josh.

* * *

The scene was attended by officers from Sheffield Central, but when the identity of the deceased was revealed it was instantly flagged as an urgent referral to Moss Way. Karen received the call in the middle of a dream that she would have preferred to continue.

Within twenty minutes she was on scene, inside a white tent staring at the man they had been seeking for the past couple of days. They'd never get to speak to him now, was the rueful thought that flashed through her mind. One side of his head had disappeared, and the attending pathologist confirmed death would have been instant.

'Somebody got to him first,' Karen murmured quietly.

'Before you had chance to bring him in?' DI Scott Townsend from Central Division appeared by her side.

She nodded. 'We couldn't find him, although a couple of his girls said he was in Majorca for a few days, would be back this week.'

'He arrived home this afternoon, according to his girls.'

'We believe he killed a teenage lad last Monday night. We managed to get fingerprints on a medication box connected to the murder, and they were his fingerprints. By the time we knew about this he'd disappeared.'

'I'll make sure a copy of the post-mortem report is sent to you, but whoever shot him was pretty good at target work. One shot, as far as we can tell, and everybody else agrees they only heard one gunshot. Saw nothing, of course, heard nothing, no cars started up, even the taxis that had brought the victim and a load of girls had decided to wait. We've got their details, and sent them on their way, but the girls are all inside the club.'

'You have their details?'

He nodded. 'The officers do. I'll tell them to send them on to you.'

'Thank you. You can let them go home, but tell them we'll be around to talk to them tomorrow.'

He shook her hand and she turned to walk away. 'I'm on an arrest job at six in the morning. I need to go home. Thank you for contacting me.'

'You're welcome. Good luck for tomorrow.'

She glanced at her watch. 'It's today.'

* * *

An expert shot. Another young lad had been an expert shot, Liam Marshall's boy, Niall. Who was presumably Freddie Earnshaw's uncle. Could Freddie have killed Gordon? But then, what did Freddie Earnshaw know about Gordon King, and why was he keeping quiet about it?

Thoughts screamed through Karen's head. Had Liam Marshall taken Niall and Freddie to the rifle ranges? Had they both become expert marksmen? Why the hell hadn't she followed her instincts and left somebody on surveillance of the caravan just until they could arrest him at the right time to be able to hang on to him for a couple of days?

Karen pulled onto their driveway, and Matt came out to meet her.

'Cuppa?' he asked.

'Hot chocolate, please. I need to sleep, even if it's only for a couple of hours.'

'Was it him?'

She nodded. 'It was. Half his head gone, lots of blood, traumatised females all over the place, taxi drivers mithering to go about their business. I tell you, Matt, if I ever had to work the Central beat, I'd resign. I suspect it's all going to be passed to me, which actually is where it belongs, but I made my excuses and legged it. Then spent the entire journey home thinking things through. Tell you what, I almost feel like yanking bloody Freddie Earnshaw out of that caravan right now, and battering the truth out of him.'

He gave their drinks a final stir and handed one to her. 'Drink this quickly, and let's get off to bed. Did you say you're picking up Rachel?'

She smiled. The hot chocolate was just what she needed. 'I am. She's a good kid. Never grumbles, just does what she's asked to do. Never flinched when I said we were going to bring somebody in at six in the morning. We're meeting Ray and Kevin at the bottom of that lane, then going up with bolt cutters in case the gate is locked. If I have to climb over it, I don't care. I will get this bloody Earnshaw out of there, never mind being protected by Granddad.'

'Liam Marshall does seem to have a lot of fingers in a lot of different pies, doesn't he? He was always a pain when I was DI, his name cropped up at some point in about half the investigations we did, but we never had anything on him that stuck. Whatever Freddie has or hasn't done, it's not going to impact on him, is it?'

'I'll make it,' she said quietly. 'Harbouring a criminal is a crime, you know. And a lot will depend on who that gun that shot Kingy is registered to. I'll bet next month's salary that it's registered to Liam. In fact, now I'm thinking outside the box, I wonder what sort of qualifications Liam has for rifle shooting and target practice. It was him that took Niall, and possibly Freddie, to the ranges.'

They finished their drinks, climbed the stairs, and Karen set her alarm for five o'clock, disgusted that it was already half past one. And still her mind wouldn't close down, she went through everything her logical mind was telling her, until finally sleep won, and she closed her eyes.

* * *

She would have sworn on oath that her phone was broken, but unfortunately it wasn't. It really was five on quite a chilly Monday morning. She dressed in jeans, a warm sweater, and took a jacket along as well. She hesitated between boots and her favourite Skechers trainers, and settled on the trainers. If she needed to chase the little runt, she would be able to run faster in trainers. She scraped her hair into a ponytail, grabbed her car keys and left the house, believing Matt to be still asleep.

He wasn't. His unease was hanging over him like a pall, and he would have given anything to be with her on what he felt was a dangerous activity. Although Karen didn't seem to believe Freddie Earnshaw had anything to do with the death of his brother, she did believe Freddie had murdered Susan Hunter for her drugs, and now she believed he could be the one to have pulled the trigger of the gun that had killed Gordon King, the man she suspected had killed Josh Earnshaw. All intermingled, and only Freddie left alive to be questioned.

Two murders potentially attributable to Freddie, and Karen was going to bring him in for questioning. He had seen her question many suspects, and had rarely seen any walk back out of the station. She was always ready, always sure, when she began her interviews, and he knew she would get Freddie bang to rights, but she had to safely get him out of that caravan and into a waiting van for transportation to Moss Way first.

* * *

Rachel was waiting for Karen, dressed warmly.

'Bloody cold,' she grumbled as she slid into the passenger seat.

Karen grinned. 'You'll warm up when we're chasing round this field after Freddie Earnshaw.'

'You think he'll click on?'

'Not if we're smarter than him. And we are.'

They began to warm up as the car heater kicked into gear, and as they approached the bottom of the lane that led to their destination field, she spotted both Ray's car and the prisoner transport van. Neither would have been visible from the field, and she breathed a sigh of relief.

Now Karen just had to hope that it was Freddie Earnshaw in the caravan, and that the open window seen on Ray's second drive past didn't just mean somebody who was of no consequence to them was actually in it.

24

Karen and Rachel got out of their car and walked towards where Ray and Kevin were standing conferring with two uniforms, who had driven the prisoner transport van.

'Good morning,' she said, and smiled at all of them. 'Lovely day for it, isn't it?'

'No, it's not,' Ray grumbled. 'It's bloody cold.'

'Same words that I used,' Rachel said. 'But apparently we'll warm up when we're chasing this suspect around the field.'

'That right, is it?' Ray asked his boss, and she grinned and shrugged.

'Okay, here's what we'll do. One of us needs to duck down behind that hedge and get up to the gate, check it still doesn't have a padlock or any other sort of lock on it. If it doesn't, we're good to go. If it does, I want one of you big tough men to go with a bolt cutter and make sure we can open that gate. This hedge is far too prickly to be forcing our way through it.'

'I'll go,' Kevin said, and they watched as he lowered himself before reaching the hedge. He arrived at the gate, gave it a gentle push and it moved. He returned to them at some speed.

'It's fine, seems to open quite easily. As soon as we go through it, we will be visible from the caravan. I assume we're counting on him still being asleep, so silence is the order of the day?'

'It is. The longer he sleeps the better. Ideally I'd like to be at the caravan before he knows we've arrived. Okay, I want you two to remain at the bottom of the field, outside the gate.' The two uniformed officers both nodded to show they understood. 'Ray, Kevin, Rachel and I will all go through the gate, with about thirty seconds between us, and head up the hill towards the caravan. Any sight of movement, shout out.'

Without speaking, they all held up a thumb.

'Okay, I'll go first. No talking from now on until we have to.'

Karen ducked down behind the hedge and moved towards the gate. She felt Rachel arrive within a few seconds and then was joined by Ray and Kevin. She slowly opened the gate and slipped inside the field. She now had her first proper sighting of the caravan and where it was in relation to the gate. The path leading to the temporary home of what she hoped was her suspect was quite clear. It hadn't been made but had clearly evolved through vehicles having been driven on it. Twin earth tracks had formed either side of a central grassed section, and she set off up the hill, walking alongside the track.

The others followed, spreading themselves out across the small field. If he ran, one of them would be on hand to stop him.

They were about halfway up the hill, still silent, when they heard the sound of an engine starting up. The noise came from the small, wooded copse, and Karen knew they had been rumbled. This was no normal rundown caravan, this caravan had security on it to protect whoever was staying in it at any given time. This was a bolthole for friends of Liam Marshall, and she guessed even Diana Marshall knew nothing about it.

She turned to look at the others, who had all stopped, and were awaiting further instructions. They too had heard the engine start.

The two uniformed officers had also heard it, and

acting on impulse were pulling the gate closed, but with them on the inside just in case they were needed to help apprehend him.

She used the same signal of holding up a thumb to say they had acted correctly, and she turned back to look for where the car was.

They could all hear it, a low throaty growl that told them it was being revved ready for flight, and Karen muttered, 'Fuck, fuck, fuck,' under her breath, knowing their problems had really escalated. This field was almost like an extra-large garden at the back of the house, and she knew Liam would have made sure there was more than one escape hatch – there had to be another route out of the field down the side of the big house. Closing that bottom gate hadn't given them any sort of advantage at all.

Kevin was the closest to her. 'Kev, get back to your car and get it round to the front gates of this house. Make sure you park across them to stop anybody from leaving.'

Kevin sprinted down the field, knowing he was battling against time. The officer opened the gate, then closed it behind him once Kevin was through and dashing along the road.

Within a minute he was parked across the main gates, and nobody was getting through.

* * *

The car was still rumbling in the cold air, and none of them could see it. Karen suddenly wondered if it was a decoy – had Freddie Earnshaw used his brains and already begun his great escape around the side of the house, but without his car? Had he started it to make them think that was how he was going to get away? She began to run up the incline to get to where the sound was, and Ray and Rachel continued towards the caravan.

Karen knew she needed answers, she needed to rule out whether he was in that bloody car or not, and if he was, did he have a gun trained on the first officer to approach him? That would be her, then, briefly crossed her mind, but her temper had risen, and she continued towards the engine noise.

And then it increased, giving her one answer. He was definitely in the car. Squirrels being playful couldn't make engines suddenly increase in volume. Only humans could do that, and every instinct told her that the human doing it in this car was Freddie Earnshaw.

Then she saw a flash of red as the car moved for the first time and she hesitated, unsure what would happen next. Then it screamed, as if in pain, and moved towards her, hurtling out of the copse that had kept it hidden from the prying cameras of the drone.

She tried to turn, to move faster than the car was moving, but it rammed her back and continued to drive over her where she landed face down.

Karen felt nothing; she didn't hear Rachel scream, didn't see Ray running towards her, didn't see the car crash into the closed gate at the bottom of the field, and didn't see Freddie Earnshaw being tasered by one of the uniforms as he was dragged from the car clutching a gun.

* * *

Matt arrived two minutes after the ambulance. Ray had rung him to tell him to get there by whatever means he could, but to get there quickly.

The ambulance parked on the road and the paramedics ran up the field carrying bags, and a stretcher. Ray had put Karen into the recovery position, but he knew it wouldn't help. The paramedics took over from him, and they used a defibrillator to try to restart her heart, but as Matt was running up the field they were shaking their heads.

'No,' he yelled. 'Keep going. You can't let her die.'

Ray went to stand by him. 'She died instantly,

Matt,' he said. 'I knew she'd gone when I turned her from her front to being on her side. I haven't left her, not for a second. I'm so sorry, boss.'

Matt dropped to his knees and allowed the tears to fall. He lifted Karen's left hand and kissed the finger that only so recently had worn his engagement ring.

'Where is he?' he said quietly to Ray. 'Where is the bastard who did this to my Karen?'

'On his way to Moss Way. I told the uniforms who've been helping us out to get him out of here. He's in the prisoner transfer van, so don't go chasing after him, boss. You getting into trouble isn't going to help anyone, especially your Harry, is it?'

Matt sank to the floor, unable to stand for a second longer. He touched Karen's beautiful face, and wiped some dirt from her cheek. 'You got him, my love, you got him.'

The forensics van arrived at the bottom gate, and Ray watched as Martin Moore arrived with his team. Ray hooked his hand under Matt's arm, and pulled him upright. 'Come on, boss, you know we have to let the pathologist do his job now.'

He led Matt to one side, and they stood watching the tent being erected over Karen's still warm body. Martin approached the two men and spoke to Matt. 'Matt, I'm so sorry for this awful loss. I'll take care of her for you, and if there's anything you want, my number is in Karen's phone.'

Matt could no longer speak. He simply nodded, and watched all the activity happening around his lady. Normally at a crime scene there would be some general chatter as jobs were handed out, photographers consulted, but there was nothing. Nobody wanted to say anything. Karen was usually one of the first detectives on scene, not the subject of the scene, and every person present was clearly in shock.

Kevin had returned from his front entrance vigil, and was valiantly trying to comfort Rachel, who was deeply distressed. She had watched everything, unable to help Karen. It had been obvious what was going to happen; Earnshaw had waited for just the right moment, probably thinking he could make good his escape while they were all dealing with their colleague. Rachel hoped that the taser, the deep gash on Earnshaw's head, and all his aches and pains would eventually kill him. But she knew it wouldn't, that was just wishful thinking.

The two uniformed officers had decided he didn't even need a doctor, and if it was proved he did, they could get one back at the station. They both recognised that with the arrival of the DI's partner things could potentially take a turn for the worse, and Earnshaw could end up needing either a doctor or an undertaker. Their thoughts had clearly been echoed by Ray Ledger, now the senior officer on site, and he had suggested they might want to get the suspect locked away back at Moss Way as soon as possible.

'Where's my grandson?' The irate figure of Liam Marshall, accompanied by his wife Diana, was standing at the top of the field, staring with some disbelief at all the activity in his field so early in the morning.

'Locked up,' Ray said, strolling over to the pair with no evidence of any rush to get to them. 'And will be for the rest of his life. Killing a police officer is life with no possibility of parole, you know, and then there's two other murders to take into consideration. So don't waste your money on a super swish lawyer for him, because he's not getting out of this one.'

Diana reached to grasp her husband's arm. 'Liam, what's he saying? Where's Freddie? Was he still in that dirty little caravan?'

Liam stared at his wife. She really hadn't a brain cell in her head these days. She must have heard every word that had just been said to him, but she seemed not to have understood any of it.

'He's locked up, Diana. We've managed to lose a son and two grandchildren in a very short space of time. I'd best go try to contact our Lynn, let her know what's going on. If I can get a straight answer from dickhead, here.'

Ray stared at him. 'That's acting DI Ray Ledger to you. And I hope the contempt your daughter feels for you comes across in the phone conversation. I'm sure it will.'

25

On that same Monday morning, Annabel Beecham was at her bank on Church Street, in the centre of Sheffield. She hadn't said a word about her plans to Dominic, but her quietness stopped when she met with the bank manager.

They knew each other well, had been manager and customer for many years, and Ben Harrison had an infinite amount of respect for this particular customer. She was careful with her money, invested wisely, and he had never hesitated to give help when it had been requested.

Knowing her aspirations for progression to a second garden centre premises, he expected the discussion to be around financial backing if it was required, and a general chat about all things plant related. The talk was about something so outside his expectations, he felt shocked.

He knew she hadn't been married for long, and he had been pleased to organise for a second credit card and a second debit card for use on her accounts, both of them to be in her new husband's name. She had explained it would make life easier if they both used the same account.

He had been the one to email her to warn her of significant amounts being transferred out of her account, and she had rung him to say it was all above board. He figured she was old enough to know what she was doing without his interference, and the issue had died a natural death. Or so he had thought.

'I want to remove my husband's name from any accounts it may be on, and I want you to cancel his debit and credit cards with immediate effect.'

He tried desperately not to sound shocked, and quietly said it would only affect her current account and her credit card, both of which he could easily comply with.

'You've separated?' he asked.

'In an hour or so we will have, I just want to sort out the finances before I spectacularly dump him.'

'I'm really sorry to hear this, Annabel. However,

I'm sure you know what you're doing, and not acting without giving it careful consideration.'

She took a deep breath. 'I knew something was wrong. I could see what he was withdrawing, and for no obvious reason. He wasn't spending anything. I bought him a brand-new car for a wedding present so he doesn't even have that as an expense, he lives in my home, which, by the way, is still my home. I didn't add him to the deeds or anything. But I did go to see a private detective who, after looking through my bank statements, wanted to actually get a feel for my husband, and went to where he works to meet him. It turns out Dominic is very friendly with Marnie, a member of his staff.'

'And your PI saw this?'

'He did. He went again on Saturday, and his partner managed to get a little video of them coming out of a storeroom, rearranging clothes. It was very obvious what had been going on. My PI then came to visit me at the garden centre and told me what was going on. It's been on my mind since Saturday, and I hoped you could find half an hour this morning to talk to me.'

'Annabel, you're a very valued customer. I'll always have time for you. So, I've cancelled his cards, and removed his name from both accounts. We can try to get some of the money back that he's taken, but as you gave permission for that to happen, it's doubtful we'd be very successful.'

'Don't worry about it, Ben. I'll write it off to experience. I'm going to burn all his clothes that are still at my place, and also dump him in front of his staff. Then I'm off to Florida for a holiday. I know it's our busiest time of year, but I have a damn good manager in the garden centre who can take care of everything for three weeks, and I've never met Mickey Mouse in person.'

She stood and held out her hand. Ben shook it and wished her good luck. 'You do know he's not a real person, don't you?' he asked her.

'Who? My husband?'

'No,' he said. 'Mickey Mouse.'

* * *

Annabel entered Meadowhall and headed straight to a coffee shop for a medium latte and a huge custard doughnut. Both items were delicious, and she sat reading her Kindle for almost half an hour before heading for the escalator that deposited her right outside her husband's workplace.

She had only been once before, and doubted that

anyone would recognise her. Apart from Dominic, anyway. She looked around the nearby shops and saw WH Smith. Oh my. Books. Maybe just a little squandering of some of her wealth might be in order when she had finished enjoying the next few minutes. And Boots the Chemist was right next door. Suntan lotion. She would need that. She could feel a proper spending spree coming on. She rarely advanced into Meadowhall because it tended to have this influence on her.

She turned right and walked into Dominic's shop. Nobody approached her, and eventually she went to a member of staff who seemed to simply be staring into space.

'Is Dominic around?'

'He's in the storeroom, won't be long.'

'Where's the storeroom? I'm his wife.'

She saw the look of horror that flashed across the young lad's face. He clearly didn't know what to do, how to deal with the situation. Eventually he gave in and pointed to the door at the back of the large room.

'That's it,' he said, 'but he's probably busy.'

'And Marnie? Is she busy too?'

Annabel didn't wait for an answer, just walked down the shop, not bothering knocking on the door. It opened easily, and Dominic appeared to be attached to the left nipple of Marnie. He turned his head as the door opened, and Marnie squealed. 'Ouch, Dom baby. That hurt.'

'Dom baby? My God,' Annabel laughed. 'Okay, Dom baby, I've come for your keys to my house.' She reached out her hand, and he unclipped his bundle of keys from a chain attached to his trouser loop. He handed her the set that was for her home, and she deliberately checked them in front of him, letting him know what she thought of his honesty and integrity without saying a word. 'You won't need them any more. I'm having a bonfire of all your clothes tonight, and the divorce papers will be prepared as soon as it is possible. Your bank cards are already cancelled, and of course you no longer have access to my internet banking.'

She turned her back on the two people currently trying to smarten up their clothing, and walked away from her marriage. Dom hadn't said a word.

She sat on one of the many seats for tired shoppers, and for a moment felt numb. It was done. She took out her phone to ring Matt and ask him to send her a bill, but it went straight to voicemail.

She tried Carol at the office, but this time the voicemail reported that the business was closed temporarily due to family matters, so she clicked off, stood and returned to her car.

The drive home seemed to take forever, but finally she was there, and she felt herself breathe a huge sigh of relief that her morning was done. Her marriage was done as well, which gave her a small frisson of excitement for some strange reason. She had thought she had loved Dominic, but it had been very easy to get rid of him, mentally and physically.

Now she had decisions to make. Should she go meet Mr Mouse and hope they fell in love, or should she first of all try to find her second garden centre? She smiled to herself. Suddenly her world had changed, she was back to being free to make her own way.

She poured herself a glass of water and sat at the kitchen table, her iPad in front of her. She opened up Google and typed in 'Florida holidays'.

* * *

Carol had locked the doors, shut down the phones and turned everything off, but she couldn't go across the tram tracks to her home. She needed to be here, where she was at her happiest, where she could think about the pain Matt, Steve, Hermia and Harry would be going through right now. She could cry.

She thought back to the previous evening's phone call when a slightly tipsy Matt had rung to break the news that he could no longer propose to her, because he was now an engaged man. She had squealed with delight, had insisted on speaking to Karen to congratulate her, and now she had the knowledge that she could never speak to that lovely woman again. They had been perfect together, Matt and Karen. And now it was over and she didn't know how Matt would recover.

And how would Karen's team accept this? Ray Ledger was always by her side, anticipating her every move, the perfect work partner for her. He would be lost without her. She didn't know the details of what had happened, just that a car had hit her, but she thought she might ring Ray later, offer her condolences and try and find out the full story. If she had the details, she would know how to avoid upsetting Matt and all his family.

She grabbed a tissue and began to mop at her tears. She didn't know how to stop them. She rested her head on her arms and gently swung her office chair from side to side. Nothing was comforting her.

Her husband would have told her to pull herself together. Those had been his instructions to her when they had discovered he had only days left to live, and she knew he would be saying the same now.

But she wanted and needed to wallow in self-pity. Her husband had lived a full life, Karen hadn't. Not by any stretch of the imagination. And Harry. How would he cope? She had watched that relationship develop and knew he would be devastated to lose her, especially as he had been so excited to hear of the engagement. Mum Two, she had been.

And where was Matt? Who was taking care of that lovely man? It had been Steve who had rung her, she hadn't actually spoken to Matt, and now she felt that it was important to have some sort of contact with him. He needed to know she was there for the whole family.

She pulled her mobile towards her and thought for a moment.

> Good night, Matt. My love to all of you. Ring when you feel able.
> Carol xxx

She clicked send and stood. Time to go home. It had been the worst of days, and she wanted to go home and get drunk, very much wanted to do that, but knew the effect one small glass of brandy had on her so decided it maybe wasn't such a bright idea, not at the moment. She set the alarm and locked the front door as she left.

She would open up in the morning, and wait to see what happened. Maybe Matt would appear, maybe

Steve would, but she knew Matt would receive comfort and love from Hermia. She would know how to handle her big brother, how to make sure he lived through each day until it felt easier. And Carol would open up each day, keep the business going as much as she could, and it would be ready one day to welcome them back into the fold.

26

Lynn Earnshaw hadn't closed her eyes at all. Mondays had suddenly become bad days in her life; the previous Monday she had lost her Josh to some murdering bastard, who it now seemed her eldest son had killed. And then yesterday some high-up police officer had arrived to tell her Freddie had also killed that lovely policewoman she had really taken to.

She hadn't really understood anything at first when the three officers arrived together. She thought initially they were telling her that Freddie had killed Josh, but gradually they made it clear that Freddie had killed someone called Susan, that he had then killed someone called Gordon King – apparently the pimp and druggie who was suspected of killing Josh – and then they topped the whole sorry saga by telling her Freddie had killed DI Nelson. And that Freddie was injured, not seriously, and was being held in custody at Moss Way.

And in the middle of it all her father had rung her, presumably to tell her the news she was in the middle of receiving from the police. She told him to fuck off and to never contact her again, and immediately removed him from her contacts list and completely blocked his number.

And now Tuesday morning had dawned, pissing it down with rain that closely matched the tears pouring down her cheeks, and she no longer required a life. The easiest thing would be to take some tablets and simply slip away. Except she only had about four paracetamol in the house, and Freddie would have taken everything he had with him. Just how do you kill yourself when the only thing you want is to join your son?

She leaned her forehead against the window and allowed her tears to flow unchecked. She thought she might never stop crying. She couldn't really remember everything the police had told her, but it seemed Freddie had shot the bastard who had killed Josh, and deep down she couldn't help but feel that at least Freddie had got one thing right in his life.

But she seemed to remember they had said he was the one who had stabbed the woman in the retail park, and then stole her prescription drugs that she had just collected from the late-night pharmacy.

Everything the police had tried to convey to her was now running around her brain, and she wished they hadn't gone. So many questions. She simply didn't understand. Just over a week ago they had been a perfectly normal family, as far as she was aware. Had Freddie deliberately overdosed her to keep her well spaced-out so that he could get Josh going out on a delivery?

They had had such a blazing row about him doing this, and she'd told him he was never to inveigle Josh into his sleazy drug deals again. Her brain was now moving up a gear. She hadn't been able to function at all last Monday, had spent the entire day in bed, hadn't been able to look after Josh when he was brought home from school because she couldn't stay awake.

She rarely took anything; if pushed she would admit to preferring alcohol, but something had happened last Monday.

Freddie had gone to that blessed party. He had needed Josh to do the delivery down at the Bath

House. It suddenly became crystal clear. She felt a swell of relief that it meant Freddie hadn't been involved in what had ultimately happened to Josh, but he had been the one who probably forced Josh to do the delivery for him, and slipped him a tenner to do it.

And maybe if Josh hadn't been struggling to breathe all day he wouldn't have died in that rain-soaked spot.

Too many maybes. She turned on the cold tap and stuck her face underneath it. She grabbed some kitchen towel and dabbed at her face and neck, then walked into the lounge.

It was quiet. Too quiet. She didn't know what to do for the best, and the sound of the lounge door opening made her jump.

'It's only me,' Netta said. 'I'm just checking you're okay. I wanted to come yesterday, after I saw the police turn up in the afternoon, but I didn't want to intrude. I'm not staying now, just wanted to tell you I'm popping round to Asda, so if there's anything you need...'

'No, I'm fine, thanks, Netta. Just trying to get my head around everything. I can't talk about it yet, but I'll come to yours tomorrow and have a cuppa with you.'

Netta stared at her friend. It was obvious she was in a hell of a state. 'I'll bring us a bun. But if you need me before tomorrow, you come and get me.'

'I will, I promise.'

Netta gave a brief nod of her head, and left.

* * *

The gloom inside the briefing room was tangible. Jaime was back at work, to face what was potentially the worst day of her life so far. It had been bad dealing with the murder of Dave Forrester, the abrupt departure of DI Matt Forrester following his dad's death, but this – losing Karen, who she considered a friend just as much as she considered her to be her boss – was unimaginable.

She felt a huge sense of gratitude that Karen had told her to stick to desk jobs for at least a week. If she hadn't, she would have been on that field with the other members of the team. She glanced across at Rachel, their newest team member, and wondered how to handle the situation. She'd only been in Major Crimes for a week, and now had lost her mentor, right in front of her eyes.

It seemed, according to Ray, that they had expected Freddie Earnshaw to still be inside the caravan and hopefully asleep, hence the early-morning visit. But Earnshaw had been alerted by something, and they would one day find out what. It was too late for Karen Nelson though.

Jaime looked across the room to where Rachel was sitting, occasionally dabbing at her eyes, and simply doing nothing. She had completed her report of the morning's activities, and now couldn't think beyond that. It seemed they'd cleared up their outstanding cases in one fell swoop. Jaime stood and walked across to her.

'Let's go get a coffee or something,' she said.

Rachel visibly jumped. 'I'm okay, thanks, Jaime.'

'No, you're not. You're a million miles from being okay, and in about the same place that I'm in, so please come for a coffee with me. If we're needed, they can put a call in to the canteen for us.'

There was a further moment of hesitation, then Rachel stood. 'Just a coffee,' she said. 'I'll be sick if I have so much as a biscuit.'

'I'm the same, but maybe we need to talk through this. This is what Karen would have done with anyone who was feeling like we're feeling at the moment.'

They headed downstairs and sat at one of the smaller tables that only had two chairs. Neither of them wanted to talk to anyone else. Jaime went to the counter, got their drinks and as she bent to pick up the tray the canteen manager leaned over and squeezed her hand. 'So sorry, love. She meant a lot to all of us.'

Jaime simply nodded. If she'd spoken, she would have cried. Thank God she hadn't let Rachel get the drinks.

She carried the tray across, and Rachel was staring out of the window, into the car park below them. 'Ray is sitting in his car.'

'I guessed he might be. He's interviewing Earnshaw later so he'll want some time out now. He's been part-nered with Karen forever, you know. Came through from the start of their careers together, but Karen pro-gressed further because Ray didn't want to.' She handed one of the coffees to Rachel, and placed the tray on the windowsill.

'Thank you,' Rachel said, and picked up the coffee. She took the smallest of sips and put it back down on the table. 'What do we do without her leading us?'

'I don't know. I imagine Ray will become acting DI until they either promote or bring a DI in, but she's definitely a hard act to follow.'

'She was first to go up that field, you know.' Rachel brushed away a tear that had leaked out.

'You didn't have to tell me that, I would have known,' Jaime smiled, and reached across to touch her hand. 'And I bet Ray was right behind her.'

'He was. He could actually have been under that car as well if he hadn't stopped to send an instruction down to the two lads manning the bottom gate. That few seconds saved his life, but Karen was right in line. The car barrelled out of the trees. We could hear it, but couldn't see it until it was virtually in the middle of us. Karen turned to run...'

'You don't have to relive it if you don't want to,' Jaime said gently. 'I just thought you could use a drink and ten minutes away from the office. I imagine the whole scene is tattooed onto your brain as you've already written your report, and I remember how that plays out.'

'I felt like a spare part. I didn't know what to do. Bringing Earnshaw in seems to have cleared everything up, we just need to get him interviewed now, and his duty solicitor isn't here yet. I'm going to ask if I can watch from the viewing room, because I haven't been involved in any high-profile interviews so far. So Ray will do it?'

'I would think so,' Jaime said, reaching for her cup and hoping it had cooled down. 'He's the senior officer, involved from the beginning. He'll be expected to walk into that interview room, be very professional, and question the suspect as if it was an everyday crime. And knowing Ray as well as I do, he will do it.

And then he will leave the room, walk out here and either punch somebody who is in his way, or punch the wall. But Earnshaw will see none of that, because Ray Ledger is a professional. And he will want the best result that he can get, especially with this one, and that means playing it by the book, every step of the way.'

The two women sat quietly for a moment. Rachel sipped at her drink and looked at Jaime. 'Thank you. I felt lost up in that office. I don't really know anybody yet, and in fact Karen was the one I'd spent the most time with.'

Jaime smiled. 'You looked lost. But we're all dealing with something we haven't had to deal with before. It's rare for a police officer to be killed on duty, and nobody knows how to handle it, how to feel, how to behave, so just do whatever suits how you are at that moment in time. We'll all understand if you need to cry – I went into the ladies' and sat on a toilet to bawl my head off when I heard the news, but when I came out, Caroline, one of the uniformed PCs, was waiting for me to give me a hug. The whole station is mourning the loss of possibly its favourite officer.'

They sat in silence for a while, finished their drinks and stood to head back upstairs. 'I'll mention to Ray that you'd like to observe the interview. Take a notepad in, he's an expert is Ray. That young man doesn't know what's coming his way, believe me.'

Rachel sighed. 'His mother is so lovely. I can't imagine how she's going to handle all of this. I was the one who accompanied her to identify her youngest lad, and she chatted constantly about him. She hardly mentioned Freddie and it was obvious Josh was her favourite. I hope she has a lot of support from friends and family.'

'She'll need it,' Jaime said quietly. 'She'll need it.'

27

Monday had been difficult, but reality day was Tuesday. Wet and miserable, it held no promise of anything. Matt knew Freddie Earnshaw would be charged with the murder of Karen, because with five witnesses to her murder being police officers themselves, Freddie couldn't deny anything.

He had been forced to break the news to Harry, taking him out of school an hour early. At first Harry had been in denial. 'She can't be dead. She was okay yesterday. She rang to tell me she was proud to be known as Mum Two.'

By the time Harry went to bed he couldn't stop crying, and the denial phase was over. Acceptance had taken its place.

Matt had spent some time on the phone with Becky discussing their son, and how to handle what he was going through. It was decided they would keep him off school for the rest of the week, and Harry would stay with Becky, as Matt didn't know what any plans would be now, what he would need to do with any matters surrounding Karen.

His brain felt numb. The whole of him felt numb. He was going from one minute to the next without remembering what had happened in the minute prior. They had spent Sunday evening discussing their future, and both had wanted an early small wedding to get the rest of their lives started.

It was only hours later that he had lost her. He hadn't been able to get to that godforsaken place quick enough to be with her at her end, but Ray had said she went instantly. She didn't suffer, and that had been some consolation to him, but this was his Karen, his love. He was supposed to protect her. And she had gone so early that morning he hadn't really been awake enough to give her his usual goodbye of 'Be careful and take care around the villains' morning banter.

And he knew without any shadow of a doubt that she would have been drawing that killer car away from causing any injuries to her colleagues.

He stood looking out of the patio doors onto the garden, the rain coming down in sheets, and didn't know what to do. He had drunk so much tea and coffee he was swimming in the stuff, but he didn't want anything that even resembled food. He felt sick, physically.

He was expected to be strong, but he knew Hermia and Steve had seen through that. Herms had held him while he poured out his feelings, telling her how lost he felt, and as he heard the front door open he knew it was either her or Steve, coming to check up on him. He didn't move, and he felt Steve's arm go around his shoulders.

'Okay, mate?'

'No.'

'You want some breakfast?'

'No thanks.'

'Okay, no problem. I'm under instructions to come and ask you and check on you. Can we do anything?'

'Not yet. I'll need to arrange Karen's funeral, but they'll not be at the stage of releasing her back to me yet. I feel like a spare part, Steve, stuck in limbo, no purpose.'

They continued to stare out at the back garden. 'Shitty weather,' Steve said.

'Shitty everything at the moment.'

'When did you last eat?'

Matt thought for a moment. 'Sunday, about five.'

'It's Tuesday morning. Okay, you're coming over to ours. I want to see you drink a full mug of tea, and eat at least one slice of toast. You getting ill isn't going to help anybody, and you've got a tough week ahead of you.'

Matt opened his mouth to protest and Steve interrupted him. 'Don't bother saying you're not hungry, I know you aren't. But hunger doesn't come into it, well-being does. And Karen would be saying the same to you.'

Matt knew when he was beaten. He slid the patio doors closed, locked them and followed Steve through to the front of the house.

On the doorstep was Ray Ledger.

'Just popped round to see how you're doing, boss.'

'You had breakfast, Ray?' Steve asked.

Ray shook his head. 'Just had this conversation with Angela, and no, don't want anything.'

'Okay, come with us. Toast all round, can't have you fading away, and going without food isn't good for you.'

Hermia was just placing Rosie into her Moses basket as they entered her hallway, and placed a finger to her lips. 'Sleeping,' she whispered.

She left the baby in the lounge with the door open, and they all headed for the kitchen where Steve proceeded to make toast for everyone, and a huge pot of tea.

'We will get through this,' Hermia said in her usual gentle way. 'I don't know how yet, because Karen was like the sister I never had. I'm going to miss her so much, but if we give in then that bastard who drove that car at her has won. We can't let that happen. I have to eat, keep myself going, for the sake of Rosie, and I want you all to be responsible and keep yourselves going for the sake of Karen. She would expect nothing less. Ray, I understand you were there?'

He nodded. 'I was, Herms. I also started interviewing the little scrote last night, but stopped on doctors' advice when he said he had a headache. The questions were getting difficult, and his duty solicitor stepped in. But today will be different. I've told them I want to restart at ten-thirty, and I'll have a doctor there to confirm he is fit to be interviewed. He picked up a small head injury when he tried to ram the gate at the bottom of the field, but it's nothing. He used it to get out of answering any more questions. He'll be charged and locked up by the end of the day.'

Hermia placed a small plate in front of everybody, and carried the mugs and teapot to the table. She filled a small milk jug and carried both that and the sugar basin to the table.

'This is posh,' Matt remarked, his face still wearing a strained expression. 'I'm used to a mug being pushed into my hand, with milk-no-sugar the order of the day.'

'Try to pretend you're civilised,' his sister said, and ruffled his hair. Her heart ached for him, she had never seen him like this before, not even when their father had died. Then he had been blazing mad, but this had reduced him to something she had never seen before.

Steve buttered the toast, and popped another four slices in to brown. He placed the first batch on the table and told them to start eating. He didn't add 'or else' but the inference was there.

Hermia breathed a sigh of relief as she saw Matt take his first bite. She was counting on the moreish qualities of toast to make him eat at least two slices.

'You have plans for today?' she asked him.

Matt lifted a blank face. 'I don't know. What should I do? I'd like to go see Karen but it may be too soon. Ray, can you find out when I can go?'

'I'll ring you as soon as I know anything, Matt. And if I'm interviewing, I'll text you. Martin said he would prioritise the post-mortem, and that must be hard for him. They got on so well. Sometimes this job can be so shitty.' Ray could hear the anger in his own voice, and he felt a tear trickle down his cheek. He brushed it away. 'I'm sorry, lost it a bit there, but nothing about this is right.'

Absent-mindedly, Matt reached for another piece of toast. 'Don't walk on eggshells, any of you. We're all affected by it, not just me. Ray, you might not have realised it, because she said she wouldn't wear her ring for work, but we got engaged on Sunday. We sat up fairly late that evening, discussing having a barbecue to celebrate, and inviting all the team and their partners to join us. We couldn't have been happier.'

Ray was visibly shocked. 'No, she hadn't said anything. But it was a case of arrive there, discuss our actions after we'd reviewed the site, and do it. We had no time for anything of a personal nature, we knew we had the advantage of surprise, except it seemed we didn't. When we arrived there Kevin went up to the gate, virtually crawled up to it to avoid being seen, and pushed on it to check if it opened or if there was a padlock or something locking it. It moved easily, so he closed it again and came back down to us. I bet our techie lads find an alarm fixed that would warn the occupant of the caravan that somebody was coming through the gate. By the time we'd sorted out who was doing what and in what order, Earnshaw had had plenty of time to get from the caravan to his car. Karen was the nearest to him and he pointed it straight at her and put his foot to the floor. That car fair screamed. She never stood a chance, bless her. And I'm supposed to be totally professional and go and interrogate him without beating him to a bloody pulp.' He finished his toast and stood. 'Thank you for that, Steve. It was very welcome. I need to get off now, but I wanted to check the boss was okay first.'

He turned to look at Matt. 'I'll find out what I can with regard to Karen, and I promise I'll contact you later, boss.'

Matt simply nodded his head.

* * *

Ray walked into the briefing room and apologised for being late. 'I called to see how the boss was doing, and he's not great. His sister has had to basically force feed him some toast. And if you think this tragedy couldn't get any worse, Karen and Matt had got engaged on Sunday. You can imagine what sort of state he's in.'

A sound almost like a moan rang around the room as they absorbed what Ray had just said.

'She would have been so happy,' Jaime said, trying to close down further threatened tears. She wasn't at all sure how any of them were going to get through this.

* * *

Matt got into the car and drove. He needed some space, some time out, some thinking moments. He headed into Derbyshire, stopped on the tops of a couple of the hills, and finally knew he needed to go down Winnats Pass, where he would find some of the peace he was craving.

The view, as always, was magnificent, and he considered it to be the best place throughout the whole of the Peak District. He got out of the car and sat on the grass for half an hour, simply letting his thoughts fly over the Derbyshire peaks and valleys. The quietude washed over him, and eventually he got back into the car, sent Herms a text to say he was okay and would be home later, then drove the rest of the way down Winnats, through Castleton and Hathersage, and eventually back onto the Sheffield road. He pulled up at a pub to buy himself a Coke to quench a raging thirst, and took some deep breaths outside before continuing.

He stopped in a layby and checked his phone to see what had created a ping, hoping it would be a message that had come through from Ray, saw there was nothing but a dental reminder, and continued his journey home. As he reached Gleadless he knew what to do. He pulled up outside the house with the blue door and rang the bell.

A minute passed and he was about to return to his car when the door opened. Carol stood there, her arms outstretched.

'Come in, lad, come in. Let's have a cup of tea and a talk.'

Freddie Earnshaw had clearly been arguing with the duty solicitor when Ray and Kevin walked into the interrogation room. There were four people in the viewing room, including Rachel, who felt a little overawed by the presence of a DCI from Central, and two other senior officers she assumed were from Central.

Ray spoke into the recorder to advise that DS Raymond Ledger and DC Kevin Potter were present along with Ethan Gardner, duty solicitor, and Freddie Earnshaw.

The atmosphere was tense, and Ray hoped Gardner hadn't advised his client to simply say 'No comment' to every question.

'You're feeling okay today, Freddie?' Ray began. 'No headaches?'

'Took some tablets,' Freddie muttered.

'Oh, good. So, we have several points we could start with, but I think we need to go back to Sunday, 19 March. Can you tell me where you were on the evening of that day, and then tell us how you can prove your answer? And this is not the Sunday that has just gone by, this is the Sunday before, just so you're clear.'

'Went for a drive.'

'Where to?' Kevin asked, his pen poised on his notebook ready to write down Freddie's answer.

'Here and there. Round the estate, met some lads up near the Frecheville pond.'

'And at what time did you go down to Crystal Peaks, to the retail park, to be precise?'

'Wasn't me.'

'What wasn't you?'

'You're trying to fit me up with that woman who was killed.'

'Freddie, you ever heard of ANPR?'

He shrugged, but cast a sideways glance at the solicitor.

'To get to the retail park the easiest route is past Moss Way, your current residence. We have several cameras recording continually around this area, because we have a roundabout that seems to have more than its fair share of traffic accidents, and we have a tram crossing, so there is a surfeit of cameras at this point. We also have ANPR cameras both here and at the Crystal Peaks traffic light junction because of the complexity of those lights. We like to know who it is if anyone causes bother by ignoring the light system instead of having some patience. ANPR stands for Automatic Number Plate Recognition, and when we put your number plate in, it showed exactly where you were on that Sunday. You arrived at the retail park at 20.38 and left at 21.28. Did you have to recover yourself a bit? You killed Ms Hunter at just after nine, and didn't leave for another twenty-five minutes or so.'

'Wasn't me.'

'Somebody borrow your car for an hour, did they?'

'No comment.'

There it was, Earnshaw's first no comment.

'Okay, let's move on to Josh Earnshaw.'

Freddie tried to stand, and Gardner put a hand on his shoulder to push him back down on to his chair.

'I wasn't here when Josh was killed. I was at a party. She checked my alibi.'

'Who did?'

Freddie took a deep breath. 'That DI woman. She knew I didn't do it.'

Ray pretended to look through his file. 'Ah, that would be the lady you killed this Monday. Who would it have been next Monday, Freddie? Your mother?'

'DS Ledger,' Ethan Gardner interrupted.

Ray shut him up with a look.

'We'll return to Josh, and what happened last Tuesday night, 21 March. You went to a party, alibi confirmed. Your brother was ill enough at school to merit a teacher taking him home. He suffered from asthma, I understand.'

'Yeah,' Freddie agreed.

'So why did you ask him to deliver the drugs you stole from Susan Hunter, the lady you stabbed at the retail park? He wasn't well enough, particularly on such a damp night. It would have aggravated his asthma, possibly brought on another attack.'

'No comment.'

'We found the tablet boxes at the crime scene, Freddie. Labelled with Susan Hunter's name. No fingerprints from your brother, because he only touched the paper bag that held the tablets, but the boxes were touched by the bloke you supplied, Gordon King, or Kingy as you know him. You see, Kingy took the meds out of the boxes, chucked them around the scene, and tipped all the tablets into the medication bag provided by Boots Pharmacy at the retail park.'

'No comment.'

'You worked it out, didn't you, Freddie?'

'No comment.'

'You knew it had to be Gordon King who'd murdered your brother. And we've taken your car apart and found a gun. You intended using this to escape if anybody ever turned up at the caravan looking for you. As we did. This same gun is the one that fired the bullet that blew half of King's head away. And it had been fired by someone who had some qualifications in shooting – oh yes, Freddie, we can trace anything, you know. You pointed that gun at the man who had killed your brother and you fired it, then disappeared, without hanging around to see the results of your work. You didn't need to hang around though, did you? You're proud of your skills. You don't miss. But your grandfather's cleverness in taking you and your uncle to firing ranges to make sure you could handle yourselves has really backfired. No pun intended, of course. You're both going to be in prison. For a long, long time.'

'No comment.' Earnshaw's voice was weak.

'I'd like to speak with my client,' Ethan Gardner said.

'Fifteen minutes?' Ray asked.

Gardner nodded.

Ray logged himself and Kevin out, and they left the room.

* * *

In the viewing room, now with visibility and sound from the interview room removed, the four watchers were joined by Ray and Kevin.

'Excellent work, DS Ledger,' the DCI said. 'He's definitely rattled. And I suspect his solicitor is about to tell him he'll get a lesser sentence if he cops to all of it without the expense of going to trial.'

Ray felt a glow shoot through him. He knew he'd done well, but he knew how hard the team had worked to get all the information they had recovered. The gun test had only arrived five minutes before the interview. And he actually felt that was the point when Earnshaw gave up.

He could have blagged his way through with an accidental death charge against Karen, saying he'd lost control of his car on the bumpy grass field, but you don't accidentally lose control of a gun that you're pointing directly at the man you believe, know, killed your brother.

And the ANPR details coming through had definitely placed him at the retail park at the time of Susan's death. But placing him there didn't show him stabbing Susan Hunter; any bright spark of a lawyer would have pushed circumstantial evidence at a jury.

He finished his coffee that Rachel had nipped out to get for him and Kevin, and waited an extra five minutes to rattle Earnshaw a bit more before going back into the room. Kevin logged them in, and Ray opened his file. He suddenly felt utterly overwhelmed in that moment – this should have been Karen's lead, and he should have been the one doing Kevin's job.

He took an extra minute to try to calm down his thoughts, then he looked up at Freddie Earnshaw.

'And now we come to what is by far the most serious part of this interview, the death of DI Karen Nelson. There were five witnesses to this murder, and all the witnesses are police officers, three of them from the Major Crimes unit itself, and therefore senior members of South Yorkshire Police.'

Earnshaw looked terrified. Whatever Gardner had said to him was enough to put the fear of God into him, and he seemed at that moment to be incapable of speech.

Ray pushed harder. 'The killing of a police officer, no matter the rank, is considered to be the worst possible occurrence. As a result it carries the highest sentence. In times past of course, it carried a death sentence, but we can't do that any more. But we can do a whole-life term without any chance of parole.'

When Freddie did speak there was an obvious tremor in his voice. 'And if I cop to it all?'

'You mean you'll admit to everything?'

'If it means I get out at some point.'

'But I don't gain anything from that. DI Nelson was my boss, my friend, and I had known her for many years. You seriously think you can barter when I'm thinking about her memory?'

'I can give you other stuff. I know I'm going to get thirty years, even if I admit to everything and blowing up parliament, but whole life with no parole means I never get out. Ever.'

'Shouldn't go around killing police officers,' Ray said, and closed his file before standing up. 'Think it over, and think over the other stuff you mentioned. I'll be back in an hour. I'm going for some lunch now, because I can walk out of here and get a Big Mac. My advice to you is if they offer you a McDonald's, have one, because once that cell door is locked you'll never ever get another one. DS Raymond Ledger and DC Kevin Potter leaving the room.'

He walked out the door, and didn't look back.

'Did you really just cinch a confession to everything on the strength of a McDonald's?' Kevin asked.

Ray shrugged. 'Might have. Let's head to the canteen and see who's there. I could do with an hour of normality. What do you think will happen when we go back in this afternoon?'

'He'll cop to the lot. That's obviously what his brief has suggested he should do, he recognised they were on a losing streak when you introduced the gun. He'll be spelling it out to our Freddie right now, and then he'll go and have a whisky and a ham sandwich across the road in the pub, before coming back to listen to his client admit to three murders, drug dealing, and unlawful possession of a weapon.'

Ray gave a dry laugh. 'Well, if he does, and it's by no means certain, it'll have been a good morning's work. He can hardly deny Karen's murder when we all saw it happen, but the others will need more than we've got at the moment.'

They opened the door to the canteen, and a spontaneous round of applause met him. He flapped his hands around in the air, mortified by the premature congratulations. 'We haven't got an admission of blame yet, so stop counting chickens,' he called out.

He sat down at the same table as the rest of the team, and checked his phone to see if any messages had come through while it had been switched off. There was just one from Matt. The pathologist had contacted him to say he could see Karen, and he was going at six that night, when most of the staff would have left for the evening. Martin would wait to escort him to see her.

Shit. Suddenly he didn't want any lunch. He wanted a full bottle of brandy to try and numb the pain he was feeling. For a small amount of time the horror of Karen being so brutally murdered had been a little bit in the background while they worked hard to nail her killer, but one message from Matt brought the full impact of it hurtling back again.

* * *

Kevin placed a cheese and onion sandwich and a coffee down in front of him, then walked around the table to sit opposite the man he had seen perform an extraordinary feat only quarter of an hour earlier.

'Everything okay, Sarge? You look... rattled?'

Ray held out his phone so that Kevin could see it. 'I had a message from the boss.'

Kevin read it, and pushed his own sandwich to one side, suddenly not hungry any more.

'How the hell are we supposed to handle this? How can we help the boss?'

Ray sighed. 'I have no idea. But I'll never regret

ringing him to get him to that field, because she was still warm at that point. I knew she had gone, but he needed to be there. I simply don't know what happens next with all of them, Harry, Hermia, Steve, even Becky, and definitely Carol.'

cing him to get him to that field because she was still warm at that point. I knew she had gone, but he needed to be there. I simply don't know what happens next with all of them, Harry Haynia, Steve own bucks and detective Caryn.

29

By two o'clock Ray and Kevin were back in the interview room, and the viewing room held seven people all keen to watch the end of what they hoped would be a confession.

Jaime was there, and she privately thought that if she was facing a minimum thirty-year stretch, before having to go before a parole board who would only say yes if she had kept a clean sheet during that entire thirty years, she would opt for suicide as soon as possible.

She stared at Freddie, taking in the fact that he was quite a smart-looking lad who didn't look much beyond about eighteen, and she reflected on what a waste of his life it was. Within the space of about eight days he had killed three people, dealt drugs to others who had the potential to die from their addictions, and yet nobody would have looked at him and believed all of that was possible.

The first person to speak was Ethan Gardner who told the two officers that his client wished to sign a formal confession to the killings of Susan Hunter, Gordon King and DI Karen Nelson. Ray's instinct was to bang his hand down on the desk and shout 'Yeah!' but he didn't. There wasn't so much as a glimmer of emotion on his face.

'Mr Earnshaw,' Ray began, 'you admit to the murders of Susan Hunter at Drakehouse Retail Park on 19 March 2023, Gordon King on 26 March 2023 and DI Karen Nelson on Monday, 27 March 2023?'

Freddie took a deep breath before answering. 'I do.'

'Then you will be formally charged after we have taken your statement. Tomorrow you will appear in the magistrate's court to be remanded in custody until you appear in Crown Court for sentencing. Mr Gardner, you will remain with Mr Earnshaw until he has been charged?'

Gardner said yes, and the room went silent as Ray and Kevin gathered their files up before departing. Ray asked Jaime and Rachel to deal with the statement and to make sure they missed nothing. They didn't want him to get away with anything on a mere technicality. Jaime nodded. 'I'll make sure, sarge, don't worry. Rachel, you done this before?'

Rachel looked terrified. 'No, but I'll just watch what you do.'

* * *

Ray and Kevin headed slowly back upstairs. It felt as if this day had fifty hours in it; the pressure had been immense. They headed for their desks and sat, unmoving, waiting for their thoughts to settle and their bodies and brains to recover.

He suspected that Ethan Gardner would stick with this one through to the end, until the truck doors closed on Earnshaw to take him away for a huge part of his life, and he knew the man would fight for a thirty-year maximum sentence. He hoped the judge, at the sentencing hearing, would look at the name DI Karen Nelson and bump it up to forty years.

He leaned back in his chair and thought about Karen, how she had touched so many lives, not least the latest mentoring of their new team member, Rachel. And he had no idea how Matt and Harry would get through the next few months without her, until finally the reality of her being gone would sink in.

Matt had stayed on scene until they took Karen away, and he had been grey. Not angry, not wanting to kill anybody, just grey. He wondered just how accepting of the situation his friend had actually been, and Ray had stayed close by his side throughout the two hours of Karen being under that tent.

And now they had the confession. He hadn't particularly wanted to go for it, he would rather have taken it to full jury trial and watched as Freddie Earnshaw was put away on a whole-life sentence with no chance of parole, but not having to go to court other than for sentencing meant that huge amounts of money were saved.

'You want to get his signature on his statement, sarge?' He opened his eyes to see Rachel and Jaime in front of him.

'Thank you. I'd better do it as I was the one who interviewed him. I'm assuming he's still in there, and not locked in a cell. I think Gardner will be glad to get this over with, so I'll just read through it, and take it down for Earnshaw's signature.'

* * *

As Ray expected, the statement required no amendments at this stage, and he hoped it wouldn't after Gardner and Earnshaw had read through it. He replaced his tie, which he'd thrown off as soon as he got back into the briefing room, ran a comb through his hair, and put on his jacket, formal attire for a formal occasion such as charging someone with three murders.

He headed downstairs, accompanied once again by Kevin. Neither of them spoke; thoughts of Karen filled their minds, and they were aware how quickly this had ended in a good result. They would both rather have had Karen back, and the idiot who had killed her still free to walk the streets. Private thoughts, that would never be voiced aloud, but genuine feelings all the same.

Ray was a little surprised at the difference in the demeanour of Freddie Earnshaw. He seemed shrunken, uncommunicative. The brashness had gone, and he guessed the enormity of what was about to happen to him had suddenly hit him. He would be taken from the magistrate's court and not taste freedom again for at least thirty years.

The two men had remained in the interview room, and had been kept supplied with a sandwich and a cup of tea.

Ray and Kevin sat down and Ray slid the typed statement from his file. He passed it to Ethan Gardner, who took his time reading it. Freddie sat, simply staring into space, saying nothing.

Finally Gardner finished, and nodded. He passed the document to Freddie who read it slowly. Ray hoped he was taking it all in, digesting just what he had done, the damage he had caused, but he doubted that Earnshaw would have any thoughts of that nature inside his head.

Freddie looked across to Gardner, who handed him a pen. He signed it, Ray took it back and witnessed it, then stood.

'Thank you, gentlemen. You will now be collected by a uniformed officer and taken to our charge office, where you will be charged, Mr Earnshaw. You will then be taken to a cell where you will be held until you are taken to the magistrate's court tomorrow. From there you will be remanded without bail, and taken to a remand prison pending sentencing.'

Ray felt his temper begin to rise. This whipper-snapper of a kid would be out in thirty or forty years still with some life left. Karen didn't have that any more. He knew it was best not to stay any longer, so turned and walked out of the room followed by Kevin.

They headed back upstairs in silence until Kevin broke it. 'You wanted to kill him?'

'Painfully.'

'Thought so. Thank God we're out of it now, but I intend being there for the sentencing. I want to see that smug little bastard go down for the maximum number of years that judge can give him.'

'And now I'm going after his grandfather. He harboured a known criminal. But first I'm going up to see Lynn Earnshaw, and then... well, I don't know. But I don't think Freddie's mother knows what's going on at all. She just knows she's lost a son, but I need to tell her the other one is going to be out of circulation for a long time.'

* * *

Ray parked outside the Earnshaw home, but instead of going in he walked across the road, past the stretch of green railings and turned onto the short lane that led down to the Bath House. The finding of Josh Earnshaw's body had been the catalyst that ultimately led them to finding the killer of Susan Hunter, but it had led on to so much more.

He stood and looked at the spot where they had found Josh lying in the rain, bruises developing around his neck where pressure from Gordon King's hands had taken his life. The lad should have had a whole life in front of him, and he couldn't imagine how Lynn Earnshaw would be feeling.

All the crime scene tape had now gone, either removed by their own officers or by the local children; he didn't doubt some of it was now plastered across bedroom doors, rabbit hutches, and front doors by kids who thought it was hilarious.

There was nothing left to remind him of the previous Wednesday morning, but he didn't need anything. His mind could recall it all. At that stage Lynn Earnshaw had only just found out Josh wasn't in school, and her world was still intact, if a worried world. She was now about to find out how much harder life could be.

He said a short prayer for Josh, then walked back up the lane and across the road to Lynn's home.

She looked thinner. He guessed she wasn't bothering to eat. With nobody else at home, food would be the last thing on her mind.

'Hi, Mrs Earnshaw. DS Ledger. Mind if I come in for a moment?'

'No... no, of course I don't. Have you come to tell me they've released Josh's body?'

'I haven't, but when I get back I'll see if they can tell me when that can happen.'

She opened the door wider and Ray stepped inside. He followed her through to the lounge and she immediately apologised that she couldn't offer tea or coffee, she had no milk.

'It doesn't matter, honestly,' he said, and waited for her to sit down before taking the armchair opposite to her.

'I have things to tell you, to bring you up to date. We have arrested Freddie.'

'It was always going to happen,' she said bitterly. 'Drugs, drugs, drugs, it's all he thought about. He didn't use, just sold, but I told him you'd get him one day.'

'He hasn't been arrested just for that,' he said gently.

He watched as her face changed. 'What are you trying to tell me?'

'Freddie has been arrested and charged with three murders. I didn't want you hearing it on the news or seeing it in the paper. He killed the lady who was stabbed down at the retail park and stole the drugs she had just collected from the late-night pharmacy down there. Those drugs were for a specific customer called Gordon King.'

'Kingy,' she said slowly.

'That's right. Freddie spoke of him?'

'He did.'

'We believe Freddie asked Josh to deliver those drugs to King because he couldn't do it himself, he was off out to that party.'

She waited for his next words.

'We believe that Gordon King then killed Josh – we found his fingerprints on some medication packets he'd thrown around on the floor. However, Freddie knew the only person who could have done it was King. He took a gun to where he knew King would be, and shot him.'

'Oh my God. He's an expert shot. All his certificates were upstairs in his room...'

'But that's not all.' Ray was relentless in his need to let her know before she found out from other sources. 'King died instantly. We suspected we knew where Freddie was, holed up in a caravan on his grandfather's property. We went Monday morning at six to pick him up, and he drove his car directly and deliberately at DI Nelson. She died instantly.'

Lynn wrapped her arms around her body and began to rock herself. 'No, no, no... what did I give birth to? Why has he turned out so wrong? Why is he so different to my Josh?'

'I don't know,' he said gently. 'Could it be that your husband influenced Freddie more?'

'No, not my husband. My man was one of the gentlest, caring people you could wish to meet, and never understood Freddie.' Her tone hardened. 'My bloody father. Josh didn't want to know his grandfather, but Freddie almost lived with him. He was the one who took him to the gun ranges, made sure him and my brother Niall were expert shots. I used to say no good would ever come of it, and now both of them are in prison.'

'I had to come and tell you, do you understand? Freddie has admitted it all, and has been charged. You will get the media descending on you, so if you can get away for a few days it might be advisable.'

'I have a long-time friend who has asked me to go and stay for as much time as I need. She lives in Gainsborough. Is that far enough?'

He smiled at her. 'I would think so. Just don't tell your neighbour where you're going, then she can't accidentally let it slip. I know this is dreadful news, Lynn, and when you start to think it through it will overwhelm you, but I'll leave my card with you. Ring if you need to talk.' He placed his card on her coffee table. 'And I promise I'll contact you as soon as I hear about the release of Josh's body. Oh, and one other thing. I'm going after your father now.'

* * *

Matt met Martin Moore at the morgue, and they walked quietly together through the building. Karen was on a trolley in the centre of the room, and completely covered by a white sheet. Martin folded it down to reveal her face, and stepped back.

Matt paused for a moment then reached out a hand to gently stroke her icy cold cheek. 'I love you, Karen,' he whispered, and bent down to place a kiss on her lips. 'Thank you for sharing my life, lovely lady. We'll meet again one day.'

He straightened and turned to where Martin was studiously looking away, giving Matt the privacy he needed.

'Thank you, Martin. I can rest a little easier now.'

Martin moved to stand by his side and shook his hand. 'I'm glad I could help with this. They've got the lad?'

'They have. Charged and heading for court tomorrow. He's admitted all three murders, so he's in for a long stretch, but it doesn't bring Karen back to me.'

30

Carol opened the office door and shivered. Despite it being late March, it felt like the throes of winter were still with them. She switched on the heating, and locked the door behind her. She didn't anticipate anybody requesting to use their appointment services, the notice she had put on the door Monday afternoon said 'closed due to bereavement'; she intended for that to be the status quo until Matt said otherwise.

But that didn't stop people leaving voicemails, and the postman delivering the post, and quite apart from that, she liked being in the office. It was her comfort setting, and she thought that with some time on her hands she would clean the upstairs flat that Harry sometimes used when he was with them during school holidays, and the little downstairs kitchen could definitely do with a bit of fettling.

She listened to the voicemails, made a couple of notes from them, and cleared everything that was irrelevant. There were five people to call back who wanted appointments, so she did that, explaining they were closed for a short time. Four of them said they would ring back in a couple of weeks and she gave the fifth one another number to call as they said there had an urgent problem.

With an empty voicemail inbox she felt settled. She began to open the post, leaving things personally addressed to Matt and Steve for them to open. The rest she dealt with, adding anything to WATSON that required adding, then she sat back in her chair. Big mistake. While she was busy she didn't have to think. Now she wasn't busy, thoughts of Karen and Matt slipped in under her defences.

He had cried in her arms. She had never felt so helpless, and she had simply held him until he stopped. She didn't bother offering the very British cup of tea, she gave him a glass of brandy.

He drank it in one gulp, and although she offered him food he said he would be sick if he ate anything.

She had never seen him looking lost before, and now he was. Completely.

'You know, Matt, I have a spare room if you want another brandy. Or even a full bottle. But I can't offer you any more if you're going to drive back home, even if it is only two minutes away.'

He shook his head. 'Nothing helps. Just being here is good, you're a very calm person, Carol, and I just needed to talk. When I get home, I'll probably carry on talking, but it will be to Oliver. That cat has listened to so many of my woes. It was so funny on Sunday night, we told him we were engaged, and he just stuck his tail in the air, looked at us and went out through the cat door. We couldn't work out if he approved or disapproved.' The recollection brought fresh tears to his eyes, and he wiped them away. 'Sorry, I suppose it will be like this for some time, every time anything reminds me of Karen.'

'Don't apologise, you should think about her. Hold on to the memories. We'll all be doing that.'

And she was. Matt had eventually driven home, and she had been left with an ache in her heart for what they had lost. Now, opening the mail, listening to messages, doing the normal routine day-to-day activities seemed almost wrong. But it wasn't. It was life.

* * *

With the kitchen spotless, the upstairs flat vacuumed and dusted, Carol decided enough was enough and she would head home. She took the letters for the two men into their respective offices, and set all the security codes. She was about to leave by the front door when the telephone rang. She considered letting it go to voicemail, but gave in to the insistent ringing.

It was the local newspaper wanting information – they had heard that the deceased police officer was connected to the Forrester Detective Agency, and could they ask a few questions.

'No,' she said, and put down the receiver.

It rang again as she locked the door, and somehow she knew it would be on her voicemail in the morning.

* * *

Hermia fed Rosie and placed her in the Moses basket, then began to load the washing machine. How could one small baby create such a mountain of laundry, she asked herself, and jumped as the kitchen door opened.

'It's me,' Matt said. 'Everybody okay?'

'We are,' she said. 'You feel any more settled after last night?'

'Not really, I feel angry. She was my wife in everything but a legal document saying so, and I don't want to be without her. She was so cold when I went to see her last night, not the Karen I've been with for quite a long time now. Martin took me in his office after, and I cried again. I'm just not handling it very well, Herms.'

'I know, but give yourself a break, Matt. It's early days. You'll cry many more tears over the next few months, every time something happens to remind you of Karen, and her funeral is going to be a huge affair, which is going to be the hardest part. But I promise you it will get easier once that is over. We're all here for you, your back-up team.'

'Thanks, sis. And I do know it. I'm popping over to Becky's house to see Harry, I don't want him to think I've abandoned him. I just knew I would have a lot to do, and it was easier to send him to his mum's for a few days. But I miss him, and I think he's old enough to understand some of the details about what happens next.'

* * *

Matt's ex-wife Becky opened the door within seconds of his knock. 'I saw you pull up,' she explained. 'Harry is in the lounge doing some of my jigsaw, and feeling a bit frustrated by it. He keeps mentioning Karen, asking if I've heard anything. I saw somebody had been charged, but I just acted dumb, and decided you're better placed to tell him what's going on. Did I do right?'

'You did. And thanks for doing it. I'll take him out for a walk, I think. An hour in the woods will do us both some good, and he can ask me whatever he wants. I went to see Karen last night, and it was so strange. I've seen so many bodies in that morgue, but seeing somebody I love is the hardest thing I've ever done in my life. I've never cried before, not like this. I was upset when Dad died, as you know, but it was different to this feeling. We had our whole life together in front of us, and now it's been taken away.'

'He's in there. I'll be upstairs in my bedroom if you need me, Florence is sleeping in her room, so I'll stay there until she wakes. Take what time you need, but if you go out, don't shout up to tell me. When Florence is asleep, it's my time of peace,' she said with a smile.

He opened the lounge door and saw the back of Harry's head, his hand outstretched trying out a jigsaw piece.

'Let's look what you're doing,' he said, and Harry jumped up.

'It's a *Star Wars* jigsaw. Good picture, but lots of dark sky. Am I coming home now?'

It caused a little glitch in Matt's heart rate as he

heard those words. 'Not just yet, pal, but I was missing you, so thought we could take a little walk through Charnock Woods, see what we can see, say what we need to say. How's that sound?'

'Does Mum know?'

'She does, so be quiet while you're putting on your trainers and your coat, because Florence is sleeping. We'll only be an hour or so, but I thought it might do us both a bit of good.'

* * *

They left the house, quietly closing the door behind them, and thus began the hardest hour of all. They walked, they talked, they cried, and Matt had to explain who had driven the car at Karen, and what was happening to him now. It poured out of him, and man and boy ended up by sitting on a log, staring at a small stream, and holding each other tightly.

They talked and talked, comforted each other, and Matt promised that he would collect Harry from school the following Monday, and bring him home. They strolled back to Becky's house, and crept in quietly. Matt hugged his son and ruffled his hair as he led him back to the table where the jigsaw was taking shape. He stared at the picture and pointed to a piece.

'That goes there,' he said, and winked as Harry picked it up and fitted it. 'Love you, Harry. Be good for your mum and with Florence.'

He left and climbed into his car. His phone pinged an incoming text and he saw it was from Ray.

Returned Karen's car to yours. Keys through letterbox. You need anything, you ask.

He hadn't even thought about Karen's Sportage, and its whereabouts. It now seemed it was parked on his drive, and he wasn't convinced he would handle that too well.

31

Ray had parked the Sportage well over to the right, leaving Matt plenty of room for the Land Rover to be parked. He locked his car and walked over to the Kia, looking through the windows. He thought he could see the strap of Karen's handbag poking out from under the passenger seat, so he went into the house and picked up her keys from the mat.

He stroked the keys, hoping to feel her presence through them, but couldn't. Inanimate objects, nothing like his Karen. He opened the driver's door and sat in Karen's seat, pushing it back a little. 'Short arse,' he said with a smile. They had always joked about how close her seat was to the controls, because she was only five feet two inches.

Reaching down, he pulled out her bag. The car hadn't been touched by forensics because it hadn't been on scene. She had left it in the police car park, choosing to travel with Ray, Kevin and Rachel in the squad car. Inside her bag was her personal phone. He guessed her police phone had been on her when she died, and would be with forensics being examined. There was also her purse, holding her cards and about twenty pounds in money. It was only a small crossbody bag, the sort she preferred for convenience, and there was very little else in it, other than a blank notebook and a pen. The front pocket contained a small pack of tissues and a lipstick and that was it. He held it against him for a moment, then cast his eyes around the rest of the car. There was a blanket on the back seat, so he took that off to take inside with him, then walked around to the boot.

The plant was flowering beautifully, a pale pink Kalanchoe in a darker pink pot, cerise Karen had called it, and balanced securely between two plastic boxes. He almost stopped breathing as the sight of the plant returned him to that day of happiness, to the day when they had visited Summertime Garden Centre and Karen had bought the plant for Jaime, to welcome her back to work.

He knew he had to take it to her. He lifted it carefully out of the Kia's boot, and took it indoors, where he gave it a gentle watering. He nipped upstairs for a quick shower and a change of clothes to repair the damage caused by his foray into the woods with Harry, and headed out once more to the Land Rover, this time carrying the plant.

He drove to Moss Way and asked the duty sergeant to notify Jaime that he was in reception and needed to see her for a minute.

'You want to go up?'

'Best not,' Matt said.

'I can give you a visitor badge.'

Matt thought it over. 'Okay. If they lock me up, I'll blame you.'

He fastened the badge to his jacket, and headed upstairs. Familiar territory, and just for a moment his heart felt extra full. The briefing room door was closed, so he knocked and opened it slowly, hoping it was just the team inside.

It was. There was a gasp of surprise, and Ray said, 'Welcome home, boss!'

'I'm only here for a minute,' Matt explained. 'I have a gift – Karen bought it while we were at a garden centre this weekend, said it was a welcome back to work gift for Jaime. So here it is.'

Jaime stepped towards him and took the pretty

pink plant he was holding in his hands. She burst out crying, and carried it towards her desk, unable to speak. Rachel moved towards her, and put her arms around Jaime's shoulders.

Matt held up a hand in acknowledgement of the rest of the team and thanked them for the hard work they had put in to get the confession. 'You'll all be there for Karen's funeral?' he asked.

'As if we'd miss it,' Ray responded. He watched as Matt turned to leave the room, and moved to follow him out. 'I'll walk down with you, boss.'

'I'm not done yet,' he said, as they walked down the stairs leading to the reception area. 'I don't care if it takes me up to my retirement, I'll have that bastard Liam Marshall under lock and key. Bear that in mind, will you, boss. Anything you might hear, I'd like to hear it as well. Any little thing, because they usually lead to bigger things.'

Matt gave a nod. 'Leave it with me.'

'It was good to see you back in that room, Matt.'

'And it's good to hear you call me Matt and not boss. It's a long time now since I had that title, and some of you still call me that.'

They reached the Land Rover. 'You'll always be boss, I suppose. I'll try to remember in future, but I can't guarantee anything. Take it easy, Matt, and text me if you need anything. Help, information, anything. You understand?'

'I understand. Speak to you soon, Ray. And thank you. You broke rules on Monday morning by ringing me, and I won't forget that favour. I owe you one.'

He started the car, and Ray watched him drive away, a thunderstorm of extreme sadness cascading over him.

* * *

Liam Marshall could never have imagined that such a conversation would have taken place between upholders of the law. His thoughts at the moment were wholly with his grandson, now locked up awaiting his trial. He'd have to put in some serious work to swing this one through as a not guilty verdict, considering there'd been coppers on site when Freddie had driven his car at that DI. He needed to start talking to some people, find out what he could during the next six months or so, and hopefully get young Freddie off. He didn't want the same thing happening to Freddie that had happened to Niall. His son had obviously been caught off guard in a weak moment and admitted to what they were accusing him of, but he didn't think for one minute Freddie would do that. He'd always had a bit more common sense about him than Niall had, and in any case he'd lined Freddie up to take on the business when he fully retired; trucks, vans, deliveries of whatever needed delivering, the whole job lot, so he needed him on the outside, not the bloody inside.

He'd find out when Freddie was going to be bailed, and he could get down there to pick him up. Then they could sort out what came next. Running over that copper was a simple accident, the car had hit a hummock on the field, and the steering wheel had shot out of his hands, hadn't it, m'lud. In fact, what he needed to know was which judge Freddie would be up in front of. That could make things a lot easier, if he got the right judge.

His thoughts began to drift, and he heard his wife moving around in her craft room. He hoped she might consider making them a pot of tea or even maybe something a bit stronger, but she'd been more than a bit off with him. She'd accused him of being the reason behind Freddie being carted off in that prisoner transporter, saying he should never have let Freddie stay in that rickety old caravan. But she'd been the one who'd thrown a wobbly about him staying in the house, shoving him in that tiny little boxroom. The caravan was pretty decent inside, scuffed up a bit on the outside to make it look rough so nobody would want to go in it, but it had served a few of his mates really well.

He wondered how the police had known Freddie was there. It had obviously been a planned visit that early in the morning. They didn't just turn up on the off chance that somebody might be there; no, they had known something.

Liam was getting a headache, thinking through everything. It had all started to disintegrate as far as he could remember with the arrest of Niall. Diana had upped her tally of dalliances, once Niall had bumped off Anthony Dawson, and at times he had wondered if it wouldn't have been better if Dawson hadn't died. She'd certainly worked her way through half of Sheffield since that had happened. And she didn't care if he knew, it now appeared. At one time she had tried to hide what she was doing, but not any more. Cutting back on his work hours had helped somewhat, be-cause now she never knew where he was, but he knew she blamed him for what had happened to her pre-cious son. He'd interested the two boys in guns.

She thought that was a big mistake and constantly told him so. Okay, so she had been proved right, but both lads had enjoyed the training, the visits to dif-ferent shooting ranges. It hadn't been wrong, just maybe not too well thought out.

His mind went back once more to Monday morning. He knew it was the idea to fit an alarm on the gate, one that sounded inside the caravan if the gate was opened, that had triggered everything. The idea was that whoever was staying in the caravan could check and see who was walking or driving up the field.

The gate had been moved early enough to give Freddie, and himself, a warning, hence Freddie being in his car when the coppers arrived to arrest him. The noise of the engine revving had made him and Diana get out of the house a bit faster and they'd arrived to see the aftermath with Freddie smashed into the gate at the bottom of the field. His grandson had already got handcuffs on by the time he'd managed to get round to the field, with Diana panting along behind him, but he knew they'd got big trouble when nobody was doing anything to assist the woman lying face down on the grass.

So Liam figured he needed to help his grandson, no doubt about that. For a start he'd get him the best solicitor, the man who had facilitated getting Liam himself out of one or two scrapes, and they'd get Freddie released on bail. That was the best thing to do.

He stood and walked across to the bar, poured himself a brandy as it was becoming very clear his wife wasn't going to do it, and drank it in one go. He poured a second one and carried it back to his chair, where he dwelt a little more on his problems.

He sipped regularly on the brandy, and eventually fell asleep. His snores alerted Diana to the possibility of her sleeping alone and she smiled. She could make good her escape the following morning without having to explain where she was going, because he never woke up early after a session on the brandy.

And where she was going was nothing to do with him. She needed to see her daughter. To see if Lynn wanted any help. And she didn't want her pig of a husband putting in his two-pennorth alongside her. No, this was going to be the beginning of the end for her and Liam, once again. Too many times she'd gone back to him, but things were about to change. She would talk to Lynn about the possibility of moving in together, getting away from Sheffield altogether. It wasn't out of the question, they could work at building a new relationship, and she could make a firm promise that they would never have to see Liam bloody Marshall again.

32

By Thursday morning the rain had passed over, although it was cold. Grey clouds were hiding any chance of sunshine at the early hour of nine o'clock, but Diana didn't care. She had got out of the house before Liam even stirred, still comatose on the sofa in the lounge.

She hadn't told her sister where she was going; she knew Liam would wear Paula down and get information out of her, so she had left a note saying she was going shopping and wouldn't be too long. She pulled up outside Lynn's house and sat quietly for a minute. She needed to take this carefully and slowly, one step at a time. She was all too aware that Lynn's final argument had been with her father, but that blow-out had caused a massive rift. It was time to put things back together.

She climbed out and locked the car before walking up to the house. She rang the bell, feeling a little relieved that it wasn't a door camera type; she wasn't sure of her welcome and her easiest option was if Lynn didn't know it was her at the door.

Nothing happened so she rang it again, and also knocked. She hoped Lynn hadn't already seen her walking up the path, so was now deliberately avoiding her.

Netta opened her door and peered out, pulling her dressing gown a little tighter around her. 'Can I help you?'

'Not really,' Diana said. 'This is my daughter's house.'

Netta turned to go back inside. 'Well, keep knocking then. She might answer in a few weeks.' She began to close her door.

'Wait. Wait a minute. Are you saying she isn't here?'

'I'm saying nothing.' Netta was about to add further words, but held her tongue.

'You know where she is?'

'Only that she's gone away until it's time for the funeral. I take it you know Josh has been killed?'

'Of course I do. It's why I'm here. I thought she

might need her mother to help her come to terms with it.'

Netta snorted with laughter. 'I can assure you that's the last thing she needs. She left a couple of hours ago in a taxi, dragging a big suitcase with her. She actually said last night she was going away for a couple of weeks but she wasn't going to tell me where in case her father came round trying to find her. She didn't actually say you, in all fairness, but she did say her dad could bully anybody into telling him anything, so she wasn't telling me where she was going.'

'Oh.' Diana didn't know what to say. It seemed her dream of them falling into each other's arms and living happily ever after wasn't going to happen. She looked around her, wondering what to do next.

'Just get off home, love, she made it very clear she wants nothing to do with anyone. She'll handle it on her own, she's a very capable lass.' Netta closed the door.

Diana stared around her. She had tried a couple of times to ring her daughter in the past, but each time the call had been cut off before it had had a chance to connect. She thought that might easily happen again. She walked back down to her car.

She wrote a little note, then walked back up and pushed it through Lynn's letterbox. She would get it at some point, and Diana hoped it would result in at least a phone call.

She drove away, feeling something that was way beyond sadness. She would almost have called it devastation. She felt that in one short week she had lost everything, and it was all down to that bullying thug she was married to, who seemed incapable of letting her go.

Things would have to change. She slipped the car into drive and headed up Birley Spa Lane. Within a minute she was heading into the Derbyshire countryside, and knew the Peak District would help her find a little peace. It always did.

* * *

Matt flashed his fob and headed through the front door of the office. Carol watched him through her reception window and frowned. Why? Why was he here? He didn't need to be.

And then it occurred to her that maybe he did need to be. Maybe this was a comfort to him when precious little else was.

He stood in the small reception area, just looking around, as if unsure what to do next now that he was here.

Carol stood and moved out to join him, slipping easily into his arms to give him a hug. Neither spoke. Neither felt words were necessary.

Eventually Matt spoke into her hair. 'You want a coffee?'

She nodded, and he released her. 'Let's go in Steve's office, he's somehow managed to get comfier visitor chairs than us. I'll make the drinks.'

She closed down the work she was doing, and opened Steve's door. She flicked on his desk lamp; it felt a little gloomy without sunshine streaming through the windows, and she doubted it would make an appearance today.

Carol felt strangely nervous. She had opened up the office without actually opening it up for business, just so that she could keep the minor activities ticking over. Why was Matt here? Did it feel like a safe place for him, as it did for her? Had something cropped up that he needed to do?

The door opened and he carried two mugs of coffee in. He placed them on Steve's desk and sat in the second visitor chair. 'Think he'd notice if I swapped these chairs for my chairs?'

'He might.'

'Best not do it then.'

'He turned up with them one day. One of his gardening clients was throwing them out because they were downsizing or something, so Steve asked if he could have them. They didn't even cost him anything, and I can't order any for you because I've no idea where they're from. The chairs he had before these are now upstairs in the flat.'

He sipped at his coffee. 'I'm obviously not officially back at work, and indeed don't want to be. I don't really want to get out of bed, but I had a quiet word with Ray Ledger yesterday. I called into the briefing room, by the way, brought back lots of memories. He mentioned it's all cut and dried with Freddie Earnshaw, full confession to three murders, they've done a brilliant job. But he knows there's more to it. Smart lad is our Ray. He's officially acting DI until they get a replacement. Anyway, I'm waffling. What he actually said on the quiet is that he's going after Liam Marshall. He phrased it a bit delicately because he can't officially ask for anything, but he said if we heard anything through anything else we were investigating, would I tell him.'

Carol listened carefully, then nodded. 'I'll create a physical file,' she said. 'We do have quite a bit about Marshall in our files, and connected to different things, not just the Anthony Dawson killing.' Carol nursed her coffee and watched as his eyes began to come back to life. They had been dead when he arrived.

'I knew you'd know what to do. My brain's not to-tally in gear, I only went to Moss Way to deliver a plant that Karen had bought to welcome Jaime back to work after illness. It caused floods of tears, and not just from me.' He looked down at his clasped hands. 'I've never cried so much in my life, Carol. Losing Dad was a walk in the park compared to this. That was probably be-cause we thought we'd lost him nine years earlier when he ended up in that damned wheelchair, and he lived a dangerous life. Yes, it was a shock, but nothing to compare to this. I turn over in bed, and she's not there. Since that first night she stayed over, we've never been apart. And now we are.'

'And how are the team taking it?'

'Badly. It's a good job the case is tied up – and it seems Ray did a hell of a job getting confessions to all three killings – but they have no other major crime to focus on at the moment, so it's giving them time to grieve. That will change if Ray gets a sniff of something to chase Liam Marshall on.'

'You miss it? Your DI job?'

'No, I like what I do now. I'm itching to get on with securing Birley Spa Bath House, but it can't be done yet. Even the volunteer group that look after it have been in touch with me to offer their condolences, and they've asked that I postpone further work on it for at least three months. I've agreed, I think Steve and I need that three months.'

'I'll make a note on their file. I'm putting people off making appointments at the moment, nobody is getting in here until you're good and ready. Some things I can deal with anyway, because I'd been handling some of Steve's work following the birth, so we're coping.'

He nodded. One day he would return, would take up the reins again, but for now it would tick along in Carol's capable hands. He stayed for just over an hour then left to go to Becky's home to spend a little time with Harry.

The jigsaw was much fuller, and he and Harry sat filling in quite a bit more of it. Matt asked him if he would like to go out anywhere, but Harry shook his head. He seemed to be quite happy doing very little, coming to terms with what they had lost.

Matt eventually drove home, feeling as though he was starting to reach acceptance of the situation. That was until he drove into the parking area in front of his house and saw the Kia again. All the careful nurturing of his soul throughout the day dissolved once again, and he slammed his way into the house. Oliver jumped, looking less like a cat and more like a startled rabbit, and he dropped to his knees, encouraging his cat to come towards him. He did, but seemingly with trepidation.

'Want some food, Ollie?'

Oliver miaowed. He knew what that meant.

Matt stood, emptied fresh food into the bowl, and refilled the water bowl. He couldn't remember doing it at all since the events of Monday, and he guessed Oliver was currently in the care of Hermia and Steve. In all seriousness, he didn't seem able to recall very much of his life since he had lain beside Karen on that grassy field, knowing she was gone. The days were melding together, the nights were long and, for the most part, wakeful.

He heard the front door open, and Hermia's voice calling out, 'It's me.'

'In the kitchen,' he called back.

She stood in the doorway and looked at the brother she loved so much. She had seen him go through some bad times – Becky leaving him for Brian Davis, Harry being so dangerously ill, them losing their father and Johnny in the same week – but nothing had affected him quite so much as losing his Karen.

'You're okay?' she asked.

'You checking up on me?' he countered.

'Yes. My prerogative.'

'Then... I'm sort of okay. Not brilliant, but getting through each day. Rosie doing well?' He felt as if he had missed out on this most important event, the birth of his niece.

'She is. Clapping weight on already.'

'How much?'

'Six ounces. I know it doesn't sound a lot, but it's enough,' she said, a brief smile flashing across her face.

'Can you put up with me coming back to yours for an hour?'

She held out a hand, and he took hold of it. 'Always, big brother. Always.'

33

And Friday brought the sunshine. Ray had arrived at work early because that's what Ray did. He had checked some emails as he was awaiting confirmation in writing that Earnshaw had given a guilty plea in the magistrate's court, who had promptly sent him on his merry way to spend a few months on remand before his scheduled appearance at Crown Court for sentencing. So everything was good with that.

He sat back in his chair and closed his eyes. He wasn't tired, he just didn't want to partake in the world at that moment in time. His mind kept flickering to Liam Marshall and he knew it would always do so until the man was either dead or behind bars. His eyes opened briefly as the word dead crossed his mind, then he closed them again.

He felt something hit his forehead, and once again opened his eyes. A screwed-up piece of paper had landed on his knee. He glared around at the others.

'Sorry, sarge,' Jaime called across to him. 'I was aiming for the bin.'

'Jaime, the bin is at the side of your desk. Are you lying to me?'

'Yes, sarge. Afraid so.' Her grin was infectious, and they all laughed. It was the first point of lightness in a long week of gloom.

'The charge is assault of a police officer. Carries a lengthy prison term,' he said, and closed his eyes again. A minute later he heard a thud, and opened his eyes to see a stranger standing in front of him, resting his arms on a huge box.

'Understand you need this, sarge.'

'I do?'

'Yes, it's stuff from that caravan. We've logged the gun taken from the car into evidence, but this is the other stuff that was brought out of the caravan itself.'

Suddenly Ray was wide awake. 'You've finished what you needed to do with it?'

'We have. Fingerprints were a nightmare, but were clear enough on the gun, which is the main thing. And the bullets still in the gun matched the one that shot the victim. My boss says to tell you he's bundled things up into packages that clearly say what part of the caravan they were in.'

'Thank you. We'll get on with it immediately, I'm hoping this will lead to much more than Freddie Earnshaw's escapades. It's the caravan owner I want.'

'Okay. Good luck with it. I'll go and get the rest of it now. I could only manage one box at a time.'

Ray watched him walk through the door. Could only manage one box at a time? Just how many boxes did he have?

The answer was four. Ray realised they would have a problem using the briefing room, things could easily become muddled, so he commandeered a conference room for a week, and the entire team moved in.

Rachel looked way out of her depth. Never in a million years would she have imagined how exciting her life would become in a mere two weeks, and now she was faced with four huge boxes of... whatever it was... to sort through and categorise. She felt a little worried that she might miss something because she simply didn't see the relevance of it, so she internally vowed to take her time; this was obviously so important, if the sparkle in Ray Ledger's eyes was anything to go by.

'Okay, boys and girls,' Ray said. 'As we all know, we have a confession of some magnitude, but there are other factors at play here. Factors that are keeping me awake at night, putting my marriage into jeopardy, or so Angela says. So for the sake of my marriage, pin back your ears.'

There was a shuffling of bums on seats as they waited.

'Right, we have two from the same family currently locked up, Niall Marshall and Freddie Earnshaw. For the benefit of newcomers to the team, Niall is the son and Freddie is the grandson of a rogue called Liam Marshall. Liam owns a road haulage company, a large one, with a base in the east end of Sheffield, close to the M1. It is a legitimate business with a good turnover that goes through the books. It is the turnover that doesn't go through the books that has given us major headaches over the years. He is closely allied to the drugs trade, and obviously with all the lorries he has, can turn his hand to carrying anything, anywhere. I want this man off the streets, and I think there's more than half a chance we'll get something from this lot. It's his caravan on his land, that his friends have been using. So concentration is going to be key. I have no idea what's in the boxes, but they're heavy, so I'm guessing lots of paperwork. Any questions?'

'Is the paperwork logged anywhere?' Jaime had raised her hand as she asked the question.

'My guess is no. I think we're meant to do that.'

'Okay,' she acknowledged. 'So if everybody logs what they're checking, anything relevant such as where it was in the caravan, I'll collate the lot at the end. We'll have a comprehensive list by the end that hopefully will make sense. Do you think we need any uniforms in to help?'

Ray thought for a moment. 'Let's see how we go. It may prove to be a walk in the park, where we find nothing, and we'll have taken somebody off their normal duties unnecessarily. Let's just get cracking and reassess after a couple of hours.'

'You've woken up then now, sarge?'

'I was awake. I was thinking with my eyes closed. Right, compulsory coffee break every two hours. When it feels as if your bum has gone numb, get up and walk around, and no singing at any time.'

They all broke out into song and he grinned. How he loved this team.

* * *

Carol had also declared war on Liam Marshall. He had cropped up in several of the Forrester investigations, not least because of his wife who seemed to have turned adultery into an Olympic sport. She was certainly participating in the training regime.

The Anthony Dawson case had brought Liam Marshall to the fore. It was strange that Marshall had known his wife was having an affair with Dawson, and yet it had been Niall who had gone to prison for the murder of Dawson. Had Marshall manipulated his son to the extent that he set out to murder Dawson, in order to get his mother back in the bosom of the family? The more Carol read about Liam, the more she became convinced he was evil through and through.

Carol began to create a document that she could print off and turn into a physical copy when it was complete; she became completely embroiled in it. She found Marshall cropping up in places she hadn't particularly thought about before, and many of them were from the Dave Forrester days. He too had suspected Marshall of deep, dark deeds, and she pulled out Dave's handwritten journal, which they had discovered after his death. If he was seriously concerned about anything he highlighted it, and she checked through for all his highlights. Liam Marshall featured in four of them.

This was added to her document, and she continued to search through WATSON for anything else that might prove to be interesting. She added everything. What she might find unusual or needing further research wasn't necessarily how Ray Ledger would see it. If everything possible was in her file, Ray could decide exactly what needed further work.

She stopped work around eight o'clock because her eyes were irritated. A good night's sleep, she figured, and she would be ready to complete the file in the morning.

Which all sounded plausible, except she was still awake at half past two. She gave in and got up to make herself a cup of Horlicks – wasn't that supposed to send you to sleep? By half past four she was mentally composing a letter to Almia Foods telling them it didn't work.

* * *

The cardboard box was labelled 'Locked file cabinet – forced entry', and Ray opened it up. He began to take out the top layer of contents, and soon realised he was dealing with manifests, items that had been loaded onto Marshalls Haulage lorries. At first glance he saw nothing wrong, and began to wonder why these files had been in a locked filing cabinet, and no key to it had been on the bunch of keys removed from the caravan tenant, Freddie Earnshaw.

Did Liam Marshall really think they wouldn't investigate the drawers purely because they didn't have a key? Was the man simple? Ray knew the answer to that; the man wasn't simple, just big-headed. He thought nobody would recognise whatever was hidden in the files.

And Ray knew, instinctively, it was about drugs.

He called Jaime over to sit beside him, explained what he was doing and where the paperwork had been discovered, and she immediately said drugs or people trafficking.

'I don't see anything that leads me to people trafficking, but drugs...'

'Okay, let's have a look.'

They worked on in silence, keeping a list of anything that they needed to remember, and reached the end of the first file folder.

Ray sat back, a frown etched onto his forehead. 'I can understand a printout for the driver, but why all of these? His business is apparently a well-respected and legitimate one, which in this day and age should be fully computerised, so why the necessity for all this paperwork? Unless this is the paperwork the accountants don't see, kind of "for my eyes only" situation.'

Jaime nodded. 'Totally agree. Look at this one. It's a manifest for a forty-four-tonne artic lorry, with six deliveries to customers of steel springs. Steel springs aren't lightweight, yet each box is listed without a true weight, just says under five pounds. All the customers are in the London area, or so it says, so I've had a quick glance at a couple of the customers and their addresses, and I can't find anything about them. It seems they're all fictional, and I suspect the steel springs are as well.'

'Do you understand what's going on?'

She shook her head. 'No, and I don't think we have anybody here who could figure this out, or even have the right contacts to discuss it with.'

'Fraud Squad?'

'I would think so. I'm going to photocopy this sheet, then I can make some highlighted notes on the photocopy. That will show them that we've at least had a go at working it out. I suspect these "steel springs" are at the very least marijuana, but more likely cocaine or heroin. And that's why these files were kept in a locked cabinet that even Freddie Earnshaw wasn't allowed to access. Something else I don't understand is why you would need a forty-four-tonne articulated vehicle to transport six items weighing just under thirty pounds.'

'I agree entirely. I don't understand it either. Definitely not steel springs being transported on this truck. I'll have a word with the DCI, tell him our thoughts and get his authorisation to send it through to the Fraud Squad. Wonder if Marshall actually realises we've stripped everything out of the caravan.'

* * *

Liam Marshall hadn't realised it until he stepped in through the door. Diana had told him to take her back inside the house, she couldn't bear to watch what was going on, knowing it had all been caused by Freddie. And he had given in and moved inside. He hadn't seen the large van arrive and take everything from inside the mobile home, so seeing it in its stripped-down state was a massive shock.

He sat down with a thud on the right-hand side seat, and felt the blood drain from him. They hadn't emptied the locked filing cabinet, they'd removed it in its entirety. He had considered it to be safer in the caravan than anywhere else. He didn't want it at work, definitely didn't want it inside his home, and thought the appearance of the rickety old van would deter anybody from investigating inside it. The system had worked for the past five years or so, but now Freddie had well and truly cocked it all up.

34

'I can't stand this any longer.' Diana stared morosely into her cup of tea, and Paula reached across the patio table and squeezed her hand.

'But you've always known he was a bad 'un. What's suddenly changed?' Paula spoke quietly. She'd no idea where her brother-in-law was, but she didn't want him listening in on their conversation.

'What's suddenly changed is that my son and my grandson are both locked up, my daughter has disappeared to God knows where, Josh is dead and all I do every day is sit and try to work out how to kill Liam while making it look like suicide.'

Paula smiled. 'There's always an answer. Maybe not murder, but don't dismiss divorce from the equation.'

'He owes me. I'd only get half of everything, and I know he'd cheat me out of a lot of it. It's in his nature, the cheating and lying. I'm just so bloody miserable, Paula.'

'You've been miserable since Anthony Dawson died. Is this a different sort of miserable?'

Diana nodded. 'Everything feels hopeless. I don't know what to do for the best, and I definitely don't know if there's anything I can do to help Niall and Freddie. That's what I mean about it all feeling hopeless. It's because I'm useless at making decisions. I shouldn't have been snotty when Freddie wanted a place to stay. I should have given him a bigger bedroom and made him feel welcome. But I didn't. I put him in the box room and made it clear I wasn't happy about the situation. So Liam took him to the caravan.'

'And have you heard anything about Josh's funeral?'

'Not yet. I think it's a bit early for that sort of stuff. There's something happened to rattle Liam, though. He hardly slept last night, tossing and turning till the early hours he was. I don't think it helped that he'd been on the brandy again. He kept me awake as well and this was when I started planning to kill him. I had two or three good ideas before I dropped off to sleep, but the problem is I didn't write them down and now I can only remember one that wasn't particularly brilliant.'

'You're not serious?' Paula looked troubled. She'd never heard her sister speak like this before.

'I'm serious in that I want him out of my life, but he doesn't necessarily have to die, I suppose.'

'So what was the idea?'

The sun went behind a cloud, and Diana shivered. 'I figured I could go away for a couple of days, or maybe we both could go but that implicates you if it all goes pear-shaped, and somehow send a text from his phone to say he was ending it all, but make it a bit ambiguous so I didn't have to come chasing back. The biggie is that before I go away I crush up loads of Tramadol or something and mix them in with his brandy. If there's one thing I'm sure of, he'll drink the biggest part of a bottle if I'm not here to watch how much he's getting through.'

'Well, the idea is good,' Paula conceded, 'but you've not thought it through far enough. The police can track phones much too easily, so your phone would have to be wherever you've disappeared to, but you'd have to be here using his phone from this location. Spot the problem,' she said and smiled at her sister.

'Hadn't thought it through enough, had I? Damn.'

'And let's make a for-instance situation. Suppose you decided you fancy a couple of days in Manchester shopping at the Trafford Centre. So, your phone is in Manchester. Yes, you could leave it in your hotel room, that's not an issue, but ANPR could track your car between Manchester and Sheffield with no difficulty, so they would know you'd booked in and headed back home. So you would come here, send the text from his phone, then head straight back to Manchester. You presumably would see him, because he's never more than a metre from his phone. I'm sure there would be a way of sending it, but it will then all be about timing, and the police would be able to tell what time all this took place.'

'Okay, so the only thing I could do in advance is doctoring the brandy? That scuppers it all, doesn't it?' Diana looked thoroughly miserable that the best of her ideas was actually a complete waste of time, and she would probably end up locked up for the rest of her life.

Paula looked around her to make sure creepy Liam hadn't materialised anywhere. 'But what if I was in our hotel room with your phone? And you drove my car back to here. You could always tell Liam you'd had to nip back home because you'd forgotten to swap your card wallet and your phone from the regular handbag. Took a different handbag, didn't you? A bigger one, to carry your new make-up and stuff we've gone to buy. Then you wait till his hand isn't attached to his phone, make it a very quick and simple text and do the deed. I can actually send some sort of jokey reply from here, as if you think he's having you on because you've left him for a night. I suggest you hide the phone because we don't want him seeing the outgoing and incoming text. Then switch it off. We can resurrect it but not switch it on when we get back, to find our most favourite person no longer with us. Dead, in fact. Ring him a couple of times in the evening from our hotel, and we can actually come home a bit early the next day because you're worrying it wasn't a joke, and you can't contact his phone.'

'Christ, Paula, I never had you down for a killer!'

'I like planning stuff like this, think I should have been a crime writer,' she said, 'I could have made a small fortune. But it is adaptable, this plan, for all occasions.'

'We should make some notes in the order it has to happen.'

'You're seriously considering it then?'

'He killed my Anthony without pulling the trigger, I know it. He manipulates people, and I think he did it with Niall. I can't tell you how much I despise him, but I can't see a way out of it other than divorce, and he won't allow that to happen. I'd consider anything before he realises I'm a bit of a liability. At the moment he still loves me, always has, but he knows I don't give a fig about him. I could easily be next on his list for disposal. Why have you got this all written down?' Diana asked, staring at her sister.

Paula smiled. 'It was the suicide aspect that interested me. It would be all too easy to kill somebody, but to kill somebody and make it look as if they did it themselves takes it to another level.'

'That's not what I meant. Why have you thought all this through, and actually made a written plan?'

'I knew what you meant,' Paula admitted with a laugh. 'The truth is we can only use this once. We either use it for you or we use it for me. I think you need it more than me, so I'll have to come up with a second plan. Once we've agreed what we're doing, I'll destroy this.'

Diana felt sick. Was this really her sister speaking these words? More than that, had this been her plan to get rid of her husband? If it worked, it would be foolproof.

Was it possible? Could they refine it so that she

didn't have to be driving backwards and forwards to Manchester?

They continued for another half hour, a second coffee helping them through the slight chill in the morning air, and then both of them went inside.

Liam was sitting in the lounge. He looked up as he heard the front door open and shouted, 'Thanks for the cup of coffee.'

Paula popped her head around the door. 'I didn't make you one.'

'Exactly. You never heard of sarcasm?'

'I have. I just try not to use it. You want one now?'

'No, I've gone past the coffee stage.' He held up a brandy glass and waved it around, sloshing some of the drink onto his fingers.

'It's not even lunchtime yet, Liam. Bit early for the hard stuff, isn't it?'

'I might have got some issues to think through,' he countered, grumpiness evident in his voice. He drained the contents of his glass and reached for the brandy bottle to top up again. 'And I can drink what I want, when I want.'

'No disputing that,' Paula said and left him to his ruminations about the way his life had suddenly become a little unmanageable.

She headed for the kitchen where Diana was adding their cups to the dishwasher.

'Give me some time to rethink everything,' she said quietly. 'I reckon we can maybe do this without going out of the door. He's already on the brandy.'

'Damn, he say anything about what's wrong?'

'Just said he'd got some issues to think through.'

'It's to do with that caravan. He said he was going to get something from it, and was livid when he came back. Said the police had taken everything. He's been an arsehole ever since.'

'Crush the tablets that you've got. How many Tramadol can you lay your hands on?'

'I've got about thirty upstairs. He doesn't know about them.'

'So when they say his body is full of Tramadol, you can run upstairs horrified, then announce that your painkillers have all disappeared?'

'I can. The doctor prescribed them when I hurt my back, but I can't take them. They have an odd effect on me that I don't like, so I just put them in my bathroom cabinet. If he passes out with all this brandy, I can get them ground up. You're thinking we just fill up a new bottle of brandy and wait until he drinks it?'

'I think we observe his behaviour for a couple of days, wait until his bottle is so low he'll need a new one, then doctor the next one he'll be taking out of the drinks cabinet. We can confirm how down he's been, how nasty to both of us. We don't actually need to lie. We can assume in front of everybody that he's died from alcoholic poisoning because he's worked his way through several bottles of brandy over the space of about three days.'

'It's certainly easier than the shopping in Manchester plan.' Diana sat down on a kitchen chair with a thud. 'Am I really discussing with my sister the best way of killing my husband?'

'Your husband is an even bigger bastard than mine,' Paula said quietly. 'He should be dead. Divorce is still an option for mine, but if I don't get a fair settlement he'll have to go as well.' She sat on the other chair, and took hold of Diana's hand. 'Be strong, Di, be strong. You don't deserve to be treated like this, and I know you're scared of him. We can make it all go away. I can't bring Niall or Freddie out of prison, but I can make your life a bit easier. What do you say?'

Diana gulped and stared across the table at Paula. 'In a couple of days? After we've watched him? I say we do it. I'll crush the tablets when he's passed out and add them to a bottle of brandy. There's easily six or seven bottles in the drinks cabinet but I'll hide the doctored one until he's ready to get a new one out.

Maybe I'll sit with him and offer to get it for him when he starts to get low on the current one. It won't matter if my fingerprints are on the bottle, I'll admit to handling it, but then going to bed because I could see he was in for a long session.'

'Excellent. Now you're thinking!' Paula stood. 'Fancy another coffee, with maybe a tot of brandy in it?'

35

In the end it was simple. The brandy bottle was so low it would probably provide one more drink for Liam, so all thirty-one of the remaining Tramadol tablets were crushed to a fine powder, a new bottle had a tiny amount of the brandy removed from it to accommodate the powder being added, and it was handled by Diana with gloves on. She also took the added precaution of wiping the bottle clean.

Throughout that day it was constantly shaken although they could see no evidence of the powder in the liquid. Diana eventually placed it so that it would be the next one removed from the cabinet, and she and Paula left that afternoon for a meal in Sheffield city centre, then a trip to the Crucible to see a musical.

Liam hadn't had a problem with them going out for the night because he figured Diana wouldn't be sleeping with someone else if she was going out with her sister, and eventually they had manipulated an already drunk Liam into suggesting they stay in the Mercure overnight to save them driving back home. He, of course, thought it was a good idea as he quickly realised it meant he wouldn't have her constantly watching what he was imbibing. He actually was the one to ring the Mercure and use his own credit card to book the room. It meant he could really get stuck into the brandy, and maybe watch some porn on television.

'See you tomorrow,' he said, and kissed his wife goodbye. He merely waved a hand at Paula, while wondering when the hell she was leaving them, and going back to that husband of hers.

* * *

The two women ate in Leopold Square at a snazzy little Italian place, then went back to their room to freshen up before strolling through the Winter Gardens and down to the Crucible.

The show was excellent, although both of them felt slightly sick worrying if everything was going to plan at home. They walked slowly back through the Winter

Gardens, stopping several times to admire the plants, and then slipped through the connecting door into the hotel. They decided to have a drink in the bar, and Paula went to get them a small brandy each. The significance wasn't lost on either of them. While Diana was waiting for Paula to return, she rang Liam.

There was no answer, so she waited a minute and tried again. Still no answer.

They drank their brandies, and headed up to the room. They looked at each other and actually giggled. 'Can it really be this easy?' Paula whispered.

'I hope so, but if we get caught I hope they put us in the same cell,' Diana responded. 'Okay, let's think this through. He's either unconscious or dead. He suggested he treat us to this outing, paid for the hotel room for us, which can be proved, but I'd already booked the tickets before we told him. He was clearly happy we were going out for the night. He'd been talking for a few days about life not being worth living without Niall and Freddie, and he'd been drinking copious amounts of brandy for at least a week. Alcoholic poisoning was possibly the best way for him to go.'

'And when they tell us the autopsy results, we gasp quite loudly and you run upstairs to check the Tramadol packs still in your bathroom cabinet, which were full when we left as far as you know, but are now empty.' Paula leaned back on her pillow with a sigh. 'Think we'll sleep tonight?'

* * *

Diana rang Liam at just after nine next morning; still no reply. She left a voicemail asking him to call her, she was feeling a little worried. She finished off the message by adding they were going to do some shopping and would be home early afternoon.

They spent some time in Marks and Spencer, Diana choosing two dresses and Paula going for nightwear. They had a coffee in the coffee shop, then headed to the car park to pick up the car.

'This is it, then,' Diana whispered. 'I'll ring him one last time.'

She took out her phone and pressed Liam's name. It rang out. Again she left a voicemail. 'Liam, we're coming home early. Really worried now. See you in half an hour or so.'

And they left Sheffield city centre by the quickest way possible.

* * *

It wasn't an easy death for Liam Marshall. He was lying on the floor, face downwards, and when the two women rolled him over he was covered in vomit. They made a half-hearted attempt to restart his heart, then rang the police. They took the half-empty bottle of brandy and poured most of it down the toilet, leaving about half an inch in the bottom. Enough to test, and enough to allow them to claim he must have died of alcoholic poisoning, not suicide by taking an overdose of a drug. It was okay to be shocked by that verdict when it was proven after an autopsy.

The name of Marshall saw the call sent directly to Ray Ledger, and he organised for forensics and everything else he could possibly need before driving out to Liam Marshall's house with Rachel Quixley and Ian Jameson.

The smell was bad; a combination of vomit, faeces, urine and brandy wasn't a welcoming odour.

An ambulance was already there, but the paramedics knew as they walked through the door that the man was beyond help. They were now standing to one side, having taken their equipment back to their vehicle, and waited for permission to head back to base.

Ray checked with Martin that he could release them, and they drove away, neither admitting to the sense of relief they felt.

Paula was in the kitchen comforting her sister, who was crying hysterically. 'So much brandy,' she sobbed, as she dabbed at her eyes with some kitchen towel. 'I told him he was drinking too much. He planned this, didn't he? He paid for us to go away for the night, then drank himself to death, because it's the death he would have chosen. What do I do now?' she wailed.

Rachel handed both women a freshly brewed cup of tea, and passed the kitchen roll to Diana. She was clearly distraught, and Rachel was rapidly coming to the conclusion that her first month with Major Crimes was definitely a baptism by fire. Everything seemed to be getting thrown at the team, and she was on a steep learning curve, a proper parabola.

'You don't think it's accidental then?'

'No, I bloody don't.' Diana's voice rose. 'I'm sure he planned it. Get them out of the house then I can top up the gallons of brandy I've been drinking all week, and proper finish the job. It's just the sort of nastiness he's capable of.' Her head collapsed on to the table and she became hysterical once more.

'How do I tell Niall? And Freddie? See what I mean? He never thought for one minute how it would affect those two boys, he just went ahead and did it because he's afraid of something. I've no idea what, but since Freddie was arrested, he's been in a proper state.

Is it just that? Or had he also done something he shouldn't have?'

She threw a quick glance towards Paula as Rachel turned to get her own cup of tea. Paula gave a slight nod as if to say well done, this is how to play it.

* * *

Ray stared at the body of the man he had grown to detest. He felt cheated. He knew they were so close to putting him away, through the paperwork that had been sent through to the Fraud Squad for forensic accounts examination. But now the bloody man had killed himself, taking away any pleasure he would have gained from seeing this underworld kingpin arrested, charged and found guilty.

He stood and watched as Marshall's body was loaded into the coroner's van and taken away for autopsy, trying very hard to squash the anger he was feeling. Liam Marshall, dead. It was almost unbelievable. And by his own hand, as well. Wife and sister-in-law at the Crucible, and staying the night in the Mercure courtesy of him, he'd definitely arranged his night to himself very well indeed.

He drove back to the station, his team in the same

car with him, and the general consensus was that they were finding it difficult to believe.

'His wife was distraught. Even his sister-in-law was upset,' Rachel said. 'I didn't really know how to help them except make them cups of tea.'

'You did well,' Ray said, 'especially as you've never had to tackle something like this before. Thank you, Rachel. We'll discuss it all in the morning, everybody in by eight, please.'

36

It seemed that everybody had different thoughts on the alcoholic poisoning theory, and Ray left a message with Martin to ask for urgent notification of the toxicology results.

He couldn't get over this feeling that Marshall had cheated the law. The man had known he was in big trouble as soon as he realised the police had access to all the paperwork in the locked filing cabinet.

He had arrived in work before seven, as a result of an almost sleepless night. He was unsure about any interactions with Lynn Earnshaw; should he tell her, or would her mother contact her? He knew she was estranged from her parents, so it was possible her mother couldn't contact her.

By the time the others started to drift in he had decided he would wait for the toxicology results, then ring Lynn. Liam Marshall had access to all sorts of stuff, mainly the illegal variety, and Ray needed all the facts before speaking to the man's daughter.

Ray passed some money to Ian and asked if he minded fetching coffees from Starbucks for everybody.

'It'll be my pleasure, sarge,' he said, a grin appearing on his usually dour face. 'I got up so late this morning I only managed a mouthful of water before running out to the car.'

* * *

They sat around Ray's desk, chairs placed haphazardly, as they all realised it was going to be a pretty informal chat. To save Ian having to remember too much, they'd all requested large lattes, and finally Rachel began to experience the camaraderie amongst this team. For the first time they were altogether, all still mourning the loss of Karen and wondering who would be brought in to replace her, but for now their boss was the man who'd divvied up for the drinks, and that was good enough for them.

He waited until they'd had some of their drinks

before turning the conversation towards the activities of the previous afternoon and evening.

'So, thoughts?'

Nobody said *on what?* They knew exactly what he was talking about.

Kevin spoke first. 'Uneasy about it. I know his wife said he'd been hitting the bottle really hard for a few weeks now, but it seems a bit odd if that's the way he chose to kill himself. There's no guarantee with alcoholic poisoning, no matter how much you drink.'

Ray nodded. 'My thoughts exactly. He obviously wanted his wife out of the way for the night because he persuaded them not to drive home after the theatre, choosing instead to pay for a hotel room for them. So was he on his own in that house, or did he have a visitor?'

'Or did he remain on his own but added something to the brandy to help his plans to die quietly? That didn't work, he was in a hell of a mess when we found him, but I think we'll find out there was something in that brandy, not just the alcoholic beverage we all know and love. We should hear any time about the contents, because Martin was starting tests last night so we get an early toxicology report.'

Jaime stood. 'Be back in a minute. I've had three

emails while I've been away from my desk, so I'll just check.'

She opened up her laptop, glanced through the twenty or so emails that had arrived since she'd last opened it, and then quickly printed one off.

'It's here,' she announced, and walked over to the printer to collect the document. She handed it to Ray, who scanned it quickly, then nodded.

'Loaded with Tramadol,' he said. 'We all know Tramadol is a prescription drug, but it commands a lot of money on the streets. He would be able to get it easily. He didn't take the chance of surviving just having alcohol in huge quantities, he added the drug to make sure of it. A large quantity of it, according to this report.'

He stood. 'Okay, we don't all need to go out to see Diana – Rachel, you seem to have the magic touch with the sympathy bit, so I'll take you.'

They didn't rush, the coffee was going down a treat, and they chatted amongst themselves as to why Liam Marshall's life had been so bad in his estimation that he had chosen to end it.

'But where's the note?' Jaime asked.

'We haven't looked for one yet. That will happen this morning, because I'm taking two uniforms with me to search for it. I'll bring his laptop and any other tech stuff he has, and you can go through it, Jaime. That okay?'

Jaime nodded. 'Delighted. I always enjoy a good rummage through other people's lives.'

* * *

Within the hour two uniforms had been seconded to the case, and Ray and Rachel were in the back seat of a squad car.

Karl and Andy, the two uniformed officers, asked questions about their role in the visit, and Ray told them to leave no stone unturned as they searched for a suicide note, or indeed, anything that might be of interest.

Ray placed a call to the grieving widow, asking her to ensure they had access through the front gates as they needed to look for specific items. She responded with a 'no trouble,' and didn't ask any further questions.

'That was the police,' she confirmed to Paula.

'What did they want?'

'They're on their way.'

'Well, listen very carefully.' Paula spoke quietly. 'We haven't slipped up yet, but we could easily do so. If you suddenly realise you've got Tramadol in the house when they tell us what was in his system, and act all droopy and tearful, they're going to take away the empty packets. And I've realised – those packets don't have his fingerprints on them, even though the tablets have gone. The bottle was never going to be an issue because his fingerprints are on that, but we need to get rid of the packets. And then we need them to arrive at a different opinion – that he went and got his own Tramadol from one of his dodgy mates.'

'I'll go and get them, there's only two packets. I'll hide them in a fish finger packet in the freezer.'

Paula laughed. 'No, if there's only two packets we'll flatten them and hide one each in our bras. They're not here to search us, they're here to find a suicide note, I reckon. Just don't let it fall out of your bra, or we'll end up in custody by tonight.'

Diana ran up the stairs and collected the empty packets, then they inserted them into their bras, laughing just a little bit as they did so.

The intercom from the gate pealed out, and Diana released the lock. They both went to the front door as if to welcome their visitors, but in reality they wanted them gone so they could actually have the tiniest of bonfires and burn the somewhat uncomfortable inserts in their underwear.

* * *

They found nothing. Rachel stayed with the two women, Ray searched the lounge that the wife and sister-in-law of the victim refused point blank to enter, and he collected an iPad, two mobile phones and a laptop.

He returned to where they were sitting quietly talking in the kitchen, none of them drinking tea or coffee, and seemingly getting on very well with Rachel.

'I can give you a contact number for a cleaning company that the police use when crime scenes need a deep clean, and it definitely needs one in there,' he said.

'Thank you,' Diana said. 'Am I okay to get them in?'

'You are now. I have more information to give you – Diana, your husband didn't die from alcoholic poisoning as you thought, he had massive amounts of Tramadol in his system.'

She forced a shocked expression onto her face. 'Tramadol? The pain relief drug?'

He nodded. 'That's right. Are you aware of the other business your husband is involved with, one that fits in nicely with his road haulage activities?'

'Other business? He's kept another business from me?'

'I doubt you would have wanted to know about it. We have considerable proof that he was ferrying drugs up and down the country as part of the genuine loads he carried. All the manifests and orders are now with the Fraud Squad, and he would have eventually been arrested. He chose this way out. He knew we had his paperwork from the caravan. He would have no difficulty getting hold of the Tramadol.'

Diana and Paula reached out to each other and clasped hands. 'He needed us to be away, didn't he? And I thought he was being nice, paying for the hotel for us.'

Andy entered the kitchen and looked at Ray, then shook his head.

'You're both done?' Ray asked.

'We are, sarge,' Andy responded.

Rachel and Ray stood and walked to the front door, accompanied by Paula and Diana.

Ray thanked them for their cooperation, told Diana he would email the contact for the cleaning company, and they climbed once more into the back of the vehicle.

'Everything went well, Rachel?' he asked.

'It did. Just two grieving women who seem to be a bit lost.'

'Well, we can pass all this technology stuff on to

Jaime, see if anything shouts out at her, then I think we can almost say case closed. I wanted to see that bastard go down for a long time, but he stopped that, didn't he?'

* * *

Diana and Paula stayed on the front steps, watching as the squad car exited the gates. Diana pressed the button to re-engage the lock, and turned to Paula.

'It occurred to me while we were in there that our shopping trip to Marks and Spencer should have seen me buying a third dress. A nice black one, something suitable for a funeral.'

EPILOGUE

SIX WEEKS LATER

Matt parked his car in the car park nearest to Karen's grave, picked up the huge bunch of flowers lying on the back seat, and then went to the boot to get a vase and a large bottle of water. Until her headstone was installed with two built-in vases, they were having to be inventive.

Abbey Lane was a beautiful cemetery, very well maintained, very green, and somewhere he visited regularly to chat to his dad and Johnny. Normally he would have visited with Karen, not to visit Karen, and he felt his stomach clench as he thought about his life as it was now.

He reached her grave that was still sporting the wreaths from the funeral of two weeks earlier, and moved them around slightly so that he could wedge the vase securely. He poured the water in it, and then opened up the bouquet. Beautiful roses, alstroemeria, tiny chrysanthemums, lilies, greenery; it looked beautiful. A beautiful bouquet for a beautiful lady. He added a single peach-coloured rose that Hermia had handed to him, cut from her own garden, saying that it was for Aunty Karen from baby Rosie.

Hermia had wanted to be with him, but he had found the courage to say he would rather be on his own, as today was Karen's birthday. She had understood, and had let him go with a sadness she found distressing. He was her brother. She should be supporting him.

But on this day he genuinely didn't need support. He needed to talk to his lady. He needed to tell her that the man who had driven his car over her entire body was locked up, probably for around forty years, that his grandfather was dead, and Ray was coping without her. Just. And not all the time.

'I'm seeing a lot of Ray, Karen. He misses you so much, doesn't want to be leading all the time, he liked it better when you were the boss. And I don't know how to comfort him, because I like it better when you're my boss, as well. So happy birthday, my lovely one. I love you so much.'

He reached forward and picked up a card that had almost become separated from its wreath. It was from Jaime.

'Jaime is doing well. Has good and bad days. She's yet another one to add to the list of people who miss you. And now it's time to tell you some news from home. Our new baby is thriving, and her name is Rosie Tamora. I had to check where Tamora is from, because I'd never even heard of it before, but obviously our resident Shakespeare expert had. It's from *Titus Andronicus*, and it's certainly different.' He reached down and moved a couple of the flowers around, aware they weren't even in the water. He'd never been much good at flower arranging.

He lowered himself to the grass, stretched out his long legs, and sat silently for quite some time. Then he broke. He felt a tear roll down his cheek that ultimately became a cascade.

'What do I do, Karen? I take out the engagement ring every night and just stare at it. It's going to remain in its box until Rosie is eighteen, then I shall pass it to her. But that will mean I will have spent eighteen long years without you, and that's inconceivable at the moment. I've never cried so much in my life.'

He shuffled on his bum to get a little more comfortable on the hard ground. 'I'm going to bring a folding chair next time I come for a chat. I have things to tell you that to me seem a bit unreal. My inbox is full every day. People checking up on me, checking up on Harry, and Carol has been a star. It seems there were more than five hundred people, mainly police, at your funeral, and I think they've all contacted me at some point. You were much loved, lovely lady. Especially by me.'

He reached across and picked up another card. It said their sadness was overwhelming, and was signed by Ray and Angela. He knew Ray wasn't handling it well.

Matt himself knew that personally he wasn't handling it at all, and without Carol he would have given up. She had been the one to tell him Lynn Earnshaw wanted to have five minutes of his time. He wanted to scream no, but he knew how unfair that was. Lynn Earnshaw had done nothing wrong apart from giving birth to Freddie Earnshaw.

'I saw Lynn Earnshaw yesterday. Her sorrow was genuine, you made quite an impression on her. It was Josh's funeral two weeks ago, and she said the crematorium was packed with all his school friends. She is totally estranged from her mother now, wouldn't allow her to go, and she completely ignored her father's funeral. No love lost there, I think. She really came to tell me she's packing up her house in Sheffield and moving to live near her friend in Gainsborough. I wished her luck. She's a nice lady with a rubbish family.'

He climbed to his feet and dusted down his bum. 'I'm going now, sweetheart, but I'll be back in a couple of days to tidy up your flowers and wreaths. I have absolutely no idea if there is an after-life or not, but if you can see all this mountain of flora and fauna, you'll know how much you are loved. And wherever you are, Karen, know I love you the most.'

He headed back to his car, stumbling over grass and gravestones, unable to see through the tears.

He pulled into the side as he reached his father's grave, side by side with Johnny's, and sent loving thoughts across without getting out of the car. 'I'll stop by next time I'm here, you two,' he promised.

He drove back through Norton and dropped down the hill into Gleadless, parking outside the office. He sat for a moment, feeling comforted by his chat with Karen, by seeing the evidence of the love felt for her by others as well as his own family, but not feeling comforted by the fact that he was still a long way off acceptance of everything that had happened.

He got out of the car and Carol opened the office door.

'Come on, I've made you a coffee. And I expect you to eat a scone, we need to start building you up again. Karen wouldn't want you to become ill because of what's happened, so let's make today the day you start taking better care of yourself, and making sure Harry does the same.'

Matt managed a smile. 'I'm listening. Your scones can cure most things, but heartbreak might take more than one.'

ACKNOWLEDGEMENTS

This book has been so difficult to write – not because of the content, not because of the storyline, not because it's the final one in a series. No, it's much simpler than all of that, I've been struggling with my sight for almost two years now, and this last year has been so troublesome. I stopped driving about eighteen months ago because I couldn't see much at all, and after deciding my eyesight was getting worse because I was getting older, I went to my opticians. It wasn't anything to do with my age, simply a matter of cataracts on both eyes. I have now had both of them removed, and next week on 26 June I go for an eye test for new glasses. One week later I will be able to see again! But this book has been written while almost blind and having to have eye drops three times a day.

Massive thanks go to the whole Boldwood team, but especially to Isobel Akenhead, who has been so patient, and who has had to reschedule her own work so that I could comply with my consultant's instructions to cut back on screen time. I am seven weeks beyond my deadline day, and she has been so supportive.

There is a special mention to send to my amazing proofreader, Candida Bradford, who has proofread all seven of my Boldwood published books. She completes the work started by the structural and copy editors, and the little comments she leaves make me smile. Thank you so much, Candida, you make me realise the struggle is all worthwhile!

I also have people to thank who lent me their names – some are carry-ons from books one and two (*Fatal Secrets* and *Fatal Lies*) such as Karen Nelson, Ray Ledger, Becky Davis and Carol Flynn, but this book is extra special because Rachel Quixley, a nurse from the eye clinic at The Northern General Hospital in Sheffield, changes her career fictionally speaking and becomes a PC. This has caused some hilarity because Rachel now believes she is a celebrity, and we are to have a meeting in the future to discuss what we will wear when we appear on *Loose Women*. Thank you, Rachel, you helped a very scared author get through an ordeal that proved to be no ordeal at all, cataract removal.

I also have to mention Kirsty Waller, my youngest daughter, for coming up with a name for a nightclub in the centre of Sheffield that wasn't already a nightclub name. I didn't want to be sued, because I knew somebody was about to meet their end outside said nightclub. That's not good promotion for them. She produced The SteelTrap, brilliant name. Thanks, Kess! Love you.

My usual thanks go to my beta readers, Alyson Read, Nicki Murphy, Tina Jackson and Denise Cutler, and to my ARC group – I hope you enjoyed this one!

My biggest thanks as always go to my immediate family. Sian, daughter number one, has been driving us to assorted hospital appointments since I stopped driving – I'm sure she must regret living only ten seconds from us. Dave, my husband, has had to put up with all my frustration, and has been the one to put in my eye drops, which has caused some hilarity in the Waller household because he also had a cataract removed a couple of weeks before I had my first one removed. His went disastrously wrong, so I was putting in his drops, then he was doing mine. It hasn't been an easy time, and he is still having treatment – laser next week. And now he's going to have to read the book! (He doesn't read psych thrillers through choice!)

My website is maintained by my wonderful grandson Dominic Kitchen, who during the writing of this book presented us with our second great-grandson, Alfie James David, brother to William. This book is dedicated to Alfie.

I have friends in the writing community who have shared my stress with this book, and I want to say a massive thank you to Judith Baker and Valerie Keogh for their encouragement and support. You are amazing.

Anita Waller

June 2024

ABOUT THE AUTHOR

Anita Waller is the author of many bestselling psychological thrillers and the Kat and Mouse crime series. She lives in Sheffield, which continues to be the setting of many of her thrillers.

Sign up to Anita Waller's mailing list for news, competitions and updates on future books.

Visit Anita's website: www.anitawaller.co.uk

Follow Anita on social media here:

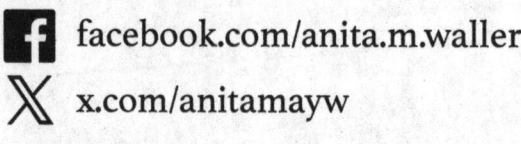

facebook.com/anita.m.waller

x.com/anitamayw

ALSO BY ANITA WALLER

The Forrester Detective Agency Mysteries

Fatal Secrets

Fatal Lies

Fatal Endings

Standalone Novels

Flash Point

The Family at No. 12

The Couple Across The Street

The Girls Next Door

Beautiful

Angel

34 Days

Strategy

Captor

Game Players

Malignant

Liars *co-written with Patricia Dixon*

Gamble

Nine Lives

Winterscroft

Kat and Mouse Series

Murder Undeniable

Murder Unexpected

Murder Unearthed

Murder Untimely

Epitaph

Murder Unjoyful

The Connection Trilogy

Blood Red

Code Blue

Mortal Green

THE

Murder

LIST

**THE MURDER LIST IS A NEWSLETTER
DEDICATED TO SPINE-CHILLING FICTION
AND GRIPPING PAGE-TURNERS!**

**SIGN UP TO MAKE SURE YOU'RE ON OUR
HIT LIST FOR EXCLUSIVE DEALS, AUTHOR
CONTENT, AND COMPETITIONS.**

SIGN UP TO OUR NEWSLETTER

BIT.LY/THEMURDERLISTNEWS

Boldwood

Boldwood Books is an award-winning fiction publishing company seeking out the best stories from around the world.

Find out more at www.boldwoodbooks.com

Join our reader community for brilliant books, competitions and offers!

Follow us
@BoldwoodBooks
@TheBoldBookClub

Sign up to our weekly deals newsletter

https://bit.ly/BoldwoodBNewsletter

www.ingramcontent.com/pod-product-compliance
Lightning Source LLC
Chambersburg PA
CBHW010700100726
47900CB00010B/2740

* 9 781835 339152 *